Death in a Half Foreign Country

James Ward

COOL MILLENNIUM BOOKS

2

First published in KDP 2018.
This edition published 2021.

A CIP catalogue record for this book is available from the British Library.

ISBN: 978-1-913851-13-2

Cover picture shows the Tube at Pimlico.

This novel was produced in the UK and uses British-English language conventions ('authorise' instead of 'authorize', 'The government are' instead of 'the government is', etc.)

To my wife

Chapter 1: Dee, Dee, Dee x n.

Forty-five-year-old Dina Oforka-Jones, known to her friends as Dee, would normally have been nervous about something like this. Desks weren't designed to take the weight of a human, even a tall, slender human with a satisfying low BMI. Stand on one, it might well collapse and you could end up looking very silly.

But given the amount of alcohol everyone had consumed, and that this was a huge celebration, well, if she ever *had* to lose a little dignity, now was the time. And sod it, England expected her to make a speech, so that's what she was bloody well going to do. A leader's prerogative. If you didn't exercise it when people thought you should, tomorrow one or two of your rivals would likely crawl out of the woodwork.

So when four junior lawyers suddenly grabbed her and swung her into the air and into place between Roger's mouse mat and his out tray, she whooped as if it was exhilarating.

Mustn't look out of the window, though. Twelve floors above the City of London, pretty heady at the best of times. Add a desk's height, and you could easily start suffering from vertigo. Then you really *would* go on your backside.

But there were enough people crowded round her makeshift podium to catch her now. At least a twenty on each side, all adoring acolytes.

Someone at the far end of the office turned off the music. People applauded her successful flight as if it was magic. Boy, they were drunk. Or maybe just ecstatically happy.

All eyes fixed on her. Silence fell.

"So ... I'm not very good at making speeches," she said. "I'd just like to thank you all for our" — She raised both fists, tensed her body gleefully and beamed — "*BEST YEAR EVER!*"

There was a rip-roaring "*HOORAAAAAAAAAY!*" and everyone raised glasses to the ceiling like they didn't care if they also threw the contents up there. She allowed the acclaim to run for a few seconds and signalled for quiet.

"Carneghan Strake may be one of the biggest legal firms in London," she went on, "but we're its most successful department by a considerable margin. It's thanks to *litigation*—"

"HOORAAAAAAAAY!"

"—that we've now entered the earnings stratosphere, the reputational stratosphere, the valuation stratosphere; turnover, eight hundred and twenty three point four *million, profit FORTY-THREE PER CENT!*"

"HOORAAAAAAAAAAAAAAAY!"

"It's thanks to *litigation*—"

"HOORAAAAAAAAAAAAAAAAAAAAY!" Men and women of all ages, in suits and party hats, high-fiving, flinging arms round each other, pogoing, fists punching the air, furious clapping; everything high octane, manic, wonderful, *wonderful!*

"—that *we're* now the go-to guys for *everyone*—but EVERY-ONE!—whose name has been unjustly—or justly!—dragged through the mud, and owns sufficient resources *to make things right!*"

"HOORAAAAAAAAAY! DEE! DEE! DEE! DEE!—"

"It's thanks to *litigation*—"

"HOORAAAAAAAAAY!"

"—that right now, you're the only guys in the entire City of London who can look at your bonuses with a clear conscience and think, '*Hey, I actually EARNED my money!*'"

"HOORAAAAAAAAAY!"

She threw her arms wide, grinned and struck an incredulous pose. "*How rare is THAT?*"

Someone offered her a glass of champagne. She waved it away.

"*And don't tell anyone outside this room those were my words!*" she yelled. "*Hey, I wouldn't want to end up getting SUED!*"

"DEE-NA! DEE-NA! DEE-NA! DEE! DEE! DEE! DEE!"

Boy, they were like a house on fire! And why not? This was probably the best, wittiest speech she'd ever given at an office party!

Still, best quit while you're ahead. She finally accepted the champagne, signalled for silence, and when she'd got it, raised her glass solemnly. "Onwards and upwards."

Everyone repeated her words like they were a solemn oath.

She smiled appreciatively and drained her glass. "Help me down, please, Sheila, Keith," she said. *"Have a great party, everyone!"* she yelled, flicking her eyes nervously between her audience and the four hands outstretched to aid her descent. *"I love you all! EVERY LAST ONE OF YOU!"*

A final roar of veneration, love and animal spirits. The music resumed.

Two hours later, the celebration wound down and the office gradually emptied. The lifts strained under a succession of cargoes of greater than the usual number of occupants, and probably more than was safe. Only a few people were sober enough to notice, and of those, even fewer thought it wise to take the stairs. Eventually, the building itself cleared. Its lights went out on every floor. The doors sealed, as if hermetically. It became one with the seemingly aeons-old darkness and silence of the nub of The Square Mile, with Mansion House at its esoteric centre.

There were mysteries aplenty here, and Carneghan Strake wasn't the least of them. Many commentators had no idea 'where it had come from', by which they meant, how it had risen to prominence and proven success so quickly. Why, they asked, given that its headquarters and base of operations was in a prestigious high-rise in one of the most sought-after office blocks in the world, did two of its five chief partners - Dina Oforka-Jones and Ian Batchelor – work almost entirely from two poky rooms in a nondescript grey pile five hundred yards away in Cheapside? And how did their particular department become so disproportionately successful?

Some claimed Carneghan Strake was so big, and built on such fragile foundations, that when it came toppling down –

which it could at any moment – the reverberations would be felt across the world. It was the Lehman Brothers of the legal world.

Other, more socially minded, observers pointed out that the British criminal justice system was in meltdown. Such a thing "can happen right under our noses," the *Guardian* journalist, Polly Toynbee wrote, "and none but judges, lawyers, the Crown Prosecution Service and prison staff know anything about it." Wasn't there something wrong, they asked, with a professional system whose most profitable sectors were those least conducive to the public good, and were sometimes actively hostile to it?

Hardly anyone cared. In this sort of area, the market ruled. And who on earth had a high opinion of lawyers anyway? They were sharks, cop-a-pleas, dirty shirts, hapus capuses. Dickens had said everything anyone would want to know about them a hundred and fifty years ago in *Bleak House*. And where the public wasn't entitled to moral expectations, its apathy was more than excusable: it was entirely reasonable.

All of which suited the lawyers of Carneghan Strake very nicely.

Chapter 2: The Return of Toby

A lot happened that summer, including Britain's longest heatwave for decades. Grass turned the colour of sand, wildfires swept across moorland, rail tracks bowed, the temperature in London's underground hit an astonishing 103F. Meanwhile, Brexit dragged on, trade wars were declared, the Europa league kicked off with a win for Spartak Subotica, and John Mordred and Phyllis Robinson left MI7's Red Department.

A catalogue of high-pressure assignments involving too personal involvements and several narrow escapes from certain death, had left John at a low ebb. 'Clinically depressed', Thames House's resident psychologist told him. It didn't feel like depression, but then, it didn't feel like anything, unless the realisation that life was meaningless was a feeling. When, after two months, the doctor certified him unfit for further work in the field, he was offered promotion to a clerical post. He chose to make a clean break. The heat didn't help. It facilitated impetuosity. Obviously, the next twenty years wouldn't always involve sitting at a desk with the office fan turned full towards his face, but that was his first mental image. Once there, it was impossible to dislodge.

Phyllis accompanied him through the exit door. Her reasons for leaving were more nuanced. She'd just been turned down as a prospective Parliamentary Conservative candidate for the safe seat of Newbury, which, had she got it, would have involved her having to leave anyway. But once she'd felt the winds of change in her hair, she couldn't stop feeling them. Although they still hadn't scooped her up and dropped her anywhere, suddenly she had to go with them, even – especially! - into the unknown. Besides, she was in love with John, and, notwithstanding his current 'gloominess' (all she thought it was, really: she didn't believe in depression as an illness like mumps or measles), without him, Thames House would no longer be fun. And she knew others who felt the same way. Not that they mattered.

Two weeks afterwards, unaccompanied by family and friends, they married in Hampstead registry office. A vicar blessed their union in St Luke's Church, then helped them celebrate with pancakes and honey in a greasy spoon café on Archway Road. Half an hour later, on the bus back to Camden, Phyllis rang her mother. She expected a row. Weddings were meant to involve massive transfers of cash to hoteliers, caterers, luxury car-hire firms and, above all, photographers: an entire industry dedicated to ensuring that, in a world where marriage was becoming less and less of a hard threshold, those who still considered it worthwhile would begin life together in penury. So it was a battle worth fighting. And anyway, she *did* have photos, just not the conventional kinds full of people wearing Glorious Goodwood hats.

But as usual, Phyllis had radically misjudged the situation. It wasn't about her. It was about her parents. And their neighbours. More ominously, it was about 'everyone'. What would *everyone* think?

John's parents were more forgiving. They'd already been through something similar with two of their four daughters – John's eldest sisters - both of whom blamed the 'capitalist trappings' of 'traditional' marriage (which wasn't really 'traditional' at all, you understand, but solely designed to fleece the happy couple) for their opt-out. John was too apolitical to appeal to ideology, but he was on their side.

On paper, the Mordred-Robinson nuptials already looked ill-starred: they were newly unemployed, one of them had been diagnosed with a mental illness, the other was a confirmed mental illness sceptic, and they'd combined to shut out their friends and family.

Still, they'd saved some money. And, for the little it was worth, they were an attractive couple. Both in their early thirties, tall, and slim, she was a former *Vogue* model with long dark hair, a wide cheerful-looking mouth, 'perfect' teeth, a small nose, and eyes that didn't just sit dumbly in her head the way most models' supposedly did; that were capable of conveying, if she wanted them to, exactly what she was thinking and feeling. John fell well short of the fashion magazine bar. He had a shock of blond curly hair, square shoulders and a strong jawline. He was attractive to the extent that his face and gestures were honest, but not much more.

She already owned a flat. He moved in with her, and began to look for work as a translator. She got a job with Conservative Campaign Headquarters collating and interpreting data from local Tory call centres. Part-time, peanuts for a wage, but it was better than nothing, and gave her time to plan. Within a year at the most, she meant to set up in the fashion industry, where she'd worked before joining MI7. Whether in design, media, retail or running an agency, she didn't yet know. She had excellent contacts, but she couldn't afford to go wrong at the outset. Couture and its attendants were ruthless masters. Strength to strength was what they liked. Strength to stagnation was tolerable, providing you didn't stay mired for too long. Strength to weakness, or worse still, strength to failure, was permanently unforgivable. You'd have to leave town that very day with your tail between your legs, and never, ever come back.

Anyway, John could help her. He had a gift for languages. He could be her ambassador to any country in the world.

If he could just pull himself together.

But that was only a matter of time, surely.

Into this sea of change and uncertainty, came Toby Mansfield, Phyllis's ex-boyfriend, who she'd dumped three years ago.

Conservative Campaign Headquarters was situated on the ground and basement floors of 4 Matthew Parker Street, just south of St James's Park in Central London. Phyllis's job involved sitting at a desktop PC three mornings a week, and providing a written report on her findings each Friday 'on one side of A4 paper only, double-spaced'. Not difficult. There were three other workers at desks adjoining hers, doing roughly the same thing: Stan, Elizabeth and Sophie. She didn't know their surnames. They all wore chinos and had sensible hair. They didn't talk much, only to exchange pleasantries, swap stationery and ask for the occasional piece of advice. And their shifts didn't always overlap.

One Friday, just as Phyllis was finishing up for the morning, a man of about her age entered the office from the door behind her, walked past her workstation, and left by the far door. He was in the room for less than three seconds, and she only caught him from the corner of her eye, but the recognition was immediate and electric.

Toby Mansfield. Skilled rugby and polo player, public school educated tough guy, well-heeled businessman, city slicker, ladies' man, one-time male model, empty headed, libidinous, vacuous tosser. What was he doing here? Nothing to do with her, hopefully. He wouldn't have breezed through the office like that if it had been.

But yes, he would. He wouldn't want to look too eager.

Be reasonable. She was thinking fast and madly now. There might be any number of reasons he was here. He belonged to the party too, didn't he? Last time she'd heard about him, yes. He might not even know she worked here. Probably didn't.

Without even wanting to, she found herself reviewing their state of play, in case the worst came to the worst and he came over. If he was some kind of regular here, then sooner or later, he would. She might have passed under his radar today, but that probably wouldn't and couldn't last.

Their last real conversation – 'conversation' – had been their break up one. She'd found a John, she told him as tactfully as she could, and a Toby simply wouldn't satisfy her requirements any more. It took roughly half an hour for him to get the message, and she'd spent the rest of the 'conversation' acknowledging that yes, *he* was breaking up with *her*, not vice-versa. He was doing it happily, easily the best decision he'd ever made. He couldn't imagine what he'd ever seen in her.

In retrospect, her acquiescence – a hundred variations of, 'Yes, you're quite right, Toby, you're the one who's calling time here' – had probably fanned the flames. He'd wanted her to become angry, maybe even cry a bit, show the appropriate good manners.

Then, a week or two afterwards, came his futile attempts to bombard her with flowers and phone calls. Which in turn petered out after a further fortnight. They'd spoken a few times since, but nothing meaningful. He'd even blubbed once or twice.

She didn't know what he was doing with himself now. She didn't want to. Her parents naturally saw him as the biggest missed opportunity of her life.

Maybe he was. If so, it was a pretty crappy future fate had in store for her.

Perhaps she should have seen what was coming. Friday was her only shift with an official midday break. Data collection and analysis in the morning, report-writing in the afternoon until 3pm, lunch 12 till 1, usually two sandwiches and a bottle of water in the park. She would read a few fashion blogs on her phone, make one or two calls; occasionally, she would skim the *Metro* or last night's *Evening Standard*. Lots of people always milled about, but being alone meant you were usually guaranteed somewhere to sit, providing you didn't mind sharing with strangers.

When she crossed Birdcage Walk to enter St James's, he was leaning against a tree. A tall man with black well-cut hair, hollow cheeks, a small chin and penetrating brown eyes. He held a large bouquet. He pushed himself to attention, wearing an ingratiating expression, as if he hoped him discreetly blocking her path with an almighty bunch of flowers wasn't an imposition, and would she please not be angry.

"Toby," she said, coming to a stop in front of him. She relaxed. It was funny in a kooky kind of way. Depending on what he wanted, obviously.

"Phyllie." He leant forward and kissed her on each cheek. "I heard you were working at Conservative Campaign HQ. Thought I'd surprise you." He proffered the bouquet. "I hoped to take you to lunch as well, if that's not too presumptuous. I hear you're married now, so no ulterior motives, just old times' sake. Having said that, you look pretty damn hot. And don't say something lame like, 'it's the weather'. You know exactly what I mean. John, is it? I mean, your husband? We never did talk about John. Not properly. I hardly know a thing about him. Before you ask, I'm just passing through."

"How lovely to see you again." She couldn't be angry. Not really. They'd been teenage sweethearts. Why sow discord? "As for lunch, I've got sandwiches. You're welcome to join me. We can even share them, if you like."

He laughed. "*Sandwiches?*"

"Yup."

"Let's at least go to the park's coffee shop. By 'buy you lunch' I didn't necessarily mean at the Ritz, although you're welcome to eat anywhere you like, any time, with me. I've got you the afternoon off, incidentally. I'm a friend of Brandon's."

"The Conservative Party chairman?"

"That Brandon, yes."

"Wowee. Don't take this the wrong way, Toby," she said, trying to put as little confrontation into her voice as possible, "but don't you think you should have cleared that with me first? I've a report to write."

"This *is* me clearing it with you. You don't *have* to take the afternoon off. It's just there if you want it. Courtesy of me and my buddy, Brandon. Anyway, no one ever reads reports. Or you can write it later, if you really, really want to. You can feed your sandwiches to the ducks."

"What do you want? Why are you here?"

"Aha," he said. "Good question."

"What's the answer?"

"I'm a messenger."

"That normally means you're acting on behalf of someone not yourself."

"Which I am."

She sighed. As usual, he was determined to string it out. "Okay, let's go to the café. Then you've got to tell me. And you can carry the bouquet, if you don't mind. I don't want John seeing me with my ex-boyfriend and an expensive bunch of flowers."

They began to walk. "Is he the jealous type?" Toby asked. "He doesn't spy on you, does he?"

"Of course he doesn't *spy* on me!"

"Your parents are pretty cut up about your marriage, you know. I've been to see them. At their invitation, before you explode. I didn't initiate it. They don't believe you and John will last. He's got 'mental problems', apparently. I'm just going by what they told me here. I'm not saying it's true. I'm sure it isn't. But they give your marriage forty days at the outside. This isn't me talking, promise. In fact, I can help. I *want* to help. These are their words. I'm just repeating them."

She shrugged. No point in appearing riled. "They're entitled to their opinion."

"I'll continue to plead your case - "

Okay, now she was riled. She stopped and turned to face him. "I beg your pardon? *Plead my case?*"

He showed her his palms. "Sorry, I went too far. None of my business. I'm a complete idiot actually. You know me. Look, I'll get to the point, shall I?"

"Yes, please."

"How would you and John like a week's holiday in Malta, all expenses paid, full approval of Tory HQ, paid leave, all that, job still waiting for you when you get back?"

"Right."

"What do you mean, 'right'?"

"All expenses paid by who? You?"

He laughed. "What makes you think *I* could afford something like that? No, no, actually, you're right. I could. Several times over. Hardly even notice it. Sorry, I'm boasting."

"You're a complete arsehole. Have you actually listened to yourself lately?"

"I don't need to. Because I'm perfect. Joke – I'm *joking!* For God sake, Phyllie, I'm not *that* bad. I just love winding you up, that's all. Look, watch this." They'd reached the café now. By some miracle, there wasn't a queue. "One meat pie, please," he told the serving woman. "Preferably in its own little tinfoil tray. Phyllie, you're having?"

She scanned the board. "A mini asparagus quiche, please," she muttered.

"Two bottles of Pepsi Cola, a bag of chips, one meat pie, one mini asparagus quiche, and a sachet of good old tomato ketchup to go, please," he declared. "That concludes our order, my good lady. Keep the change." He handed over three ten pound notes.

"Thank *you*, sir," the serving woman said, making Phyllis despise her.

They took their food to a bench next to the lake. They had to squeeze up at one end because it was already occupied by a middle-aged couple who'd taken up residence at the seat's centre, obviously to deter others from joining them. Toby took out his phone and talked loudly about stocks and shares. After a few sour expressions, the middle-aged couple left.

Toby stopped mid-sentence and thrust his phone into his pocket. "Quick, Phyllie! To the centre! Before anyone else gets here!" He sprang to the middle and spread himself out, putting his pie and drink on his right, and patting the empty space on his left where he wanted her to sit. "Winners take all."

She laughed. She couldn't help it. He was awful, but then, so were the middle-aged couple. They'd also wanted the bench to themselves. The only difference was, they hadn't been as ruthless.

"Paradise," he said, taking a large bite of his pie. "Bloody *gristly* bloody *British* paradise. Wait till the ketchup goes on. Rapture plus one. What's your quiche like, chica?"

"Pass the tomato sauce," she told him.

He laughed. He raised a clenched fist. "Up the workers!"

She held her quiche aloft. "Long live the revolution!"

"I love you," he told her.

She swallowed a weary sigh. They sat in silence for five minutes and ate. He was nice, in a stupid, objectionable kind of way, but nothing like John. She should probably have met his 'I love you' with an 'It's not reciprocated', but what did it matter? He knew where he stood. He must do. Otherwise, he was beyond saving. And she certainly didn't need to tell *herself*. Yes, they were having fun, of a kind, but she'd far rather it was her husband sitting next to her right now.

"So who's the messenger?" she asked when they'd both finished eating.

"Aisling Baxter."

"Aisling - ?" For a surreal moment, her mind went blank.

"Baxter. Your parents told me all about it. Not that they needed to. It's common knowledge. Yes, Phyllie: *Aisling Baxter*, the woman who pipped you to the post as the next MP for Newbury. Having said that, I hear you cut quite a dash in the interview. One in the eye for Cynthia 'the crook' Cartwright. You should have got it. I'd have voted for you. But I'd also have given you a priceless piece of advice before you went in. *Be boring*. Start off boring, continue boring, and end boring. Question: how do you see yourself fitting into the constituency, Phyllis? Answer: I'll attend all the agricultural shows, Cynthia, and raise lots of money for the Rotary Club."

She clicked her tongue. "Back a bit. You're trying to tell me Aisling Baxter's prepared to pay for John and I to go on holiday? Sorry, Toby, you need to explain why that's funny. I'm not kidding. It's such a feeble stab at humour, I'm not even annoyed. I just feel vaguely sorry for you."

He scoffed. "Bitchy, bitchy!"

"Yes, keep saying stupid things. Remember, you don't have an audience. It's just me."

"I'm not - "

"If you want to raise the matter of the Newbury interview where, in fact, the best woman won – and it wasn't me – just do it. On the other hand, if you want to make fun of me, just do that. But don't try to combine the two things. You don't have the necessary brainpower for that level of multi-tasking. And it may have slipped your attention, but I don't have to take it. Unlike you, I'm an adult, and there's nothing whatsoever to tie me to you."

"Bitchy, bitchy again."

She stood up. "Bye."

"*Sorry!*" he yelled, making everyone around turn and look. "Please, honestly, I'm sorry. Sit down. I'll explain everything. Sorry, I was just annoyed because you didn't believe me. It's true. It really is Aisling Baxter. Look, get your phone out. Put it to stopwatch. Give me one minute. I'll explain everything, and if you're still not convinced, you can go. But you'll find out it's true later, because if I don't pass the message on, she'll do it in person. Then you'll see this conversation in a different light, and you'll feel sorry for me. I mean, given how utterly pathetic I am. And always was. I'm sorry."

He was apparently hyperventilating. She experienced a moment of indecision then sat down. "Go on, then," she said. "You've got a minute."

"Taylor's the travel agent in Newbury town centre. It's also got branches in Basingstoke, Wokingham and Reading. The owner, Ted Taylor, recently made a hefty donation to the Conservative Party. He's part of a consortium hoping the government will clamp down a bit more on the Trivagos and the Expedias of this world. Lost cause, if you ask me; too late in the day. Part of it's in the form of fifteen tickets for a week's holiday in Malta. Officially, it's for a fact-finding mission about internet holiday provision. But you know how these things are. Officially, they're worthy investigations. In reality, they're jollies. Of course, you've got to go through the motions to a certain extent, especially when the taxpayer's footing the bill. But that's the beauty of this one. The taxpayer isn't footing the bill. Ted Taylor of Taylor's Travel Agent is."

"Is Aisling Baxter going?"

"Definitely. Although, in her defence, she's actually taking it seriously. So is her husband. So am I. And so is my beautiful French girlfriend, Sabine. That leaves eleven spare tickets left. Nine, when we've factored you and John in."

"Sabine, eh?"

"She's *magnifique*."

"Great. And it's all expenses paid?"

"Flight, hotel, meals, everything."

"So why am I hearing this from you? Why not Aisling Baxter?"

"Long story. Aisling says you and she talked before the interview. She rather likes you, and she's wise enough to recognise that, potentially, if not actually, you're a big noise in a small constituency. In theory, you could be very useful to her. But even if you're totally embittered by what happened, and determined to block her every step of the way, you know the old saying: keep your friends close and your enemies closer. Anyway, she'll be very difficult to block. I mean, just how *do* you block the attending of agricultural shows and the raising of money for the Rotarians?"

"Let's not disparage her, please."

"No." He folded his arms. "Okay."

"And you still haven't answered my question."

"She likes you, she needs you, yet she's a bit scared of you. But I'm not. And I'm Newbury born and bred too. A good many local people, truly wonderful people actually, remember the *item* that was you and I with affection, and, touchingly, they think I've still got a lot of influence with you. Damn my aching heart, I've done nothing to discourage that notion. So I was their natural choice for goodwill ambassador to Phyllis – *Mordred*, is it now?"

"That's how I'm writing it now, yes. It's way, way more interesting than Robinson. So what if I accept? When will this holiday be?"

"No time like the present."

"Meaning?"

"Tomorrow afternoon."

"And I've been given a week off work?"

"Don't take this the wrong way, Phyllie, but your work's not very important. You're hugely talented. You should be doing something more with yourself."

"Yes or no?"

"I've spoken to Brandon. He says yes, absolutely, go for it. If you want to."

"So… what's the catch?"

"*Nada.*"

"Really?" She laughed. "Sorry if that sounds cynical."

He frowned. "What sort of 'catch' do you have in mind? Spell out your worst fears."

"Okay, are my parents coming?"

"Not if you don't want them to. Consider them barred."

"Will John and I be left alone?"

"You don't have to spend *any* time with *any*one else in the party if you don't want to. Look, here are some other catches you may not have considered. Let's cross them off the list. Will John and you be sharing a room with anyone? No. Have Toby and Sabine got the room directly above yours and will you hear the bedsprings going all night? No. Do you have to eat at the same table as everyone else? No. Is it a one, two, three or four star hotel? None of the above. It's a five star hotel. What's the weather forecast like? Sunny. All week? Yes. Is it the real Malta, or just a pretend version, located in an industrial estate just outside Milton Keynes? It's the real one. Are buckets and spades provided? I don't know and I don't care. Will you be travelling first class? Yes. Will Toby take the slightest interest in your beach body? No, I've got Sabine. Okay, scratch that. Yes, I'm only human. Will Toby make a nuisance of himself, like he has in the park today? No. Will Toby belittle John, or interfere with John's marriage in any way, shape or form? No. Toby will be invisible, except, hopefully, to Sabine."

"Er, what does Toby get out of inviting John and Phyllis then?"

"This conversation, today. And the knowledge that I've done something nice for you. And that when the forty days are over and you're alone again, naturally, you might need a big, manly shoulder to cry on."

"I see, yes. So much the worse for poor Sabine then."

"She'll survive. It's a gamble, in other words. That your parents are right. I hope they're not, but they might be. And remember: this is for you and John. As a couple. From me. I'll keep one hundred per cent out of the way. I both hope you make it and hope you don't. I'm a psychological mess."

"I must say, a holiday sounds very appealing. I'll talk to John about it when I get in. Supposing he says yes, though? Where do we pick up the tickets?"

"Do you think he *will* say yes? I mean, your parents said 'mentally ill'. I don't mean to pry, but there's no smoke without fire. I don't want you building your hopes up."

She laughed. "Oh yes you do. Our entire conversation has been you building my hopes up. And no, he's not 'mentally ill'. He's a bit depressed, that's all."

"Text me either way. If it's a yes, I'll get in touch with Aisling and she'll call you. Then Ted'll call you. Then it's full steam ahead. You can pick up the tickets at the airport tomorrow. That simple. Don't forget your flowers, by the way."

"I'll use them to brighten up the office a bit. I'd better be getting back to work now. I know it's not much of a job, but I don't like leaving loose ends."

They stood up. "Till the next time, then," he said.

"Toby?" she said, turning back to him as she was walking away.

He shot her an inquiring look.

"Thank you. John and I could do with a holiday."

She immediately regretted her words. She should at least have said, 'honeymoon'.

He smiled and nodded knowingly, as if discerning an underlying meaning.

Chapter 3: The Magic Cure

John Mordred sat at a table with a Hungarian novel in front of him and an unopened *Angol-Magyar Szotar* in two volumes. Dictionaries were a bit like condiments. You always thought you wouldn't really need one, but as soon as you put one out, it demanded to be used.

Phyllis's living room – he hadn't yet begun thinking of it as *theirs* – was twice as long as it was wide, with a dining table next to a window that looked out onto a well-tended communal garden. The sofa and armchairs were minimalist, discreet and compact in muted colours. On the windowsill, and dotted on flat surfaces all around the room, were twenty-three cards from family and friends congratulating them on their wedding. All well-intentioned but meaningless.

He looked at the clock. 3.30pm. Phyllis would be in soon. He looked into his head. How depressed was he, on a scale of one to ten? Would she notice? How could he stop her noticing? Did it matter?

Of course it did. They loved each other.

He put his elbows on the table and his palms over his eyes. What was even making him 'depressed', really? The lethargy - was that a cause or an effect?

Breaking out of the mire was about getting a purpose. Yet how could you when you knew that all purposes were phoney? That nothing was worth the effort? All the world's books and music and TV and people and places and food and drink and days, weeks, months, years – they were all the same. Nothing to get excited about anywhere. He certainly wasn't making a difference. Because he *couldn't*. No one could.

He was probably dragging Phyllis down. Ideally, he'd crawl away somewhere and lie prone, and do nothing for the rest of his life.

The strange thing was, while he definitely didn't feel happy, neither did he feel particularly *un*happy. He certainly didn't feel sorry for himself. He had no thoughts of suicide. He simply felt jaded. Like he'd seen everything a thousand times too often, and there was nothing more the world could offer him.

Looked at disinterestedly, it was a mood, that's all. It would pass. He just had to give it time. In the interim, no medication. Just a healthy lifestyle. A walk in the morning, meditation after lunch, a bit of translation, shopping, cooking in the evening, a routine. It was just unfortunate that he'd become 'ill' now. Right at the beginning of his married life.

Mind you, Phyllis might not have proposed otherwise. There was definitely a sense in which she felt sorry for him, even with her 1900s approach to the problem: cold showers, regular bedtimes and cod liver oil. She'd cancelled his subscription to *Private Eye*, assuring him, plausibly, that any effective treatment for depression had to involve not continually reading about the hideousness of the world on their doorstep. Hopefully, she wouldn't leave him when / if he got better.

And anyway, wasn't everyone depressed right now? The world had gone to pieces. The internet had created an army of trolls. For a while they'd contented themselves with merely making nasty comments online, but then they'd somehow combined, and now they'd grabbed power just about everywhere. Once the genie was out of the bottle, there was no putting it back. The future didn't look great anywhere at all. Even the world's oceans were full of rubbish.

He wished he'd been a physicist instead of a spy. Humankind's only hope, when you thought about it: colonising the solar system. Putting intelligent, sensitive people up there, and leaving all the trolls behind on Earth, which they'd probably proceed to blow up.

But that wouldn't happen in his lifetime.

Still, it might one day. The thought cheered him up a bit. Not the world being blown up. Just the extra-terrestrial colonies.

And there was God, that was a source of comfort. Although what God was doing was a complete mystery. Actually, a lot of the trolls were die-hard God-fans.

At least everyone was going to die in the end. That was a good thing. Maybe orthodox Christianity was right and you'd have to account for your behaviour. That would also be good. Unless you had to account for something stupid, like why you hadn't been a Roman Catholic or a Mormon. If you had to explain why you'd been a venomous ball of scum, making the world worse for everyone else to live in, that'd be just super.

He realised, not for the first time since leaving MI7, that he was talking aloud to himself. He could hear Doctor Chakladar saying, 'That's right, John, let it out. It's called the talking cure. It'll do you good. Don't bottle it up. You're angry.'

He sighed.

He heard the door open. Phyllis. She came into the living room. They put their arms round each other and kissed.

She laughed. "Were you talking to yourself again? And don't deny it. I overheard."

"I'm afraid so."

"Saying what? Come on, sharing's part of the cure."

"I don't know. But I did have one clear thought. About how, what I'd like more than anything else is for us to get in a rocket, right now, both of us, and leave this planet behind for ever and join a colony of nice fellow earthlings – people like William Shatner, Louis Theroux and Nadiya Hussein, maybe – at the far reaches of the solar system. In a purpose-built space station."

For some reason, his eyes got wet while he was speaking. His voice became wobbly.

"What about our parents?" she said.

"Yes, I suppose they'd have to come. And Ruby Parker, and Annabel, Alec and Edna, and all the other people at MI7 who we'll probably never see again. You're right. When you start to think about it, it's unworkable."

They sat down on the sofa.

"No it isn't," she said. "Not in principle. It's just a bit more complex than you thought. Anyway, you'll never guess who I saw at work today."

"Theresa May."

"No one from the Conservative Party. Well, that's not strictly true, but no one famous."

"Someone I know?"

"You've never met him. I don't know what I'm even asking you for. You'll never get it. Toby. Toby Mansfield. My ex-boy-friend. He was waiting for me outside St James's Park with a big bouquet of flowers. We had lunch together. Sorry, I realise this isn't sounding good, but I haven't finished. He's under absolutely no illusions about us: I love you, you love me, and that's the end of it. But he'd been sent on an errand by Aisling Baxter – the next Conservative MP for Newbury, the woman who slew me in the interview that day – and Aisling's got fifteen tickets to an all-ex-penses paid holiday in Malta. We're invited. Toby's going, but we won't see him. We can spend all day, every day in the hotel room, if you like."

"Where did Aisling Baxter get fifteen tickets for Malta from?"

"A big Tory donor. And yes, I know it sounds very *Private Eye*-ish, but look at it like this: you and I can have no conceivable impact on government policy, and if we go, we're stopping some-body else going, who maybe could. Probably some trough-snuffler."

"So the taxpayer's not paying?"

"No, that's the great thing!"

"Okay, when do we leave?"

She turned to look at him. "What? You're *okay* with it?"

"Unless you're going to run off with Toby. But if that was going to happen, it'd have happened today. Has Toby got a girl-friend?"

"Sabine, she's called. French. I haven't met her."

"Repeat: when do we leave?"

She threw her arms round him. "I love you, John. I'm so glad you're not the stupid, jealous type. We depart tomorrow after-noon."

"What did you do with the bouquet? Just out of interest?"

"I used it to embellish the office. Sorry, I draw the line at bringing Toby's flowers into our flat in any case. But it would be pointless bringing *any* bouquet home, even one from you, if we're going away. Imagine coming back to a roomful of dead flowers."

"Well, I would, but the doctor advised me against it."

She held him at arm's length. "Hang on, did you just crack a joke?"

"I – I think so."

"OH MY GOD! YOU'RE CURED!" Her phone began to ring. "That'll be Ted or Toby or Aisling. Sorry, I've got to answer. You're out of the woods now. Look after yourself."

Chapter 4: Angelo's Party

Fomm ir-Riħ, Malta

In a spacious first floor lounge dotted with antiques on display stands and hung with abstract paintings, twenty men and women, Maltese, Azerbaijani, British and Russian, all dressed in formal evening wear, mingled amiably, drank sparkling wine and ate canapes. A pair of French doors leading onto a broad patio framed a perfect Mediterranean sunset. Chamber music played. Four waiters slalomed discreetly between conversational groups, attempting the impossible: remaining invisible whilst fielding queries about where the toilets were, or asking, 'Can I offer you a refill?' or 'Would you like a savoury profiterole?', and occasionally saying, 'Allow me', in a cheerful, indulgent tone, when anyone spilled or mislaid anything. The waiters were all in their early twenties: two women, two men. The guests were also equally divided by sex, but, with the exception of four elderly men huddled in a conspiratorial group outside, they were middle-aged, expensively attired and vaguely attractive in the peculiar, easily detectable way that only significant wealth, with its known capacity to rectify physical defects, can achieve.

The host, Angelo Bonnici, was seventy-six. Bald, perpetually smiling, straight-backed and unusually tall and thin for his age, he wore an old-fashioned smoking jacket and carried a silver-tipped cane. Like the waiters, but not so obviously or ingratiatingly, he moved from guest to guest on a seemingly everlasting quest to discover if everything was satisfactory.

The answer: it both was and wasn't. In one sense, there was nothing he could do to make it any better: the company, the setting, the outstanding ocean view, the food and the drink were all perfect. What wasn't perfect was the Sword of Damocles hanging over everyone's head.

He'd invited them here to assuage their anxieties in the general way he alone knew how. They, in turn, had faith in his ability to 'fix matters'. Over the course of his life, he'd proved an expert at standing on a stepladder and cutting Swords of Damocles down with stainless steel shears. He probably had a whole collection in his basement, all long forgotten and gathering dust. No one needed to know the details of what he intended, and certainly not that, in a moment, he'd repair to his study for an interview with a hired thug called Marchus Grubfeld. They simply needed reassuring that he took the matter seriously.

Eventually, he stopped to talk to two of his oldest friends, the London solicitors, Dina Oforka-Jones and Ian Batchelor. A slim ex-fashion model with straightened hair, cut into a bob, and a grey-haired man with a long face.

"I've been talking to a few acquaintances," Dina said. "I thought we had nothing to worry about. Until now."

"Before the unexpected addition to the 'landing party'," Ian said ominously.

Angelo smiled. "We're already ahead of them. I'm not sure what they're looking for, but the British government must think it's worth the effort. You don't add a couple of top spies to your jolly little 'fact-finding' excursion unless you're fairly confident of bringing home some sort of major prize."

Dina shuddered. She looked past Angelo and out to the sea.

Angelo beckoned one of the waiters over. "Miriam, could you ask Claudette to close the French doors a little? It's beginning to get chilly." He turned back to Dina. "You're worried."

"I love my life here," she replied emotionally. "Everything about it. I couldn't bear for it all to come tumbling down."

Angelo laughed. "They're looking in entirely the wrong place. The mere fact that they've sent spies in shows they know they can't get what they want through the normal channels. And what are spies going to find? Unless they can access written records, which they can't, or they're prepared to engage in a spot of burglary, which they won't be - "

"How do you know they won't be?" Ian asked. "Sorry, I didn't mean that to sound brusque."

Angelo laid a forgiving hand on his arm. "Think, Ian. Think about it. If they were going to burgle anyone – and how would they know who, what or even *where* to burgle? *I* wouldn't! – they'd have arrived by dead of night, on a fishing boat, dressed in black. They wouldn't join the sort of outing that was actually here to ask questions. They've put themselves in the middle of a group of people that everyone's going to cold-shoulder!"

"Which begs the question, why?" Dina said. "There must be something we're missing."

"It doesn't pay to underestimate your opponent," Ian added. "Angelo, you've just pointed out that what they're doing is, on the face of it, completely stupid. But we know they're *not* completely stupid. So the question arises, what are we missing? Because we must be missing something!"

"Keep your voice down, Ian," Dina said irritably. "This is a party. And Angelo's our host. You're being rude."

"Sorry, Angelo, sorry again," Ian said. "I'm nervous, that's all. I'm getting too old. I should have sent one of the junior partners along."

"Not at all," Angelo said, although a little less gracefully this time. "You're asking why they're here, Ian. It's only what everyone else here tonight is asking. And let me say, you're not the jumpiest person in the room." He paused for a smile, as if to slow the tempo. "Why they've decided to come ashore as part of a very obvious *prying team*? The answer is surely clear. This is the *advance* landing party. If they find anything, others will follow. If they don't, they won't. From what I understand, it's very much the group leader's idea: Aisling Baker?"

"Baxter," Dina said.

"Her personal crusade," Angelo said. "The British government is probably tagging along because it's free, and money's tight in the UK nowadays. All we have to do is make sure it's a disaster from start to finish, and, if necessary, remove her from the equation."

"What do you mean by that?" Dina said. "I hope you're not suggesting - "

"More than a mere scare," Angelo interrupted. "An accident of some kind. Not fatal by any means. Just enough to make her want to go home. And not come back."

"I don't see why that should be necessary," Ian said. "We've already said she can only make progress by accessing written records of the type that are under lock and key."

"I didn't quite say that, Ian," Angelo replied. "I said that's what *spies* would need to do. An ordinary woman, going around the countryside asking questions, might well turn up enough to make a return visit worth her while. *In her view.*"

"It's subjective, Ian," Dina said. "It's how Aisling Baxter *sees* the whole thing. And there are always some local people willing to talk. Even when they're spouting rubbish, it can still have a profound effect on an impressionable mind."

"Of course, if Aisling Baxter gets hurt and has to go home," Angelo went on, "I can't see the rest of the party picking her truth-seeking beacon up. They'll either follow her back to England post haste, or knuckle down and enjoy the free holiday: sunbathing, fine dining, day trips to Valletta and Mdina. Even the two spies. Spies are only human after all."

"I hope so," Dina said.

"We've got one huge advantage," Angelo said. "They don't know we know they're coming. They don't know we've got measures in place to frustrate them."

A waiter stopped in front of them. "You asked me to remind you about your guest, Mr Bonnici," she said.

"Thank you, Marama," Angelo said. He turned to Dina and Ian. "I hope you'll excuse me? It's been so lovely to see you both again. I'll be in London next week. I'll look you up and hope you're not too busy."

"We're never too busy for you," Dina said.

Angelo smiled and bowed slightly from the neck. Marama was already holding the door, a few metres away on the far side of the room.

Dina watched him stride away and disappear from view. Then she swept her eyes about to check no one else was within earshot.

"Much as I love Angelo," she told Ian quietly, "I'm not sure we can rely on him a hundred per cent. He's getting old. I've made a few arrangements of my own."

Ian's eyes widened. He didn't look pleased. "What do you mean?"

"I've arranged to have the excursion's rooms bugged."

"Wh – What? Are you *mad?*"

"Keep your *voice* down, Ian! I've told you that once tonight already! I haven't bugged all of them, just the chief players: the Baxters, the Taylors, the spies. A private security firm I hired. Horvath. We get the tapes. They won't even look at them, scouts' honour."

"But the victims are professionals! At least, the MI6 agents are! They'll do a sweep of the room as soon as they get in. What the hell were you *thinking?*"

"Oh, do be quiet, Ian. It'll be good to put the cat among the pigeons, anyway. Spook the spooks a little. It can't do any harm, and it may well do a lot of good."

Marchus Grubfeld walked briskly across country and arrived at Angelo Bonnici's villa twenty-five minutes before the party began. For just under half an hour, he hid in a copse by the entrance and clandestinely photographed the arriving guests. He recognised two Azerbaijani oligarchs, a Russian politician and a middle-aged Maltese actress. The remaining faces were unfamiliar. Not that it mattered. He could look them up later, if need be.

This particular contract was his big chance to become an influencer. He'd learned the hard way that, to rise to the top, brawn wasn't sufficient, nor courage, nor any amount of killing. Rather, it required a meticulous plan and lorry load of information about specific individuals, including which locations they'd visited, when, and in whose company. Right now, he was optimistic. Armed with detached forethought, incontrovertible intel and his natural adaptability, he could conceivably progress to some sort of operational inner circle somewhere. Alternatively, if things went wrong, a selection of the right sort of photographs might enable him to transform an uncomfortable police interview into something more congenial.

In any case, he didn't like to be late for appointments. He liked to be welcomed grudgingly as someone whose allotted time-slot was still some way off, so he could be shown to an out-of-the-way room where he could sit alone and methodically assess his surroundings.

He knocked at the big oak front door and gave his latest name to the greeter, a woman about ten years his junior with tied up brown hair, a long neck and a tray of snacks. She looked bemused, asked him to please wait while she checked the guest list, and returned thirty seconds later with a compensatory huge smile.

"Mr Bonnici asked if you'd be so kind as to wait in the study," she said cheerfully. "Follow me."

Grubfeld had dark curly hair, a thin coating of stubble and a cream suit. His small eyes underneath brooding brows, thin mouth and heavy build all gave him the look of a stereotypical bad guy. Light coloured clothing was meant to mitigate that, and he wore it when he was trying to create a favourable impression.

But such an impression wasn't for his host. Bonnici already knew about him, or thought he did. It was for whoever answered the door, and any guests that might inadvertently stray into wherever his host chose to put him, thinking it was the rest room, or somewhere to talk or behave privately.

The greeter led him to a small room lined on three sides with bookshelves. Two armchairs stood either side of a window whose heavy grey curtains had been drawn. An antique desk and matching chair were the only other articles of furniture.

"Mr Bonnici will be along in about ten minutes," she said. "Can I get you a drink or something to eat?"

He shook his head. She closed the door on her way out without turning her back on him.

He sat on the chair farthest from the door. He wanted to get a good look at his host as he came in. He was interested to find out, as he sometimes could just by looking, how it would feel to kill him.

Because Bonnici wasn't the only one paying out, although he probably thought he was. The Kremlin was stumping up most of the cash. The Azerbaijanis had contributed about a fifth. Grubfeld's opportunity lay in driving a wedge between the two state entities on the one hand, and the private investor on the other, then eliminating the latter. Bonnici was definitely the dispensable party, for all his posturing. Typical of his type, really. People like him always had ideas way above their station.

According to what the Russians had told him, there were a couple of spies in the English party. They'd have to be killed, but not yet. Not for several weeks. The good thing about this job was that, right now, everyone involved was on board with that.

Angelo Bonnici left his guests in each other's company and walked alone along four corridors to his study on the opposite side of the house. He let himself in and closed the door behind him.

A man sat slumped in one of the armchairs, looking like a mafia chauffeur or a gigolo. He didn't stand up when his host entered, nor did he extend a greeting. Rather, he regarded him as if he were a dog who'd pushed the door open with its muzzle and was coming in for a stroke.

"Marchus, yes?" was all Angelo said. No point in making small talk. "Come over to the desk," he said in response to his guest's nod.

"I've been briefed by the Russians," Grubfeld said, but he got up anyway. "I need it from you too, though."

Angelo unlocked the desk. He took six photographs out from the top drawer and laid them side by side on the leather surface. "Aisling Baxter, Robert Baxter her husband, Phyllis Mordred, John Mordred her husband, Millicent Taylor, Ted Taylor her husband. These are your concern."

"Which are the spies?" Grubfeld said.

"These two."

"And you want me to dispatch all six?"

"Over a long period of time," Angelo said. "So that no one will think of them as a group that's being killed off. By 'long', I mean *long*. Up to a year. In as many different places as possible. And as 'accidentally' as possible. We don't want any of these deaths to look like murders. I suppose that goes without saying."

"Pretty much," Grubfeld replied. "Right now, I need payment."

Angelo reached into the bottom drawer of the desk and took out a small rucksack. "It's all in there," he said. He could feel himself sweating now. Always the same when it came to the money, because that's when they were most likely to turn on you. They didn't always want the second or third instalment, and they weren't always the consummate professionals they made themselves out to be.

But that wouldn't happen this time. One of the chief benefits of a shared contract was its joint enforcement. The best kind of insurance. However high Grubfeld's opinion of himself – and some of these types had ideas way above their station, infantile fantasies about turning the tables on their masters - he'd know he couldn't outrun the Russian GRU, not to mention the State Security Service of the Republic of Azerbaijan.

Comfortingly, his gait was wholly consistent with that awareness. Sullen. He slunk out and his footsteps gradually faded.

Angelo immediately forgot about him. The enormity of what had just transpired hit him for the first time. He sat down at the desk and put his head in his hands. He'd just killed six people. Including collateral, maybe even more.

Never easy, however often you did it. And never pleasant.

He'd have nightmares tonight, as he always did after this sort of meeting.

Chapter 5: Cameras, etc.

Phyllis and John arrived at Gatwick at 3pm, made their flight just over an hour later, and cleared Malta International Airport customs just after 8pm local time. They met none of Ted Taylor's other guests, nor saw sign of them. Somehow, that felt spooky, even though Aisling Baxter, when Phyllis had spoken to her the night before, had assured them they'd be left completely alone if that was what they wanted. "It would be lovely if we could meet *sometime*," she said, "but I know you've just got married, so it'll probably be really romantic for you – hopefully! fingers crossed! - and you won't want all sorts of boring schedules to obey. Enjoy!"

After the plane's air conditioning, the heat outside was like walking into a ship's engine room, but not much worse than in England right now. Ted Taylor had laid on a taxi direct to their hotel. The room was on the seventh floor of the Dolce Christie in Marsaskala. A view of St Thomas Bay, a double bed, polished oak furniture, a pastel blue deep-pile carpet and an *en suite* with a Jacuzzi. On the coffee table, a bottle of champagne in a silver ice bucket. The bell boy helped them in with their suitcases. Phyllis had no idea what counted as a generous tip here. She gave him ten euros.

"Do you want to go in the shower first, or shall I?" she asked, when they were alone.

They combined sex and the Jacuzzi, then got changed. Somehow, they took it for granted they'd be going out tonight. Whatever Aisling Baxter had said, good manners required that they make themselves known personally to Ted Taylor and his guests. The earlier they did so, the sooner it'd be out of the way.

"We should probably try the hotel lounge first," Phyllis said, when she was drying her hair. "Although, Aisling and Toby apart, I've no idea how we'll spot anyone. I don't even know what Ted

Taylor looks like. I imagine him being a bit like Swiss Toni in *The Fast Show*. Remember that? What are you doing?"

He was looking under the coffee table. He'd already run his fingertips along the inside rim of the wardrobe.

In fact, what he was doing was obvious.

"This is a holiday," she told him. "And we're not spies anymore."

"Sssh!" he replied.

She suddenly realised he was right, like waking up from a pleasant dream. Why hadn't she seen it earlier? Clearly, he hadn't either, not right away, but at least he'd adjusted now. Once a spy, always a spy, and, God help them, Toby probably wasn't beyond setting up some kind of webcam. She joined the search.

He prised something from behind the TV cabinet and held it up with a solemn expression. A microphone.

Her heart plummeted. She nodded an acknowledgement and resumed the hunt.

She quickly discovered another microphone under the bed, and a camera hidden on top of one of the picture frames. Suddenly, they were in the middle of a nightmare.

She turned to John. Time for a serious discussion.

But John didn't look well. He stood in the bathroom doorway, hands limply by his sides. The colour seemed to have drained from his face.

"What's the matter?" she asked, despite herself. Not the kind of remark you were supposed to make in these sorts of circumstances: you should pretend everything was okay, for the sake of the microphones. But there were cameras too. Whoever was on the other end would already know they'd twigged.

He took her hand and led her into the bathroom. Above the sink, an accessory shelf; then, a mirror; then, an ornamental ledge with a cascading plant in a ceramic pot.

And in the middle of the pot, partly disguised by the foliage, and looking from afar like a decorative jewel, a miniature camera of the same type she'd discovered in the bedroom.

She saw it in three stages: firstly, that it was a camera; secondly, that it was pointed at the Jacuzzi; thirdly, in the role it was destined to play in her future.

She would become one of those people who has a sex tape on the internet.

She might already have joined their ranks, actually. The MP4 might be playing and re-playing, all over the world, right this very moment. Ex-*Vogue* and *Vanity Fair* model, Phyllis Robinson, surprise porno queen of the year, who'd have thought it? How the mighty are -

She rarely panicked, but for a moment, she couldn't breathe. It didn't matter that she was married, and that this was her husband. Sex tapes didn't come in grades of respectability. In any shape or form, they were normality-wreckers. You might not care – you might even welcome it - if you wanted to be a celebrity, but she didn't. All she'd ever wanted was to be taken seriously. She'd taken it for granted that she was, and would always be. Now this.

Her parents – what would they say? And – *everyone*.

She knew what that word meant now. How final it was.

She suddenly heard herself. Like John recently, she was speaking aloud without realising. She was saying *Oh God* over and over again.

John stood on a chair. He removed the camera and put it on the accessory shelf.

"You call the British embassy," he said. "I'll call the police, then the hotel manager. You need to get in touch with Aisling Baxter." He clutched her to him. "Come on, come on. Calm down now. We can deal with this. Don't cry."

Weird, weird feeling: right now, she actually *hoped* it was Toby. She'd literally murder him, but it might just – *just* be containable.

The British High Commission was eight miles away in Ta' Xbiex. John had second thoughts about making the police his first phone call. He rang Ruby Parker in London on the secure line he thought he'd never need again. She had two agents in Rome, she said. They could be in Valletta in two hours. "Don't tell the police," she went on. "Not yet. I'll get the High Commissioner out of bed. You go over there. If you're in your hotel room, you're vulnerable." When she'd hung up, he felt stupid, but that was what he'd expected.

He and Phyllis strolled casually out of the hotel, walked several blocks in case someone was waiting for them, and got into as random a taxi as they could. They sat on the back seat feeling bombed out. The driver didn't speak. On the darkened, bumpy roads, they had a feeling of not being entirely safe. He put his arm round Phyllis. She'd stopped crying now. She was in shock. But she'd come round. She was trained to cope.

The truth was, he hadn't thought he and Phyllis were important enough to be targeted by surveillance operatives any more. Who sets up recording equipment for two ex-spies on an innocent holiday abroad?

One answer: it wasn't widely realised that they *were* ex-spies. Someone believed they were here on behalf on The Realm.

Another possible answer: internet travel firms who didn't want the likes of Ted Taylor taking them down.

The best answer by far, however: Toby Mansfield.

If he could find out where Toby was staying, he could probably put things right straight away.

But who was he kidding? If Toby had been filming them, he'd know they were on to him. He'd have stashed the evidence by now.

But as a solution, Toby didn't really make sense. If he'd wanted a sex tape of Phyllis, there were any number of ways he could have duped her before now. He'd probably at least have broached it with her at some point, pre-John.

And he was here with 'Sabine', whoever she was. How did Sabine fit into this?

Well, she might be a made-up person.

And when would Toby have installed all the equipment? He'd been in London yesterday. The room hadn't become available till this afternoon.

Still, several hours. That was enough time.

What was he hoping to get? Maybe just a few shots of Phyllis naked. He couldn't have known they'd have sex in the Jacuzzi.

Maybe he realised he'd gone too far then. He must know they knew. Presumably, he'd also seen how upset she was. He probably – maybe, possibly – felt guilty. He couldn't be *that* bad. He might actually be erasing everything, right now, in a fit of contrition.

But of course, it might not be him. It could be anyone, come to think of it.

Aisling Baxter wasn't entirely beyond suspicion. She'd pipped Phyllis to the post in the interview, but this might be her way of ensuring there'd be no comeback.

Or MI7. Not Ruby Parker. But Blue or Grey departments, they probably had it in them. Years in the future: "We hear you're going to Moscow for a fashion show, John. There's something we'd like you to pick up for us while you're over there. Because remember that video file of you and your wife? It'd be a terrible shame if it ended up in the wrong hands. Phyllis is doing so very well for herself lately, and it's so awfully vulgar."

An entire roomful of suspects. *Murder on the Orient Express.* But without a killing.

The taxi pulled up in front of a long Edwardian-type building with bay windows fronting a marina. Phyllis paid, watched the car drive away and got on the phone. "Yes, Aisling, it's me. We're in Marsaskala now. Or rather, we're not. We're in Ta' Xbiex on our way into the British High Commission… There were hidden microphones and cameras in our room… That's right… Yes, that's right. Horrible… *Look* like? You'll know them when you see them… John spotted one by chance. You know his oldest sister's Hannah Lexingwood? The press are always bugging her hotel rooms, wherever she goes… Yes, he's got a bit of an eye for them… No, I'm pretty certain he's not mistaken. It wasn't just one, either… No, don't apologise. It's certainly not your fault. I'd better get off. I'm going to ring Toby. Call me back if you find anything. And if you do, the official advice is, get over here before you do anything. They'd like some of their experts to check it over before we get the police involved."

She hung up and linked arms with John. "She doesn't believe me. She thinks I'm crazy. I'm going to ring Toby now. I'm going to put it on speakerphone. I want you to tell me whether he's lying. It is one of your supposed talents, after all."

"I was hoping you'd ask."

"If he is responsible, he'll have seen us looking for the cameras and microphones. He'll know he's been rumbled. So he'll have rehearsed sounding shocked and indignant. Do you think you'll be able to see past that?"

"Absolutely."

"Okay, here goes." She pressed 'call'.

"Hello? Phyllis?" Toby said.

"How are you?" Phyllis asked.

"Not great, but at least we got here. Bloody two hour delay. Listen, I was hoping we might meet up sometime, you and me and the big 'J' and Sabine, but I think Sabine and I are just going to crash tonight. Two hours! Are you in Malta yet? Don't tell me you're ringing to cry off. Where are you?"

"Ta' Xbiex."

"Come again?"

"*Ta' Xbiex*. It's where the British High Commission is."

"Right. So what are you doing there? Is everything okay?"

"Not really. Our room was bugged."

"*Bugged?* Er, what do you mean? With *microphones?*"

"And cameras."

Pause. He gave an incredulous scoff. "Sorry, have you taken something? Say that again. *Your room was bugged, with microphones? Are you sure?*"

"I'm stone cold sober. And I wish to God I was mistaken."

"Have you told Aisling, or Ted Taylor?"

"I've just got off the phone to Aisling. Ted Taylor's next on my list of people to speak to."

"Who the hell would bug your room with microphones and cameras? Oh my God, it's obvious, yes. Someone who knows who you are. Like, who knows you're the ex-fashion model. I mean, you *were* pretty damn big in your time. Not Kate Moss or Cara Delevingne big – though I suppose you could have been: you're attractive enough – but famous enough for someone to want to film you, make a quick heap of cash on the dark web. Good job you spotted it in time. Shit, have you told the police, though? What a downer. Are you okay?"

"I'm coping. We're probably going to be flying back to Britain tomorrow. I'm only telling you because you need to check your own room when you get in."

"What do they look like, these microphones?"

"Just pretend you're in a spy film. Look under surfaces. You'll know if you find one."

"I'll look, but I don't expect to find anything. I'm obscure and so is Sabine. Although I suppose it could be the internet travel companies, listening to find out what we're up to. Bit of industrial espionage. Seems unlikely, though, in comparison with the perv-with-an-eye-on-the-main-chance possibility. Thanks for the heads up. Anything I can do to help?"

"You could ring Ted Taylor for me."

"Consider it done. God, I'm sorry. I wish I hadn't asked you over here now. There's some bloody slimy bastards in the world."

She hung up.

"He's not lying," John told her. "And I'm pretty sure he's at the airport. You could hear the tannoy announcements in the background."

Her phone began to ring. She picked it up without looking at the screen or switching speakerphone off.

"Aisling here," came the voice. She didn't sound as assured as last time. In fact, she sounded like she might be crying. "There's

– you were right. Oh, my God. You were right. The room's full of tiny bits of recording equipment. I'm in a taxi with Robert. You did say not to call the police, Phyllis, didn't you? That's what you were told, yes. Oh, my God. My God, this is the end. I've made the biggest mistake of my life."

She hung up.

Chapter 6: The Wisdom of Toby

The High Commissioner, Harold Finch, was in his late forties with brown gelled hair, a flat nose and a blazer. He stood in the doorway of the High Commission, waiting to greet John and Phyllis in person. His staff had been called in at short notice and the building was as much a blaze of lights and activity as it probably ever became.

"There's been nothing remotely like this before in all my time here," he said, as he led them upstairs. "Nor, I'm pretty certain, any of my predecessors'. I've sent a member of staff over to your hotel room to keep an eye on it till the investigators get in from Rome. I understand that should be two hours. Unfortunately, you're not alone. I've just heard from two other members of your party: a Ms Baxter? And a Mr Taylor? How many are in the group in all?"

"I was told fifteen," Phyllis said. "But I'm not in charge. Mr Taylor is. I don't even know him personally."

"We'll discuss it together when the others get here. I was given strict instructions not to call the police. Yet. *Let us take care of it*, London said. Meaning them, that is, not us. High level security, apparently. Sounds like something from *The Osterman Weekend*, the way they're treating it, but that's probably just me. In the meantime, you can stay here. If you need to sleep, we can put out some Z beds and get you some blankets. How about a pot of tea in the meantime, and some courgette cake?"

A man of about Mordred's age bounded up the stairs after them. "Excuse me, Mr Finch," he said, "there's another call from a member of the same party. A 'Mr Mansfield'. Identical complaint. Shall I tell him to make his way over here too?"

"Asap," Finch replied. "And send someone to his room to make sure it isn't compromised while we're waiting. Get a guest list from Mr Taylor as soon as he arrives. My God, this has all the makings of a major national scandal. It's going to be a long night by the look of things."

Finch showed them into a high-ceilinged room lined with book-cases and furnished in the style of a country house seventy years ago: deep red carpet, overstuffed large armchairs and a variety of low tables, some topped with plants, others with magazines and books. An air-conditioning fan on the ceiling whirred lethargic-ally.

After ten minutes, Aisling Baxter and her husband arrived. A thin woman in her late thirties with long hair and an outdoors-y face, she looked to be about ten years younger and several stones lighter than her husband, whose pot belly and double chin made him appear doubly defeated. Cursory introductions were effected, then both couples sat down in silence, on opposite sides of the room.

Ten minutes later, Ted Taylor entered with his wife. He had a huge white bouffant, a white moustache, large ears and a walking stick. His wife, Millie, had a side pony, lots of make-up, and a floaty pink dress. She was at least half his age. Ted apolo-gised profusely to everyone for five minutes, then sat down and looked at his feet. The only sound in the room again was the fan.

Then, as if it was a show where the cast of a murder mystery night had been told to enter at regular intervals and give the audi-ence time to adjust, Toby came in with Sabine. She was tall and thin and grinned a lot. She wore a T-shirt with 'I love Australia' on, denim shorts and flip-flops. She was definitely the youngest person in the room, probably in her early twenties.

"Pleased to meet you, man," he told John, pulling him close as he shook his hand and patting his back. "Take care of my ex. So what's the news?" he asked the room. "Anyone heard whether the investigator guys have arrived yet?"

Everyone looked at each other but no one replied.

"We haven't heard," Phyllis muttered eventually.

Toby looked as if he couldn't quite figure out what was going on. Then as if he'd just realised.

"This is only a guess, yeah?" she said. "But did you guys - ? I mean, was, like, the first thing you did when you got into the room - ? Like, me and Sabine might have - ? But, er, that because we'd been warned..."

Phyllis sighed. She and John exchanged looks, then she turned back to staring at the ground. "Guilty," she said.

Aisling and Robert joined hands. "Guilty," they mumbled. Aisling wiped her eyes.

"Guilty," Ted said.

"Ted!" his wife said. She laughed. "We did *not!*" She cleared her throat. "I arranged some dried flowers on the chest of drawers. Ted had a can of lager and a poo."

"It wasn't a *'poo'!*" Ted said vehemently.

Toby shrugged. "The footage will tell us later, Ted. Sorry, I'm not making light of it. I wonder if the seven *other* members of the party have been filmed having sex? Or a can of lager? You got off lightly, my man."

"I'm mortified," Ted said. "Someone's trying to discredit me. And they've used you two lovely couples, and God knows how many other members of my party, to do it. I'm finished."

"Let's not jump to conclusions," Toby said. "I really don't think it was about making a few pornos. Sex tapes are ten a penny nowadays. If it was only Phyllis and John, yes I get that. Just. Phyllis was a one-time major male fantasy, and, with respect to her new status as a married woman, she's probably still got one or two unable-to-move-on fans. But no one's going to want to watch fifty minutes of Aisling and Robert Baxter rutting away on the duvet, or Ted and Millie Taylor, or even Sabine Meunier and Toby Mansfield. Not when the whole web's awash with professionally produced 1080 HD stuff starring the actual Kardashians, and any number of nubile Hollywood wannabes. Porn's moved on, people. Anyway, with respect, Aisling and Phyllis, and Robert and John – and I'm just trying to put your minds at rest here – a camera of that size is probably going to give low quality images. The hypothetical viewer might not even be able to tell it's you. More: whoever's thinking of posting it *anywhere* is going to be taking a risk, since – and I don't know about Maltese law, but it's probably similar to British, because this is only a half-foreign country – it's probably been obtained illegally. You can't just film people without their permission. No one's going to risk jail for a crappy ten-pixels-per-square-metre video that's likely to get handful of hits at the most. Pornography's about advertising revenue, not idealism. YouTube won't touch it for a start. And if it affects the tourist industry – let's say people start thinking twice about coming on holiday here because they don't want to be secretly filmed by a pervert – then the Maltese Mafia – which I don't know whether it exists, but since we're close to Sicily, let's just imagine it does: it's plausible – is going to go absolutely AWOL. They'll find out who did it. They always do. They're like the Mounties. They always get their man. And that man will be sleeping with the fishes. After they've cut his balls off, probably, and made him eat them."

Silence. Phyllis sat up and swept her hair back. "That actually makes me feel a whole lot better, Toby. I really mean it. Thank you."

"Yes, thank you," Aisling said.

Millie and Sabine had started giggling halfway through. They were clearly embarrassed but couldn't stop. They got up and went to sit next to each other, as if they'd been ostracised.

"It's not funny, girls," Toby said.

They tried hard to stop, but began weeping with the effort. Millie buried her head in a cushion.

John put his arm round Phyllis. Toby had made a good speech and she'd been comforted. She might even get an hour's sleep out of it. But he'd missed the point, and she'd see that pretty soon. Whoever was behind those cameras, their purpose probably hadn't been 'making a porno'. Blackmail was more likely. Which worked by its emotional hold. What mattered wasn't facts about the market, or the film quality, or anything, but about what worst case scenarios the victim could envisage, and how effectively she could be manipulated to fixate on them. Her nightmares. As Phyllis had already said, sex tapes didn't come in grades of respectability.

Four hours later, Harold Finch announced that the investigators were done, and on their way over to share their findings. Everyone had fallen into a doze. They sat up. Toby blew his nose. Sabine and Millie checked their phones. Phyllis crossed her legs and tried to look upbeat. "I need a shower," she said.

The investigators were dressed in warm-weather business attire: shorts, button-up blouses and white brogues, no socks. Melanie and Laurel, both in their mid-thirties. Presumably, they worked in MI7's Red Department, but John couldn't recall seeing them before. After the introductions, they switched on a laptop, plopped it on a table facing the eight holidaymakers, and took up position either side. The screen filled with a black and white grainy video of the two investigators moving about in what was obviously one of the hotel rooms.

"We're assuming you were all filmed at some point," Melanie said. "This is the sort of visual quality those cameras produce."

"It may not be very good," Aisling said, "but we can still see who you are."

"Did any of you do anything you'd rather... hadn't been filmed?" Laurel asked. "I mean, *really* rather hadn't?"

"John and Phyllis had sex," Toby said. "And so did Aisling and Robert. Ted defecated."

Ted closed his eyes as if he'd just been hit. "No, Toby, I didn't." He sighed miserably. "All right, bloody hell, yes, I did."

"It'll probably come to nothing," Laurel said, "but we've informed the police in both countries. Everyone's taking it very seriously indeed. Needless to say, we don't know who's behind it yet. But it's early days."

"The key is not to submit to blackmail," Melanie went on. "Not that we believe it'll come to that, for reasons we'll explain in a moment. But any whiff of it, we've got a special number you can call. We can't rule it out entirely."

Laurel nodded her agreement. "More likely, the point was simply to find out what you're up to. I understand you're on a fact-finding mission. Internet travel companies? There's a lot of money in that, and if there's a possibility you might uncover something, it'd definitely be worth their while to keep tabs on you."

"The police have launched the investigation by questioning the local representatives of those companies," Melanie said. "Assuming they are behind it, once they know they're in our sights, they'll probably destroy everything they've gathered. If they leave anything intact – even on the so-called dark net - there's always the possibility it can be traced back to them."

"That would make more sense than almost any other hypothesis," Laurel added. "As far as we can discover, none of the other members of your party – seven in all – have been targeted for surveillance. You're the leaders. You're the ones driving the whole thing. It would be rational to target only you, if that was the purpose."

"And there are no cameras elsewhere in the hotel. Between us and the police, we've checked every room. So the point can't have simply been to garner sex footage. It's not an opportunist crime, in other words, some spiv and his mates out to earn a fast buck. It's likely industrial espionage. And if that's your area of expertise, you're probably not going to branch out into peddling MP4s. You'll stick to what you think you're good at. You'll delete anything that might take on a life of its own, so to speak. Unpredictability's always the criminal's worst enemy. If they're in any way sensible and professional, they always try to eliminate it."

"We hope we've set your minds at rest," Laurel said. "Any further developments, get straight back in touch with the British High Commission. We've been ordered to stay in situ until you've finished your holiday, and we're keeping a very close eye on the local investigation. Any developments, we'll let you know."

Melanie switched off the laptop. "Any questions?"

"I think I'd like to change rooms and possibly hotels," Aisling said. "I can't face the thought of going back to the Dolce Christie. No offence, Ted."

"None taken," Ted said.

"We'll arrange new hotels, courtesy of the British government," Laurel said. "And you can choose your own rooms. How does that sound?"

"Very good," Aisling said. "And thank you for your explanations. You've set my mind at rest a bit, I must say."

"Ditto," Phyllis added.

Everyone stood up to go. John had to admit it: Laurel and Melanie had done a good job. They'd analysed the situation with razor-sharp precision and they'd been highly convincing.

Time to get some sleep now, and maybe head for the airport.

Depending on how Phyllis felt.

Chapter 7: A Day of Trying to Act Normally

John awoke at five am. Phyllis lay asleep, facing him on the other side of the bed. No point in getting up, so he turned to look at her for an hour or so. It was allowed: they were newlyweds on holiday. Probably normal. Romantic, some might even say.

That she was 'beautiful' didn't matter at this point, any more than whether he was 'handsome'. Hers would be the face he looked at every day now, hopefully for the rest of his life, and he could hardly believe the enormity of his good luck. She had a *good* face, though. Moral. Nothing mean or judgemental there. And her skin was as smooth as an advert. If you were a stranger and you were making comparisons, yes, you'd definitely say she was astonishingly attractive, even without make-up. Everything about her was exemplary: eyes, nose, mouth, ears, and the exact shape of the head in which they all sat: each in a class of its own, the whole more than the sum. And why was it that when hair was long and soft and there was lots of it, it looked pleasing? It was just strands of keratin, after all. And her neck and shoulders. Her eyebrows. Her hairline. In fact, the more you looked at her, the more perfect she became. Painful to keep on, really. It was likely natural to seek out the flaw that offset the faultlessness. Unable to find it, you might well feel uneasy.

It didn't make her a better human being, of course, all this 'beauty'. It was just luck. A bit of genetics, a healthy diet, not habitually pulling censorious facial expressions from an early age.

And in some ways, it was wasted on him. Because he didn't love her for her face or her body. At least, as far as he knew. He loved her for her conversation and her wit and her intellect. And, if some psychologists were correct, probably because she resembled his mother in a way he hadn't yet discerned.

But who was he kidding? Could he honestly say her looks were so secondary? Biology was powerful. A person might think he was above it, especially if he fancied himself as some kind of superior cosmopolitan intellectual, but he probably wasn't.

And in any case, *was* she so perfect? He saw her through his own eyes, and he couldn't step outside them to look at her with anyone else's. He loved her. For all he knew, that might make her perfect.

And who was to say it wasn't *entirely* subjective anyway, every last bit of it? In all likelihood, the idea of a man or a woman simply *being* beautiful was an invention of the media. *These* celebrities, above all *these*. And after that, anyone who could make themselves resemble them. These *photographs*, to be honest, not these actual people. Because all faces were perfect from some angle. It was about who set the standards. The criteria didn't just exist, out there, like trees or mountains. They were made-up.

Would he love her if, say, her face got terribly burned in a car accident? It hardly bore thinking about, but yes. Yes, he would. He might not lie in bed, gazing at her, trying to fathom her half-erotic, half-aesthetic aura, but he'd still want to be with her in perpetuity. After a certain point, the friendship thing trumped everything. They'd long since passed that point.

A car accident. His thoughts were becoming maudlin again. Overthinking. He'd been told all his professional life it was his biggest problem, he'd always denied it, and hey, guess what? It was true. He slipped out of bed and went outside the bedroom onto the veranda.

They'd probably be going home today, depending on how she felt. Melanie and Laurel had skilfully set everyone's mind at rest last night – better than Toby, although he'd made a good effort, and he'd come across as a decent guy – but Phyllis would make the final decision. And he'd go along with it whatever it was.

Because it affected her more than it affected him. It seemed scandalous, when he thought about it, that there had been four people in the room last night, all of whom had supposedly been filmed, and yet only two had really been devastated: the two women. Because something like that still had the potential power to wreck even the most modern woman's future in a way it wouldn't wreck a man's. *Shame* was the power's name. All over the world, it was still thought fitting for females to feel it in an absurdly wide variety of circumstances. Even in more enlightened places, it still lingered as a kind of historic expectancy. Men were in a different boat. They were expected to feel *remorse*. But remorse wasn't the same. It was about what you'd actually done, concrete things you could have changed, your activity. Shame was about who you *were*. It was passive. It found you already enmeshed in a web of relationships, most of which you had no choice over. Your moral luck, in other words. Or lack of it. *It was your fault you were attacked, you should have been more careful.*

They'd get out of here if she wanted to. And if she wanted to stay, they'd do that too. She probably didn't need protecting – she was old enough and strong enough to take care of herself – but something about his own uselessness in this context made him despair. And as Doctor Chakladar had repeatedly told him, that was the root of his 'depression': morbid feelings of powerlessness. Too much in the world was too malign, and he had four sisters, two living parents, a wife he loved, and a large collection of work colleagues whom he admired and whose company he enjoyed. He couldn't help feeling that, sooner or later, they were all going to be engulfed, and there wasn't a blind thing he could do about it. It didn't help that, as a spy, he was on the front line.

Stupid, really. He probably could have kept his job had he been willing to take antidepressants, but he wasn't going down that path. Far too many people were walking it, and it was part of the problem not the cure.

The sun was already beginning to warm the air, and down in the street, men and women parked vans and languidly set up stalls. Four men sat down on the pavement and opened briefcases to reveal petite shelves of wristwatches and jewellery. Beyond the rooftops, the Mediterranean glowed azure and already the sky was almost completely dominated by the sun. A strong smell of pine and diesel wafted up. Cicadas chirruped, but not yet deafeningly. In the distance, a lorry honked.

"John?" Phyllis said. "Where are you?"

He went back into the bedroom and got back into bed. "Just admiring the view."

She laughed.

"What's so funny?" he said.

"*Just admiring the view*. It's the sort of corny thing a man says when he's staring at your cleavage. Then I realised you were *actually* admiring the *actual* view, and my respect for you was renewed. Boring story, but you did ask. Well done."

"Redeemed. Even though I'm your husband, not just 'a man'."

"What shall we do today?" she asked. "What time is it?" She picked the bedside clock up. "*It's bloody half past five, John! I thought it was about ten! No wonder I'm talking delirious nonsense!* Can't we sleep in, for goodness sake?"

"I didn't wake you."

"Yes, you did. By getting out of bed. Go back to sleep, and that's an order. See you in four hours' time. Sweet dreams. Although there's not much chance of that, given yesterday."

"Do you still want to go home?"

"I will if Aisling Baxter does. But I don't want to look like a weakling. And my guess is, it'll simply make her more determined. The kind of woman who gives up when the going gets tough's hardly the kind who's likely to cut it in the House of Commons. Can we talk about this later? I love you, but I'm not going to be much use to you if I don't get my eight hours. Not when we're on holiday."

They were awoken at nine by a knock on the door. John opened it to reveal a man in a red waistcoat standing behind a trolley loaded with croissants, several pots of jam and honey, some butter and a tea set. "Compliments of the hotel," he said gloomily, as if he wasn't quite sure what sort of reception he'd get. "Sorry to disturb, but no notice is on the door. Manager says to enjoy."

"Thank you," John said. He helped wheel it in and tipped him. Phyllis sat up and pulled the duvet around her but didn't speak.

This was the sort of thing that happened in a film when someone was out to poison you. They both thought it and ignored it. They ate four croissants between them, had a cup of tea, changed into their bathing suits, and went down onto the beach. Phyllis donned her sunglasses and read a novel: *Eleanor Oliphant is Completely Fine*. John bought a copy of *The Malta Independent*. Every hour, they went in the sea.

"How are you going to find out what Aisling Baxter's doing?" John said, when they were drying themselves after their third swim. "She might already be on the way home, for all we know."

"She said she'd contact me today," Phyllis said. "She won't just clear off without saying anything. It'd be rude, apart from anything else. Still, I know what you mean. It does feel a little as if we're in limbo. Just as it would seem impolite of her to go without telling us, so it'd seem the same for us to stay if she's gone."

"We're Ted Taylor's guests, not hers. He seemed pretty cut up about what happened yesterday. If everyone clears out, how's that going to make him feel? Sorry, I realise that's a pretty good argument for staying, and I didn't mean it to sound like that's what I want. I'm happy to go with your preference."

"I'm pretty sure we'll be staying," Phyllis said. "We're British and she and I are Conservatives, so we're insufferably smug about things like stiff upper lips. We're not going to let a few microphones and a possible sex tape put us off. Sorry, *two* possible sex tapes."

"Laurel and Melanie helped me sleep last night better than if they hadn't done that spiel."

"Ditto. But YouTube infamy or not, that many cameras and microphones is pretty serious stuff. If someone's going to go to those lengths to scupper Aisling Baxter's investigation, such as it is, the question is, what more can we expect?"

"Maybe nothing at all. Whoever was behind the camera-microphone extravaganza probably realises they've bitten off more than they can chew."

"I hope so. Is there anywhere you'd especially like to go in Malta, John?"

"What do you mean?"

"Any particular sites of historical interest? Any shows? Any sights? I only ask because you've cheered up a bit since being here."

He suddenly saw what she was driving at. "Whereas you want to go home."

"I've been lying on my back reading a novel for three hours, John, and I've barely said a word. That's not me. Especially not on holiday. What happened last night creeped me out. I'd like to say it didn't, and I've been trying to pretend, but it did. It really did. I'm sorry if this ruins the trip, but - "

He hugged her hard. Them both being in their bathing costumes, it probably looked like something from *Love Island,* and he could already sense the prurient interest from some quarters of the beach, but it didn't matter. "I love you," he told her. "It wouldn't be normal for something like that not to have some effect. I'm getting better now, I can sense it. We'll rendezvous with Aisling Baxter and go home. You can go back to Conservative Campaign Headquarters and I'll go back to trying to translate *The Book of Margery Kempe* into Hungarian till something better comes along. Which it will. Back to normality. I love you, Phyllis."

"Anywhere you want to go, we can go there now. Today. I haven't actually got a stiff upper lip right now, and I'm willing to bet Aisling Baxter hasn't either. There's more to this than she's letting on, I know there is. I haven't been in MI7 for however many years it was for nothing. I can sense danger."

"Okay."

"So I'll ask you again: is there anything in Malta you'd particularly like to do?"

"I'd like to see the Megalithic Temples."

"Let's go right now, then. Forget the beach. Let's get changed and find a coach station or a taxi."

They spent the next six hours switching from bus to car to foot, latching on to a variety of guides with different tour parties. *These were built between 3600 BC and 700 BC and are internationally recognised as the oldest buildings on Earth. They are older than the Egyptian Pyramids! They are older than the English Stonehenge! They are older than the Scottish Skara Brae!* Phyllis finished her novel on their third bus journey, a hair-raising hurtle along a hillside road with a sheer drop apparently inches away. The driver kept swerving for no apparent reason. Then, as the tourists recovered, some of them looked behind and saw the chasm in the road they'd presumably just avoided. The sun beat down, the invisible insects continued making a din, men and women in shorts and sunglasses and baseball caps drank bottled water and took photos with their phones. No birds flew. Nothing in the landscape moved. Everything seemed both cheerful and dead.

After a while, John and Phyllis realised they were being watched. By Melanie. Then later by Laurel. Neither made any attempt to disguise her presence, although neither did they attempt to make contact. Nevertheless, it was reassuring to know you were being looked after.

They arrived back at the hotel at 6pm, exhausted and ready for dinner. When they checked in at reception, there was a message from Aisling Baxter. *Please join me and Robert for dinner tonight at our hotel. The LKX International at 7pm. Hope to see you there.*

They groaned in unison. Then realised: perhaps some of the Baxters' friends were watching. "Oh, look," Phyllis said. "There's another note here... *in addition to the first one.*" She nudged John. "It's from Aisling Baxter."

John pretended to read it again. "That's nice. I'm already looking forward to it."

"I'm pretty starving," Phyllis said, when they were alone in the lift. "I wasn't banking on waiting another hour to eat. Still, I suppose we both need to go in the shower, and a lie down wouldn't go amiss. Better set the alarm, I suppose, in case we fall asleep."

They scoured the room for devices. Nothing. They showered and by the time they'd changed for dinner, it was time to go out. She wore a blue print summer dress and heels. He donned his oxford shirt and ironed chinos.

"I could sleep for a year," Phyllis said. "I'm not even hungry any more. Still, at least we'll get closure. If she's going home, that's it. So are we."

"Do we know where the LKX International is?"

"No, but that's why God created taxis."

Toby and Sabine were waiting by the entrance. The LKX was a concrete block, four floors high, ten identical bays wide, in a slight arc facing a huge planter with hardy evergreens. Its front doors were up three steps. Toby and Sabine moved infinitesimally towards the arriving taxi, as if they'd been expecting Phyllis and John, but didn't want to look too eager.

"Hi, Toby," Phyllis said in a tone of undisguised irritation. *"Bonsoir, Sabine. Est-ce votre hôtel aussi?"*

"Are you here for dinner with the Baxters?" Toby said before Sabine could reply. "Hi, John. Because *we* are, and they've gone off to rendezvous with someone. They asked us to meet you."

Phyllis looked at her watch. "We're not late. We didn't even know you were coming."

"We didn't even know you were coming either," Toby said. "But I guess we'll both just have to make the most of it."

"I didn't mean it like that," Phyllis said. "Sorry if I sound tetchy. I'm very tired. It's been a great day, but last night took it out of me, and I'm still not back to normal. Who's she gone off to see? Am I allowed to ask?"

"I don't know. Someone connected to the bloody internet travel agent thing, I guess. She's taking it way too seriously. Here, she left this for you." He passed her a small sealed envelope.

"What is it?" she asked.

"Inside, there's a list of names of journalists who've investigated the internet travel business and somehow been warned off. Yeah, I know. Sounds like something from Monty Python. I promised to pass it on. I didn't promise not to make fun of it, though. Personally, I think she's got the whole thing totally out of proportion. Still, she needs something to make into her 'bag', I suppose, once she gets into politics. Make her stand out on the green benches. And Ted Taylor's a big donor."

"When you open the envelope," Sabine said, "you've got thirty seconds to read it, then it self-destructs. Poof!"

They all laughed politely. It was nice that Sabine had a sense of humour.

"Let's go into the bar and get some drinks," Toby said. "We've got to do something till the Baxters get back. I'll buy the first round. What are you having, John? Are you a cider or a lager or an ale man?"

"Ale, please," John replied.

"Girls?"

"We're not 'girls'," Phyllis said. "And I'll have ale."

"Ale for me too, please," Sabine said.

Toby grinned. "Any particular *kind* of ale, Sabine?" he enquired sardonically.

"Fizzy?" she replied, after a pause.

"Fizzy for me and John too, please," Phyllis said. "I wonder what time Aisling will be back," she said, before he could renew his sarcasm.

"I hope it's soon," John said for the same reason. "I'm getting hungry."

They'd reached the bar. "Four pints of ale," Toby told the barman. "Fizzy, please."

The barman gave a nervous grin. "Er… excuse me, sir?"

"*Fizz-zee*," Toby said. He turned to Phyllis. "You did say that's how you like it, yeah?"

Phyllis shot the barman a smile. "Sorry, my friend here doesn't really know much about beer. Three pints of Amstel, please. Toby, my 'friend', will have a Rossini: prosecco and pureed strawberries. Just a small one, please."

"Technically, I win again," Toby said as the barman went to get their drinks. "Amstel's lager, not ale."

"*Malheureusement*, something of a hollow victory, Mr Mansfield," Sabine said in a gruff voice, after they'd all thought about it. She walked up and down with tiny steps.

He suddenly laughed good-naturedly. "That's Sabine's Poirot impersonation. She does street theatre. And before you say anything, we do know he's Belgian, yeah." He threw his arms wide. "You're right, Sabine, I'm an utter arsehole."

When, after an hour of relatively small talk, and two more beers, Aisling and Robert still hadn't returned, Sabine suggested they order food.

"Do you think we should be worried?" Phyllis said. "I mean, you'd think they'd have contacted the hotel and left us a message by now. Maybe something's happened to them."

Toby took his phone out. He looked disapprovingly at the screen, pressed call, and sat looking solemn for a few seconds. "Hi, Aisling," he said, "this is Toby. We've decided to go ahead and order grub. When you get this, you might like to get something outside, because they're going to stop serving here soon. Sorry we missed each other. Give me a buzz when you're free. We can meet up tomorrow if you like. At least let me know you're okay. I know I'm not your mum, but I do care. Ciao."

It seemed wrong to get a formal meal when their hosts weren't there. They ordered a selection of pastizzi, filo pasties filled with ricotta or mushy peas, and four glasses of Kinnie, the local orangeade. They ate in guilty silence and when they'd finished, nothing seemed more natural than that they should separate and go back to their respective hotels.

"Bloody hell," Phyllis said, when she and John were back in their own taxi. "I'll give the Holiday from Hell this: it certainly carried on true to form tonight. If I have to hear any more about Toby's Maserati, his cryptocurrency portfolio, and his bloody polo injuries, I'll take a knife to him. God, I'm so glad I met you, John. Imagine being married to that! I mean, what the hell did I ever see in him? Who even *was* I?"

"He's not that bad," John said. "A bit monotonous, true, but in many ways, rather like Alec."

"What? The Alec? *Our* Alec? You mean *MI7 Alec?*"

"Keep your voice down. And yes, that one."

"Sorry, I've had three ales, and I'm in the indiscreet phase of inebriation. I suppose you're right. But Alec's much less of a prat. Was."

"On the other hand, he's ten years older."

"Was."

"Still is."

"I'm desperate for a wee," she said.

"We'll be back at the hotel in a minute."

"Sorry to mention that, by the way. I hope it hasn't taken the magic out of our marriage. Bloody hell, I was hoping for an in-depth conversation with Aisling tonight. I *really* want to go home now. I mean, I had no idea Toby would be there. He'll probably be there again tomorrow. Oh, God, *why? WHAT THE HELL HAVE I GOT US INTO?*"

He chuckled. "Keep your voice down."

The taxi pulled up outside their hotel. He paid while she ran straight inside and into the ladies' on the ground floor. When they got upstairs, he checked the room for devices again, while she went into the bathroom to take her face off. He was getting used to performing the regulation sweep now. When they got home, he'd do it there as well. After all, they'd have been away for a few days, and they still had no real idea who was behind the first and, so far, only batch. He might end up doing it for the rest of his life.

He heard Phyllis's phone ring and her pick up. Nearly 9.30 now, and Aisling Baxter had probably just got Toby's message. So a repeat invitation to the LKX was likely on the cards; although, the way Phyllis was feeling, she'd probably want a serious conversation right now. To stay or not to stay.

Given how long Aisling had been out tonight, though, she'd probably found something. Which meant she'd be staying. And that Phyllis would have to stay too, for appearance's sake. Like it or not, she'd have to dust off her stiff upper lip and back it out of the garage. Which, in turn, meant they needed to brace themselves for more Polo and Bitcoin and Maserati talk, tomorrow night.

Great.

Phyllis came out of the bathroom and stood in the doorway. Her eyes looked at nothing in particular. Her mouth hung open slightly. She looked far paler than removing her make-up should have left her. She adjusted her focus, scanned the room weirdly, and fixed her husband with an imploring look.

"John, that was Toby," she said. "Just now, on the phone. About Aisling and Robert Baxter. He says they're both dead."

Chapter 8: Upshot of the Very Bad News

According to the subsequent police report, Aisling and Robert Baxter had been driving along the coast road from Valletta at 8.30pm when their car swerved for no obvious reason and breached the metal barrier separating the thoroughfare from a long, rocky incline. The sole witness saw it collide with a felled tree on its way down, somersault, and, two seconds later, impact roof-first on a huge boulder. The two occupants probably died instantly.

The cause was quickly identified as a large pothole in the road. It caused the front tyre on the driver's side to rupture and, as an almost instantaneous consequence, the wheel axle to buckle slightly. Malta was notorious in this regard, and even a long-running internationally supported Facebook campaign - 'Fix Malta's Roads' - had failed to improve matters. The authorities had better things to spend their money on, many people grumbled. Like themselves.

Ted Taylor called Phyllis and John in their room, half an hour after they'd heard the news from Toby. "I've been asked by the High Commissioner to get everyone together in the hotel lobby of the LKX in an hour's time," he said in an ashen voice. "The police may want to speak to some or all of us, just as a formality. We're getting directions from the Foreign Office in London. Obviously, we'll all be packing our bags now. God, I can't believe it. I really *cannot* get my head round it."

Phyllis sat on the bed with her head in her hands for ten minutes. She'd been in the army, then she'd been in MI7, so death didn't necessarily shock her rigid in the way it often did other people. And she hadn't really known Aisling Baxter, much less her husband. They'd met briefly at the Newbury interview, then at the British High Commission, and they'd spoken briefly once or twice on the phone, that's all.

And yet she *was* shocked. Ironically, because it hadn't come completely out of the blue. It had come on top of last night's camera and microphone debacle, and that made it suspicious, however reliable Ted Taylor might believe the police verdict was.

After fifteen minutes, John walked across the room and held the door open. "We need to talk," he said.

She nodded and followed him outside. He'd reached the right conclusion a few seconds before her, but she hadn't been far behind. The entire thing was suspicious with a capital S. And they couldn't really be certain there were no bugs left in this room. If your microphones and cameras were compromised at the outset, you wouldn't necessarily react by scrapping your project. You might simply reduce the size of your devices, make them ten times harder to find.

As they walked through reception, the man at the desk gestured as if to say something. He clearly knew what had happened. He might even have been briefed to intercept them, although there was nothing sinister in that. Harold Finch had probably been in touch with the hotel manager. Besides, it might even be on the TV by now. They ignored him and kept moving.

They walked for five minutes and arrived at the marina. 10pm. Couples strolled with their arms round each other, families sat outside cafés and ate Bragioli and stuffed aubergines, fully-lit shops sold souvenirs and beach paraphernalia, and played folk music on MP3 speakers. A full moon shone above the silhouette of a church.

They sat down at a restaurant, so as not to draw attention to themselves. John ordered a loaf of sliced Maltese bread and a carafe of white wine.

"Have you still got that envelope Toby gave you?" he asked when the waiter had gone.

"I left it in the hotel room," she said blithely.

"Er, what?"

"But not before I took a photo of it and posted it on a variety of social media. I also texted and emailed you with it. And I put it in six different locations in the cloud. I know what Ted Taylor said about a pothole, but that's bullshit, and I'm pretty sure you agree. Things haven't been right since we got here. I'm not just talking about the cameras. I mean, why did she even give Toby that envelope to pass on? Why use him as an intermediary? There's only one possible answer."

"She thought something might happen to her tonight."

"And by 'coincidence', it did."

"And so now they'll be coming after us."

She scoffed. "How can you say that? We've made ourselves safe, if anything. We don't have any classified information that the 'bad guys' have to stop us disseminating. It's out there on the world wide web now."

"So they know we've realised it's significant in some way. Unless you've linked it to Aisling Baxter's car accident – which might cause both of us all sorts of credibility problems – there's no reason for anyone else to think it's remotely interesting. The web's full of that kind of stuff. It's information overload, if anything. In other words, the list might get lost. The fact that we think it's important may not."

She poured herself a glass of wine. "I did tag it, as a matter of fact."

"Saying what?"

"*Aisling Baxter gave me this, just before she died. Does anyone know what it means?* Words to that effect."

"Oh, boy. The police are going to have a field day."

"I'm sure she'd have done it herself if she'd known how soon it was going to end. The only reason she didn't is because she probably hoped to add to it tonight."

"Big assumption. But probably correct. So what do you expect to happen now?"

"I expect we'll go back to our hotel room and find the envelope's gone. I doubt whoever's behind this is looking at the internet right now, so they'll miss the fact that I've posted it here, there and everywhere. When we've discovered the physical envelope's gone, we've got something to tell the police. It might even throw new light on the 'accident'."

"I admire your optimism. The police are on our side, like they are in every country we've ever been to. For all we know, the names on that list might be part of some database she obtained illegally. Publishing it might have landed us in big trouble."

She took a deep breath. "I admit, I hadn't thought of that."

"You might be legally obliged to take it down. And *then* the bad guys might come after us."

"Yes, always look on the bright side of life, John. Look, here's how I'm going to play it, okay? I tell the police what I've done, and that the envelope's missing - "

"Which it isn't, at least as far as we know."

"*Yet*. Either way, I cry my way through the whole interview. I am actually very upset, to be honest. And it wouldn't be remiss of me to behave irrationally in the circumstances, which would explain, and if necessary possibly excuse, me posting a confidential inventory on Instagram and Pinterest. I don't like weeping in public; it betrays the feminist cause, apart from anything else. But I'm damned if I'm going to do time in a Maltese prison for the sake of Aisling Baxter's crusade against online travel agents. I say we get out of here, and put the whole thing behind us as much as we can."

"I agree."

"Really?"

"Whatever this is," he said, "we're probably way out of our depth. And at no point did we commit ourselves to any investigation. We came on holiday, and the sole reason we got an invite is because Toby fancies his chances at the end of the forty days. You've got to choose your battles in life, and this isn't ours."

"So we're agreed then?"

"We turn up at the LKX in fifteen minutes' time, express our sincere condolences, listen to what Ted Taylor and Harold Finch have to say, answer any questions the police feel like asking, make ourselves super-amenable to all the relevant authorities, then catch the first available flight to Gatwick or Heathrow or Stansted or Manchester. The FCO will probably smooth our way. It's probably chartering a plane as we speak."

"Settled, then. Finish that wine. We've got to go back to the hotel room before we repair to the LKX."

"I thought we said - "

"We have to check whether the envelope's gone. That's reasonable. If it is, we can tell the police, and no one can expect any more of us. We'll have done our duty."

He sighed. "Okay."

What did she have in mind? He couldn't put his finger on it, but she probably wasn't planning some jolly *Tommy and Tuppence*-style adventure. She knew it was serious, and she'd seen enough of the world to realise that, if they decided to play at being private detectives and their worst speculations were accurate, they'd likely be mincemeat within a week.

But still, he could see there was something on her mind.

And then he realised. Because it was on his own mind.

None of this was over.

Not because of anything he and Phyllis were planning to do. No, they'd played their parts. Now the die was cast, and all they could do was sit and wait. And tremble, if they thought about it.

Because whatever came next, it almost certainly wouldn't be something nice.

Twenty minutes later, thirteen tourists, six in tears, sat on padded armchairs in the low-ceilinged hotel lounge of the LKX listening to Ted Taylor's speech: one third personal apology, one third practical advice, and one third eulogy. Afterwards, Harold Finch relayed the official advice from the Foreign and Commonwealth Office, mostly about everyone cooperating with the Maltese authorities and liaising closely with himself whenever necessary. No mention of a special plane being laid on, although everyone said they wanted to leave within twenty-four hours. "We don't want it to look like an evacuation," Finch explained. "It could offend the hosts. We'll pull all the stops out to accommodate any request to go, however. We can virtually guarantee you'll get what you ask for - within reasonable limits, obviously."

A team of police officers had been corralled to complete the formal questioning process as swiftly as possible. When Finch finished speaking, they entered the room like they were on tiptoes, and set about their task in the same painstaking manner.

Phyllis and John had been back to their hotel on the way here. Phyllis had left the envelope on the bedside table where it could be easily spotted – she didn't want to come back to find everything turned upside-down. As she expected, it was gone. Even so, her stomach lurched. It was one thing to believe something sinister might happen; another for it to have occurred precisely as you expected, recently, with the evidence right before your eyes. Yes, someone had been in their room. Whoever it was had watched them go out, then calmly entered, intent on one thing. And now he or she had disappeared back beneath the skirting boards. Very professional. Very unsettling.

When Phyllis told the police officer – a young man with a thin nose and very black short hair – he wrote something down in his notepad, then went to consult his superior, a Sergeant Major Grade II; another man, but much older and stouter with heavy-looking hands and small eyes under a protruding forehead. They conversed for a while, the younger man doing most of the speaking, the other nodding occasionally or uttering a terse sentence. Eventually, the constable returned.

"Tell me all you can about the theft," he said, "and where you have posted the pictures. We will take care of the rest."

"What if it's confidential information?" Phyllis asked. "Could I get into trouble?"

"There will be no 'trouble'. Something like this, we make allowances. Not that it happens very often, obviously. No, the whole thing is tragic enough. I have spoken to Sergeant Major Camilleri, as you saw. He gives you his personal word that you can forget the whole thing. Let *us* find the thief and get to the bottom of what it means. You have enough to concern you."

"Thank you," she said.

Twenty-four hours later, they were back in London.

Chapter 9: Conference at the Indian

When John and Phyllis returned to Britain, the newspapers were full of reports of the accident, but only for a day. Forty-eight hours after their bodies arrived home, the funerals of Aisling and Robert Baxter took place in the Church of St George the Martyr in Newbury. Ted Taylor and his wife weren't invited, nor anyone else from the Malta excursion. Aisling's parents made no secret of the fact that they blamed Ted and his 'holiday' for her death. She'd been running about on a wild goose chase, looking for evidence to support his silly campaign. She'd died in the most stupid, tragic way possible on an island whose government was too inept to even take proper care of its own transport infrastructure. In sum: if she'd never met him, she'd still be alive.

In the meantime, Phyllis returned to her job at Conservative Campaign Headquarters, John got a job translating legal documents online for a solicitor in Chepstow. The holiday had left them both dispirited and disjointed, as if they weren't sure where they should be at any given moment or why any of it mattered.

And yet, it drew them closer. Neither had really known Aisling and Robert Baxter; even so, it was a timely reminder of the fragility of life. Anything could happen to anyone at any moment, so you'd be an idiot not to make the most of your little time together. And it *was* little. The universe had been just fine before you were born, and it'd be fine after you died. There might or might not be an afterlife, but you certainly couldn't guarantee you'd be together there. To hell with the expense: they ate out every night for a week, each time in a different location. At the weekend, they went ice-skating at Lee Valley. Life to the max.

Meanwhile, Toby dropped out of their lives as suddenly as he'd re-appeared. From the little Phyllis picked up from her parents, he and Sabine had split up. Right now, he was bombarding her with flowers and texts in his usual ineffectual manner.

At 8pm, exactly one week after they'd arrived back in Britain, they went to an Indian restaurant whose grey paisley wallpaper was dotted with framed Persian miniatures and where sitar music played quietly in the background. Mordred had a glass of lager; Phyllis had a blackcurrant juice. They'd toyed with the idea of going to a club later. She wore trousers and a white halter neck blouse, he wore a charcoal suit minus the tie. The waiter took their order and disappeared, leaving the room virtually empty. Then a middle-aged man and woman came in, looking miserable. The waiter reappeared, took their coats and guided them to a table by the opposite wall.

"What shall we talk about tonight?" he asked.

She took out her phone, tapped her 'random topics' app and rolled her eyes wearily. "*Sausages*, apparently," she said.

"I think that's something best discussed when you're in a group," he said.

"Why?"

"Because what can you say that hasn't been said before? Continental vs British, vegetarian vs meat, how inhumanely they treat pigs in most places, how intelligent pigs are, how in the olden days sausages used to be gristly but - "

"You see that man and woman who just came in?" she whispered.

He adjusted to the sudden tangent. "They're the only two other people in the room. So yes."

"I..." She blushed and looked at the tablecloth. "God, I'm sorry. Have I gone red?" She switched her phone to selfie mode and looked at herself. "Right, I have. Sorry."

"Are you okay?" He reached across the table and took her hand.

"They – you don't notice anything unusual about their behaviour? I only ask because you're good at body language."

"I can tell you what I think, if it'll help. I'm pretty sure they had a row within the last hour. They asked for a table away from us so they could talk. She's less comfortable about being here than he is. He's - "

"They couldn't be watching us?"

Another readjustment. "What's going on?"

"Someone's watching me. I haven't yet managed to catch sight of them – him, her - but I can feel their eyes on me. I mean, watching me go to, and come back from, work. And at lunchtimes. Occasionally, at weekends. I felt them at the ice-rink, for example. Now, yes, I know this sounds paranoid. Maybe it is. But we've both been trained to pick up on subliminal signals and to trust our instincts. Sometimes we 'know' these things before we can consciously confirm them. And I'm pretty sure about this."

"You think it's linked to what happened in Malta?"

She flicked her eyebrows. "I can't think of any other reason. Not a specific one. But given what we both used to do for a living, it could of course be anyone, for any number of reasons. Maybe it's some private security firm, looking to recruit me. It could be a test. Or anything. I'm not ruling paranoia out completely, by the way."

"It should be fairly easy for us to find out. Whether you *are* being watched, I mean. But it would probably still leave open the question of who and why."

"We've both still got contacts at MI7. You rang Ruby Parker from Marsaskala and she didn't take it lightly. Between us, we've got a lot of information, and someone might pay through the nose to get his or her hands on it."

He chuckled. "We haven't got that much information. MI7's not set up like that. But it's irrelevant, how much or little we have. If someone *thinks* we've a lot, we could be in trouble. Maybe I should call the big RP again."

"I don't think that's a good idea. If I'm wrong, we'll look stupid. And if it happens again, and again, I don't want to end up being the woman who cried wolf. One day, it might be real. Did you know that Ted Taylor has disappeared?"

"What do you mean?"

"Just took off abroad somewhere. No forwarding address or anything. His daughter's been to see the police. She tried to report him missing, but they weren't having any of it."

John shrugged. "I'd imagine he's still upset. I would be, in his position. And I'd definitely want to get out of Newbury. What happened wasn't his fault, but technically he was in charge. That can have a very negative impact on your ability to sleep at night."

"Why not go and see a counsellor? And if you've got to get out of Newbury, why not just move house? Why not at least tell your own daughter where you're going?"

He nodded. "I see your point."

"Really? Let's hear you spell it out then, just so I know we're on the same page."

"He thinks someone's after him. And maybe he's right."

"Check. Or, even worse, someone *was* after him, and they caught up with him."

"You think he could be *dead?*"

"I'm not discounting the possibility, John. And I doubt his daughter is, either."

"Okay," he said. "We've got to find out whether you're being followed as a matter of urgency. The obvious solution would be, come Monday, we set off from the flat together. Then separate. If it is connected to Malta, they'll probably have someone detailed to follow me too. The only reason I haven't had your problem might be that I work predominantly from home. Like a hermit. But a working hermit."

"As in, 'Before we let you into the country, do you have a work hermit?' Sorry, I'm delirious."

"It was really funny. Anyway, I can lose anyone that follows me. They won't be expecting me to take evasive action."

"It might set alarm bells ringing if you do."

"What alternative do we have?"

"None. Okay, carry on."

The waiter arrived with their curries, and put four pop-padoms and a selection of pickles and chutneys in the centre of the table. He interlaced his fingers on his stomach, smiled, told them to *enjoy*, then retired.

"Afterwards, I disguise myself and come back to where I know you'll be," John went on. "The park at lunchtime, the tube to Camden after work. You can take a bit of a detour, string them along, make it easier for me to spot them. If someone *is* following you, I'll find out."

"Has it occurred to you that our flat might be bugged?"

He grinned. "I've been checking every day. Just to be on the safe side. When you've gone out. I didn't want to scare you."

"I've been checking too. When *you're* out of the way, getting changed, or in bed at night. My reason's different. So I didn't look mad."

"So it's agreed: we love each other."

"We *care* about each other. There's a difference. Luckily, it just so happens that we love each other too, so isn't that sweet?"

"Has it occurred to you that your watcher might turn out to be Toby?"

She deposited a teaspoon of mango chutney on her curry. "That would be truly creepy. No, I don't think he'd do that. He'd have no reason. If he wanted to stalk me – which is unlikely – he'd do it with flowers and texts and maybe removing his shirt to blind me with his *Poldark*-standard abs. He wouldn't follow me to work every morning, *incognito*. Besides, he doesn't want me anymore. He wants Sabine."

"He's got *Poldark*-standard abs?"

"So have you."

"Thanks."

"Don't thank me. It's a scientific fact."

"Let's consider Malta again. Someone definitely came into the room and removed that envelope, right?"

"Unless you think I'm making it up. But that's grounds for divorce, and the forty days aren't even up yet."

"We went to the restaurant at the marina and you said you'd left the envelope in the room because you wanted it to be 'over'. You thought if you simultaneously put everything out there on the web, then relinquished the hard copy, you'd make it pointless for anyone to come after you."

"What could I give them? Theoretically, they might want revenge. I mean, in a child's world. But from the outset, it didn't have the ring of that. As Laurel and Melanie said at the British High Commission, we were likely dealing with professionals. Whoever started it wasn't looking to blackmail anyone with sex tapes. They were after something else. And they were highly methodical in their approach."

"Okay, so you surrendered what they were looking for. They've got the envelope and its contents. And now you've shot every arrow in your quiver, and they're still standing. You haven't even scratched them."

"I've an empty quiver, yes. And they're still upright and unscathed. But they're wearing a helmet with a visor, and the visor's down, so I can't see who they are. Now, what do they do? Attack me? That would be a risk. I might pull their helmet off. They wouldn't like that, not one little bit. Their best bet is to walk away. After all – I haven't mentioned this yet, but it makes sense – there's a mighty river between me and them. Crossing that river is also risky. *I'm* not going to cross it because I don't have any weapons. Just an empty quiver. *They're* not going to cross it because they know I'm effectively out of the picture now, having no arrows. So why would they bother? I'd put all my hopes in my archery skills, you see. Now I'm kaput. What's your point, John?"

"Well done for extending the metaphor so creatively."

"Thank you for the compliment. We aim to please even our most patronising clients. The answer to my question is?"

"What the envelope might 'prove' is that Aisling Baxter trusted you to receive and safeguard information. Now what if the chap with the visor thought, 'This looks strange. Exactly like she expected me to come into her hotel room and take it. She must be trying to fob me off. She must have something even *more* important in her possession. She's dangling her empty quiver because she's got a huge trebuchet hidden behind that foliage.' Sorry, I didn't mention it earlier, but there's a large shrubbery behind you."

"Well then, why not just kill me? Why waste time following me?"

"Because you've shown a certain cunning. You disseminated information in ways that they didn't anticipate. Who knows what you might already be planning for your trebuchet?"

"Sorry, John. You said earlier that you checked our room for bugs while I was out."

"What about it?"

"On the perfectly reasonable grounds that you *didn't want to scare me*. So can I just ask: what the hell do you think *this* is doing? Because what you're suggesting might be a very good reason for them to kidnap me, torture me to find out what I know, then dump my corpse in a lime pit."

"Yes, I can see that. Sorry."

She sighed. "On the other hand, I am a feminist and not some fragile little milksop who gets petrified by bumps in the night. Congratulations, therefore: you're no longer our most patronising client."

"Hurrah. Sorry again about the nightmares we'll both be having tonight. Just to put a more optimistic spin on matters - "

She laughed. "This, I've got to hear. There's a global shortage of lime?"

"If they've done their research, they'll know we're ex-spies. Unless they want to bring the full weight of HM Government down on them, they'll have to tread very carefully indeed."

"The 'full weight' of Theresa May and Jeremy Hunt. They'll be quaking in their boots."

"MI7's not always answerable to the likes of Terri and Jimbo. I mean, if I had to choose, I'd say Ruby Parker was closer to Tony Soprano than any Prime Minister we've ever had."

"There is a lot of resemblance, yes. Is that your tenth beer, by the way? Let's talk about something else."

Chapter 10: A Bit of Shadowing

Monday, 10am. John left the flat in a suit and carrying a large briefcase. At 10.10, he boarded an underground train at Mornington Crescent. He stood next to the exit doors. Four minutes later, just before they closed at Tottenham Court Road, he pulled a face as if he'd forgotten something and abruptly disembarked. He mounted the escalator two steps at a time. At the surface, he got straight into a taxi. Three minutes later, he paid the driver, entered a department store, took the lift to the fourth floor and went into the gents'. He locked himself in the far cubicle. He opened his briefcase to reveal a change of clothing and a haversack. He swapped his suit for a grey sweat shirt, jeans, and trainers. He rubbed dark colouring into his hair before donning an NYC beanie and sunglasses. He methodically dismantled the briefcase and thrust the pieces into his backpack along with his folded suit and his brogues. Four minutes total, not bad. He came out of the gents' and walked leisurely across the floor of the men's wear department. He descended four flights of stairs to the store's rear entrance.

He still hadn't seen anyone watching him, but he couldn't afford to be complacent. Once outside, he rounded the corner, broke into a sprint, and hailed another taxi. Ten minutes later he was in Southwark Park. He sauntered into a café, bought a coffee and a croissant and sat two seats back from the window, where he could observe the exterior without necessarily being seen in return.

If anyone had been following him, he'd lost them. But it didn't pay to be complacent. He finished his breakfast, went into the toilet and another cubicle, and changed into a short-sleeved yellow T-shirt, a baseball cap, and a different style of sunglasses. He applied a kids' temporary tattoo to each of his forearms. When he left the café, he walked to the middle of the park, put his back-pack on the grass to use as a pillow, crossed his hands behind his head, and lay looking at the clouds for half an hour.

Eleven-thirty. Time to make his way over to St James's Park. He put the grey sweat shirt back on. It was getting chillier and yellow stood out too much.

He spotted Phyllis as soon as she crossed the road. Of all the people who might be following her, he singled out ten. Difficult to assess. She was attractive, and naturally drew glances from passers-by, not just men. Anyone else, the field would have been narrower and his job easier.

Nine men and a woman followed her across the level cross-ing to the park. When she turned left, four went the other way. Another stopped to talk on his phone. Which left four men, plus the woman.

Of course, her watcher probably wasn't following her that closely. Otherwise, she'd have identified whoever it was herself. Back to scanning the circumference of her visibility.

He logged twenty new possibilities. Men, all firing looks of varying degrees of readability at her. He made a mental effort to fix each in his memory, then crossed the road to walk away from her. Observation Number One complete.

Five minutes later, he double-backed and walked to a spot ten metres from where she'd agreed to sit. He came to a halt as soon as he caught sight of her, and pretended to speak on his phone, grinning. He scanned the surroundings.

One guy he recalled, yes – probably. Memory being the im-perfect thing it was, he couldn't be 100% certain; nevertheless: ten minutes ago, on the roadside? Tall, well-built, mid-thirties, weather-beaten face, black curly oiled hair, dark coat, collar, tie and respectable brogues. He sat on a bench beside a couple, closer than was probably discreet – there were several inches between him and his end, whereas they were right up against theirs. Every few minutes, he talked to them. Obvious, if you were looking for it, that they didn't actually know him yet didn't find him horribly objectionable either. He offered them cigarettes. They smiled and took one each. He produced a lighter. All three smoked together. They became more sociable.

He was using them as camouflage. Enough of a pro to know that the best place for a tail to conceal himself was amongst 'friends'. Shadows were loners, and if you suspected you might be dragging one, you'd probably scan the anti-social types first. Giving the real one time to melt into the background.

And he kept looking at Phyllis. Since she was at an angle to him, he could do so freely. Despite that, he wasn't taking any chances, not even turning his head most of the time, just his eyes. When she got up, he casually made his excuses to the couple, exchanged a few pleasantries – he obviously wasn't in any hurry – and departed, adopting a wide arc to his quarry and, to all appearances, not eyeing her at all.

John started to walk away in the opposite direction to both of them. He looked at his phone. 12.40, precisely as arranged. In ten minutes, he was due to pass her as she walked southeast down Warwick Street. He'd better get a move on.

Then, two things he wasn't expecting. Two more shadows.

But they weren't following Phyllis.

Or rather, they were, but only indirectly. They were following the guy with the dark hair. Tailing her tail.

More, they clearly had no mutual awareness. They were so focussed on the dark haired guy, they hadn't registered each other's existence.

One was a woman, small with blonde hair and oversized sunglasses; the other a stocky man of about sixty with a grey moustache and a homburg.

The woman. My God! It was Annabel! His MI7 ex-colleague.

Suddenly, he felt a lot more secure – at least, on Phyllis's behalf. Obviously, he couldn't afford for Annabel to spot him. She'd recognise him instantly, even with his sweat shirt, sunglasses and trainers. A miracle she hadn't clocked him already, but she obviously hadn't. She'd never have entered his sight-line otherwise. He'd better be damn careful at the next rendezvous.

Who was the old guy, though?

At their next agreed point of intersection, Warwick Street, he solved the problem of effective concealment by finding a minicab and asking the driver to stop at the kerbside for a few moments so he could 'pick up a friend'. They pulled in to the side just as Phyllis walked by.

The dark haired guy passed a whole forty seconds later, at such a distance from her that anyone else would have been frantic about losing the scent. Forty seconds! A lifetime in the shadowing business. It smacked of supreme confidence. Uber confidence.

Then came Annabel and the old guy. Somewhere between St James's Park and here, the old guy had changed into a Green Day T-shirt. And he wore a newsboy cap.

Funny old business, the spy thingy.

Anyhow, time to get a few photos, then home to make the dinner.

Phyllis came in at 3pm, roughly as arranged. He heard her close the door and put her shoes in the cupboard, then she came into the living room and sat down on the sofa.

"So what you got?" she asked.

He showed her the photos he'd taken. Her incredulity mounted, then plateaued, then she laughed. "You're a bloody genius," she said. "Do you know, I actually looked for you at one point. I couldn't help myself. And I couldn't find you. But I didn't lose faith. I thought, 'He's here somewhere.' And you were. I feel a whole lot better knowing Annabel's out there, though. Don't take that the wrong way. You're good at detection, which is always handy. But in this sort of situation, you might require someone highly trained in martial arts and the use of machine guns."

"We may be getting ahead of ourselves here."

"Maybe, but I don't like the look of that guy. If I was directing a film, and I needed a baddie, that's who I'd cast."

"Appearances can be deceptive. We've no idea what he's doing yet."

"You know what I mean, though. What's our next move?"

"We trap Annabel and co-opt her."

She nodded. "Sounds like a good move. In theory."

"You mean, how are we going to trap her without alerting the other two?"

"I don't want to go running to Ruby Parker. We're adults now and we've flown the nest. Besides, she must have put Annabel on the case. She didn't bother to tell us."

"We need to act quickly, though," he said.

"Obviously. This guy's probably sitting outside our flat right now. He must be watching me for a reason."

"To see if you contact anyone from the media is my guess. You might decide to make a big thing of Aisling's list with a journalist or two. And they're probably planning their next move. They've made a few mistakes so far. They probably weren't banking on us finding those snooping devices so quickly, for a start. And one thing led to another. They need to get it right this time. Like we said the other day, you're an ex-spy. If anything happens to you, a lot of people will 'remember' the cameras and microphones and the list Aisling Baxter gave you and the car accident. Whatever they're doing now, there's a huge chance that if they don't deal with you *properly* – which might mean leaving you alone, since you've clearly no intention of going to the BBC or Channel 4 or anyone from the broadsheets – it could all blow up in their faces. My guess is that this guy will disappear in a week or so, and that'll be it."

"It's a very comforting conjecture, but it's not very convincing. Firstly, the old guy – let's call him Mr Kidd: sorry, we can't just call them 'old guy' and 'young guy', it's too generic - and Annabel already knew about the young guy, let's call him Mr

Wint. As you say, Mr Wint might intend to go away if I don't look like a threat any more. But then Mr Kidd might move in. Mr Kidd might be just waiting for Mr Wint to withdraw."

"So what's Mr Kidd want?"

"I don't know! That's the whole point! Neither of us know anything!"

"Okay."

"We need to get in touch with Annabel, like we've just agreed. Have a conference. As you say, 'co-opt' her. The problem is, I've no idea how to go about that without tipping off bloody Mr Kidd and Mr Wint. And why should she talk to us anyway? She might just run back to Thames House, report that we're on to her, and get Ruby Parker to assign someone else. Someone we've never seen before, and who'll therefore be much more invisible."

"Have you wondered why that isn't *already* so? I mean, someone other than Annabel on the case?"

"I'm too busy wondering about all the other stuff, thanks."

"There's a good chance she actually *asked* for this assignment. She is on record, as I recall, as saying you were her best friend. She'd probably want to look after you."

"That cheers me up mightily, with its not-so-subtle implication that she knows I'm in serious danger. Look, John, this sort of thing was different when we worked at Thames House. We don't anymore. I'm not in the mood for being shadowed by Mr Kidd and Mr Wint and someone who used to be my colleague and who wants to protect me. And my husband, since we might as well add you into the mix. Four shadows." She laughed darkly. "Add another and I'll be Cliff Richard."

"Okay, here's what we'll do. Annabel might not *want* contact from us, but right now she doesn't know about Mr Kidd, and that means we've got information she needs. If we don't show our hand, but show that we've *got* a hand, we can probably draw her in. By that, I mean she won't automatically hare back to Thames House. But *I'll* have to make contact with her, not you. Right now, Mr Wint doesn't know about Annabel, and he doesn't know about me. You're his sole interest, and if you meet her you'll flag her up, likely sabotaging all her work so far. She's not going to welcome that. We'll do it next time you go to work. Once I've buttonholed Annabel, I'll text you, and then I want you to get in a taxi and go straight home."

"Or go somewhere public and meet someone."

"But not a newspaper editor. And not Toby, because he's connected to Malta."

"And he's probably in Newbury, and he wouldn't want to meet anyway. Okay, I'll come straight home. Although I'm not sure I feel entirely safe here, alone."

"Why not ask your parents down?"

"Are you joking? No thanks."

"Alec."

She drew her chin back a millimetre. "Alec *Cunningham? MI7* Alec?" She laughed. "How do you think you can make that work?"

"I can't. Annabel can."

Chapter 11: Lucy Staveley, Ace Reporter

Lucy Staveley didn't want to work long term at *The Newbury Echo*, but she wasn't sure the feeling was mutual, not any more. When she'd started as an intern, eighteen months ago, she was going nowhere. She wasn't even getting paid. But then she'd got a break: an anonymous bundle of documents by post, addressed to her at her parents' house, detailing the council's confidential plans to axe the area's biggest sports centre. As luck would have it, a group of researchers had just published a report into obesity amongst local primary school pupils, and their findings weren't good. Ten percentage points above the national average. Roger, the editor, had encouraged her to write the article, then he'd put it on the front page. She was a natural, he said. There'd been a follow-up in *Private Eye* and then apparently, a council 'inquiry' to find out who the leaker was. Meanwhile, in the wider world, protests were organised, online petitions generated, and the sports centre survived.

Then, six months later, another scoop. Once again, direct to her home address. A council grant to a local rugby club, registered as a loan, and whose repayments were 'inadvertently wiped' from encrypted financial records each time they fell due. Five occasions, in all. Corruption, and this time it was a matter for the police.

In the end, it had all turned out to be a 'misunderstanding'. Or that was the official conclusion/whitewash. But in the meantime, Lucy Staveley's reputation had soared. She'd become the local superhero journalist: socking it to the bad guys.

Only four foot six inches tall, long hair down to her waist, fashionable black plastic frame glasses and a liking for jeans and woolly cardigans, even in hot weather, she was beginning to set her sights on the national dailies. She probably wasn't ready for

The Times or *The Guardian* yet, but *The Daily Mirror* or *The Sun* might have her. She wouldn't need to live with her parents any more. She was twenty-five now. But her CV was getting longer every day. Simply a matter of time, really.

One more major scoop would swing it. Something midway between the sports centre (which had been embarrassing for the bad guys, but no more), and the rugby club (which had potentially been their downfall). But it had to come soon. Six months down the line, she might start looking like she'd lost her touch.

Which is why she was so excited when her mum knocked on her bedroom door that Tuesday morning and told her there was a parcel downstairs for her on the kitchen table. "Not an Amazon one. I haven't opened it, obviously." She took out her phone, and showed a photo of it.

"Why didn't you bring it upstairs?" Lucy said.

"Because you need to get out of bed."

"Why?"

"Because lying in bed at your age breeds bad habits. Come on. I'm not being unreasonable, Luce. It's gone half past eight."

Lucy didn't have an office to go to. She was a junior reporter now, but even so, everything she did was from home. Online, and on the phone when she needed to speak to Roger. Face to face meetings were as rare as hen's teeth. Most days, at least when her mum was in a decent mood, her working day began at 10.

She went to the toilet, walked downstairs, gave her mum a goodbye kiss at the front door, and entered the kitchen.

And there it was. A B4 size Manila envelope, bulky and important-looking, and the tell-tale orange 'Signed for' sticker.

It was important, she could already feel it. Maybe even enough to be what she was looking for: her ticket to London and complete independence. No more living with mum and dad in their boring semi on Salesdean Drive. She looked at the postmark by way of savouring her anticipation, and poured herself a bowl of wholegrain cinnamon Malties. You couldn't rush something like this. If it was what she thought it was, and anything like the last two, it would require hours of reading. It wouldn't interpret itself. She'd be lucky to finish it today. But she'd work through the night, if need be.

God, she was getting ahead of herself. It might be anything.

She went to the drawer beneath the sink and took out some scissors. Within thirty seconds, she'd cut the top off. A pile of documents and a USB pen. She laid the papers out on the living room carpet and put the USB on the mantelpiece for later. She wasn't interested in her Malties anymore. Let them go soggy.

But then, that was stupid. You needed food in order to think. She rushed back into the kitchen picked up the bowl, and shovelled them into her mouth, walking back into the living room.

Okay, so what was it? Laid out before her like a road map to a new life, it looked to be made up of about five bits. She got down on her hands and knees, the better to scan it.

The first was a copy of the minutes of an interview at the Glenmoran Hotel in Newbury, very recently. The candidates: Keith Sutherland, Aisling Baxter, Rory Jupp, Phyllis Robinson, and Steven Waite. The interview panel: Sir Anthony Hartley-Brown, Cynthia Cartwright, Innes Mount, Nick O'Connor and Vanessa Parkinson.

Aisling Baxter – wasn't she the woman from the news? The crash victim in Malta?

The second section was an accident report. My God, it was the same accident! The other night's crash in Malta! Talk about hot off the press. This was real goose bumps stuff. She couldn't actually feel the presence of whoever had sent it. They must have posted it – when? They must actually have *been in Malta* to get hold of it! And with pretty high-level access! It was a police report!

Calm down. Breathe.

The third was a copy of a letter written by a member of the Young Conservative movement, someone called Moira de Winter. It described a meeting she'd had with Phyllis Robinson and Sir Anthony Hartley-Brown and two other YC's, on the top floor of a pub in Central London. A secret meeting, by the look of things.

The fourth was a list of guests of a local travel agent called Ted Taylor, in Malta. The car-crash excursion. There she was again, the common denominator: Phyllis Robinson. Only now under a new name: Phyllis Mordred.

As if to ram the point home, the final category of documents was a variety of clippings from magazines going back about ten years, but none more recent than three. Pictures of Phyllis Robinson as a model.

She went upstairs and retrieved her laptop from under the bed. She was breathing so hard now it felt like she was going to pass out. This was big.

She put the USB pen in and double clicked on the MP4 file.

Yuck. A fat bloke having sex with his middle-aged wife in what looked like a hotel room. Pretty clumsy, both of them. The woman, underneath, reached for her phone on the bedside table. She glanced at it and put it back.

My God. The woman. It was *Aisling Baxter*.

Okay, this revolved around *Phyllis Robinson and Aisling Baxter* in some way. Time to start reading.

Four hours later, she had it. It had been staring her in the face from the start, really. Not exactly a smoking gun, but enough to be going on with. She picked up her phone and pressed call.

"Lucy," Roger said. "Tell me you've got something more interesting than, 'bus driver makes eleven-year-old boy walk six miles home in the dark after ten pence shortfall in fare.' If not, at least give me some notion of how to shave the word-count."

She laughed. "Seriously, that's our front page?"

"Unless you've got a better idea. It's been a slow week."

"Not anymore," she said. "It's got the makings of the best seven days of both of our careers."

"Right. Well, I like what I'm hearing. Unless you're on drugs: carry on."

"Have you ever heard of a 'Phyllis Robinson'?"

Chapter 12: Annabel's Great Escape

John watched Phyllis go by from inside Pizza Hut on the Strand. The sun shone from behind a thin white film of cloud that made the entire sky a slightly paler blue than it would have been without it. In fifteen minutes, it'd have burned away.

He had to concentrate carefully, because Mr Wint might not be along for another half a minute or more, and not anywhere obvious. How he did it was still a mystery. Annabel and Mr Kidd were always much closer to him than he was to Phyllis. Thirty or forty seconds for Mr Wint to appear, then merely an additional ten or twelve for the other two. Given how good Mr Wint was, it seemed odd he hadn't latched on to what was behind him. Like most shadows, he'd probably developed a degree of tunnel vision. An impairment in most walks of life, it definitely helped in this.

Or maybe he *had* latched on, but didn't care. Which would be highly disturbing, but of a piece with his profound aura of self-assurance.

Maybe he even knew about John.

But no, that was crediting him with too much. Quasi-supernatural powers. Easy to do that when someone freaked you out. More likely, he'd simply been in the business for a long time and he'd never done anything much else. He probably couldn't do crosswords, for example, or roller skate. He might not even be able to fire a gun.

But that was too much to hope. Not that he *would* fire a gun, however. This was Britain. Only wannabe drug barons used guns over here, and there weren't that many of those, thank God. Professional assassins weren't so crass.

Oh-oh, here Annabel came. He put on his sunglasses, went out onto the street and strode towards her, trying to disguise his natural gait. She was moving quickly and scanning the middle-distance behind him.

"Excuse me, Miss," he said as he passed by. He grabbed her arm. He had to: she'd ignore him otherwise.

She looked at him in the same moment he removed his sunglasses. A millisecond later she'd probably have felled him. As it was, her face transformed from one variety of shocked outrage to another. *Who the hell do you think YOU are?* to *Bloody HELL, it's YOU, you MORON!* Slightly different around the corners of the mouth.

But he was prepared for this too. "Looking for someone?" he said, simultaneously thrusting a photo of Mr Wint into her hand. You had to do a lot of things simultaneously with Annabel if you were to avoid a serious injury.

She looked at it for a second as if she thought it might be a religious tract. Then her mouth dropped open, her wrath evaporated, and, for the first time ever, he saw her look confused. "What the - ?"

"Into Pizza Hut."

"I'm not hungry." Her confusion had deepened. She was still mentally readjusting. "Okay, I didn't mean that. Obviously you're not dragging me in here to satisfy our appetites. But what's going on, John? We don't work together anymore!"

But he was on the phone to Phyllis. "I've got her," he said. "Go to the agreed spot." He hung up.

"Who the hell are you talking to?" Annabel said.

"Who do you think?"

"She's going to be in danger if I'm not following her. We can talk about this another time."

"You've already lost him now."

"Who?"

"Good try. Ring Alec and tell him to meet Phyllis in The Ivy Grill on Henrietta Street, in ten minutes' time. He's paying."

She sighed. The resistance went out of her. They were already standing in Pizza Hut, behind the little sign that said, 'Please wait here to be seated.' Two couples stood in front of them; another sidled up behind while they were arguing. Annabel took off her beret and shook out her long blonde hair. She was small, with blue eyes, and she exuded toughness. Looking into that face, you knew instinctively not to tread lightly.

She took out her phone. "Annabel here," she said wearily. "Drop your case files, Alec, and get over to The Ivy Grill on Henrietta Street. Your dream's just come true. You're taking Phyllis to lunch on the company tab. That's right. *The* Phyllis." She hung up. "What's this about, John? Where did you get this picture?"

"I've lots of others," he said, taking his phone out and showing her his collection of pictures of Annabel in various states of disguise, taken over the last few days.

"Very clever," she said.

"If I'd been an enemy agent and you were in hostile territory, you might well be dead now."

"Nice of you to rub it in. But, hey, that's *Call of Duty*," she added, for the benefit of eavesdroppers. "I told you we should have bought a board game."

"I only like computer games," he replied, seeing what she was doing. "We could play Mario tonight, or Sonic the Hedgehog."

She lowered her voice. "Okay, that's enough, John. Why have we even come in here? Can't we talk on the street?"

"Because Mr Kidd might go past any moment. I don't want him to see you."

"A friend of yours?"

"In the same way that Mr Wint is."

"Nice to see you haven't changed," she said. "I mean, not making any sense at all."

"Mr Kidd and Mr Wint. Phyllis's made-up names for her two shadows. Taken from *Diamonds are Forever*, I believe. And before you ask: neither's a nickname for you."

"Phyllis has *two* shadows? In addition to me?"

"Yup."

"Who's the other?"

"Wouldn't you like to know?"

She smiled. "Yes, please."

"It was a rhetorical question."

"I know. I take it you can *prove* what you're claiming."

"Affirmative."

"And that you're looking for some kind of information exchange. I tell you who Mr – 'Wint', is it? – is, and you reveal the identity of Mr Kidd, thus making it less likely that Mr Kidd will kill me. How kind. How considerate of the life of your close ex-colleague."

"Mr Kidd doesn't know who you are. Or that you even exist. He's as ignorant of you as you are of him – or were of him, until a few moments' ago."

"Are you sure of that?"

"Absolutely. I'm a body-language expert, remember? I definitely wouldn't try to exploit a situation in which your life might be in danger. You weren't just my colleague. You were my friend. You still are, insofar as it's possible to have a friend the Official Secrets Act makes it impossible to see on a social basis."

"Or any basis at all."

"I'm seeing you now," he said.

"Yes, and we're probably breaching it."

"Flirt."

She sighed. "We're getting off the subject with all this hilarious banter. What are you proposing?"

"You give me information about Mr Wint. In exchange, I give you information about Mr Kidd."

"The trouble is, you've actually played all your cards."

"Meaning?"

"Now that we in MI7 know there *is* a 'Mr Kidd', it shouldn't prove too difficult for us to locate and identify him. All we have to do is put another shadow out there with a brief to discover who's *one:* following 'Mr Wint', and *two:* isn't me. So I think we're done here. Thank you for the pizza we almost ordered, but I really ought to be getting back to Thames House now."

Good God, she'd outplayed him. The ground quivered beneath his feet. She coolly broke free of the queue, and he followed her outside the restaurant. They stood against a drainpipe. A bus roared past making a little breeze. Another pulled up and hissed.

"Before you go," he said, "can you at least tell me how much danger Phyllis is in?"

"I honestly don't know. Phyllis is your wife. You and she are connected, in other words, so I wouldn't underestimate the danger to yourself. Look, John, even if I hadn't just outflanked you, I wouldn't talk. An exchange of information can't just happen, not here. Thousands of miles from base, maybe, but in London, I'd have to clear it with Ruby Parker. I can plead your case, however. I might well be in touch again."

"Plead my case? How convincing can you make it?"

"I can tell Ruby Parker what's obvious: that you and Phyllis discovered something we didn't know. Entirely off your own backs, with no help from the extensive machinery of the state. Which is pretty impressive. The trouble is, she probably wouldn't agree to an 'exchange of information' with a pair of amateurs. I don't mean that in a derogatory sense, so don't take offence. She'd probably want you on the inside if we were ever to work together at all. Now, are you sure you'd be up to that? Because you were unwell last time I saw you."

"I'm better now."

She laughed. "People always say that when they want something. Apologies if that sounds brutal, but it's true."

"The reason I was mentally off-colour is because Phyllis and I were up in the air. She'd already turned down my marriage proposal. She was about to leave MI7. I suddenly realised how fragile everything was. I wasn't cut out to be an MP's husband, which seemed like the best case scenario. Being The Ultimate Londoner appeared to disqualify me as a spy. It was a disquieting time."

"And now you're married, that's made it all better?"

"Yes, it has."

"So can I tell Ruby Parker you'd like your old job back?"

"It's not just about me. It's about Phyllis."

"Talk to her then. Nothing would make me happier than for you to return. Phyllis was probably the best friend I ever had, and I miss both of you terribly. And I know Alec and Edna do. I probably shouldn't say that, incidentally. Look, put it another way. Let's say I'd actually told you who 'Mr Wint' was, a moment ago; let's say I'd told you all about him. Where would you be? What could you and Phyllis reasonably expect to do with that information? How would it help you? You're just ordinary citizens now. You know she's being followed. You've probably worked out Mr Wint's not necessarily friendly, otherwise why would *I* be there? What sort of an endgame do you envisage? Or even middle game? Admit it: you haven't the foggiest notion. You'd be one more piece of useless information worse off. Because jigsaws are only fun if you can do them. Otherwise, they're just useless scraps of cardboard."

He reached into his pocket and passed her his wad of photos. "That's 'Mr Kidd'."

She transferred the collection to her bag, as calmly if she'd expected this outcome all along. "Thank you. Obviously, it'll make it easier when I speak to Ruby Parker if you've been kind and cooperative."

Her phone rang. She took it out of her bag, listened to the speaker and hung up. Her expression had changed.

"That was Alec," she said. "Phyllis hasn't turned up."

John's phone rang. He looked at the screen. *Phyllis.*

Thank God. "Hello?" he said.

"Something terrible has happened," Phyllis said. "I didn't go to The Ivy Grill. I'm at home. Can you get back quickly? I need you here."

"I'm on my way."

She hung up before either of them could say any more.

"That was Phyllis?" Annabel said. "She's okay, then?"

"I, er, believe so. I'd better go."

But she was already walking away. "I'll tell Alec. Nice seeing you again. Take care."

Chapter 13: Something Even Worse

John left Annabel at the Strand and ran. As he entered Charing Cross Station, he called Phyllis back.

"I don't want to talk over the phone," she said. "I've reached the level of paranoia where I'm not sure who's listening in. But I'm not being held hostage. Where are you?"

"Central London. About to board a tube train. I'll be back in a few minutes."

"See you then."

Ten minutes later he walked through the front door on high alert. He didn't think he was walking into a trap – her voice hadn't suggested that – but he was definitely walking into the unknown. The hairs on the back of his neck stood up in the conventional way. His adrenalin pumped.

"I'm in here," she called from the living room.

She stood alone by the window in a white blouse and jeans, with her hair tied up. As far as he could tell, they were the only two people in the flat, which might constitute the beginnings of a relief, depending partly on what she said next. On the table, a teapot, six cups and saucers and a plate of biscuits suggested visitors, and since everything was meticulously arranged, they were more probably on their way than just departed. The furniture looked subtly different from this morning, so she'd likely done another sweep for bugs.

"The police are coming round," she said. "They want to ask me some questions. And I've got a firm of lawyers on the way. And possibly my parents. Okay, here's what you need to know," she added as if she hadn't already told him.

She paused, apparently for air. He hugged her. She hugged herself. They sat on the sofa.

"Begin again," she told herself. "Right. There's this journalist called Lucy Staveley. I don't know anything about her except that she works for a paper called *The Newbury Echo*. Newbury, where I was born and grew up. What she thinks she knows is that I was behind a plot to murder Aisling Baxter."

"What?"

"On the dark web, apparently. Where it can't be confirmed and I can't disprove it."

"How the hell's she got that idea into her head?"

"She's got 'evidence', apparently. 'Lots' of it. And she's got a reputation – albeit a minor one right now - as an effective crusader. What she knows that *is* true – and I've no idea how she got hold of this - is that, a month or two ago, after Aisling Baxter beat me fair and square in Newbury, Sir Anthony Hartley-Brown asked me to a meeting on the first floor of The Red Lion in Parliament Street. Technically, I suppose, it was a 'secret' meeting. Just me, Sir Anthony and the leaders of three Young Conservative groups. To be honest, I can't even recall that much about it."

"I remember you mentioning it, though. They said they might try and parachute you into some other constituency on the grounds that your political programme was so attractive. You said you didn't want to run as an MP anymore."

She put her hands on her head. "Two things about that meeting. Firstly, Sir Anthony had a copy of the minutes of my interview, which he'd shared. That's probably illegal in itself, but incidental here. Second, I'd made a big thing about devolving much more power to locally placed bodies: parish councils, town halls, provincial charities, that sort of thing. So I said I wasn't happy about being 'parachuted' into another constituency. Newbury was where I was born and grew up, and I'd missed my one and only chance there, so that was it: I was out. For good."

"I see, so you had a motive to kill Aisling Baxter, and you went on holiday with her, so you had an opportunity, but that's just circumstantial. It's not enough to go to publication with."

"It might be. If you're very careful about what you say. *We're not saying anything, just presenting the facts*, and leave the readers to draw their own conclusions. Obviously, Aisling Baxter being dead probably entails another round of interviews for Newbury's safe Parliamentary seat at some stage. I wasn't intending to stand anyway, but since the question hadn't yet formally arisen…"

"You haven't been able to state that publicly."

"She's only been in the ground a few days."

"And now, when you do recuse yourself, it'll look like a reaction to *The Newbury Echo*'s insinuations."

"Except that there aren't going to be any. Somehow, Sir Anthony got wind of the entire thing before it went to press. He called my parents. They've hired a firm of libel lawyers called Carneghan Strake, based in the City of London. The best in the business, apparently. Carneghan Strake's persuaded the courts to slap an injunction on the *Echo*. It hand-delivered a letter to *The Echo*'s office, this morning saying that what it's proposing to publish is 'an entirely untrue attack on a woman of impeccable moral character and therefore grossly defamatory'; all that kind of thing. If it goes to press, it faces 'ruination in the courts and the possible imprisonment of its principal initiators.' It names Lucy Staveley, the investigative journalist, and Roger McGregor, the editor. But obviously, they're not going to go down without a fight. These sorts of people never do. They think they've got justice on their side."

"How did Sir Anthony find out about it?"

"He's an influential figure. He's got connections. I guess someone at the *Echo* must have spoken to someone in Newbury who was a Conservative, and they must have talked to other Conservatives, and, since it involves Sir Anthony directly, someone told him. It makes sense."

"And he got on to your parents. And they got on to Carneghan Strake."

"For which, thank God," she said absently. "Just in the nick of time, apparently."

"The big question is, who wants to ruin you? And why?"

"What did Annabel say?" she asked. "Because it doesn't take much to see that this is connected to Mr Wint. God, I feel stupid calling him that now. Why can't I ever take anything seriously? It's your influence, John."

"Mine?" He sighed. "You're probably right."

"It's a good one, most of the time. Anyway, getting back to the subject: they've sent someone out to keep an eye on me, but that's probably expensive, and they can't keep it up for ever. Far better to go on the offensive. Load me down with so many problems that I forget all about Aisling Baxter and her little project."

There was a knock at the front door. They looked at each other.

"That'll be the police or Carneghan Strake," she said. "Or possibly, my parents."

"Look through the spy glass before you open the front door. It could be Mr whatever we're calling him now. Assuming it isn't, would you like me out of the way?"

"We're married," she said as she left the room. "You live here. So no."

He stood up. If it was Carneghan Strake, handshakes would probably be expected. If it was the police, less so. If it was her parents, he'd probably have to defend himself. They still hadn't said congratulations for getting married, and now this. It'd be difficult to make *The Newbury Echo* his fault, but they'd had the whole journey down to find ways.

When Phyllis came back into the room, she was alone. She'd put her shoes on. She had her bag over her shoulder.

"It's a taxi," she said. "Courtesy of Carneghan Strake. They don't do home visits, apparently. It's a dedicated ride and I've just had a text confirming the sender, so it's okay. You wait here, otherwise you'll just be dumped in a waiting room with *The Law Society Gazette* and a pile of car magazines. You know how these people work: their office, their rules. Put the dinner on. Before I go, you didn't tell me earlier: what did Annabel say?"

"Nothing of interest. She'll put in a good word for us with Ruby Parker, but if we want to get to the bottom of this, we probably need to re-apply for our old jobs."

"Not the worst thing I can think of right now. Depends whether you can persuade them you're better. Which you probably are. And whether you want it. We'll talk about it later."

She kissed his cheek and closed the front door softly as she left.

What next? Apart from putting the dinner on?

He picked up his phone and went to photos. They'd only taken one in all the time they'd been in Malta, and it hadn't even been with his camera. She'd sent him it, in addition to putting it in 'six different locations in the cloud'.

Here it was. A list of names of journalists.

It would take a while, but he needed to find out who they were and where they were now. Then he needed to speak to them. He'd show Annabel what a fully determined amateur could do. He'd show all of them.

Chapter 14: We're Here to Help

As she left the flat, it occurred to Phyllis how easy it might be to fake a text from a solicitor's *We politely request your immediate presence at our Westminster office. RSVP.* And how odd if it was real.

But then, her parents had warned her something like this might happen. No ordinary solicitor's, her mother said: they didn't like wasting time, for a start. Which, unless their client was actually in custody, meant making him or her come to them. A free ride wasn't actually what it looked, of course. It would appear on the invoice later. Plus the travel time.

It took twenty-five minutes to reach Carneghan Strake's offices, set within a dour grey building on Cheapside, just round the corner from Mansion House. Plenty of time for Phyllis to speculate about who'd got it in for her, and why. What sort of 'information' did Lucy Staveley actually have? Would Carneghan Strake tell her? Would they even know? What kind of a meeting was she even going to? Wasn't she supposed to be seeing the police at some point? And what did the police want? And exactly how close was she to becoming the doomed victim of some sort of airtight frame-up?

Pointless thinking about it. At the worst, Carneghan Strake might simply want a hello-goodbye meeting designed to tick a box. But she had serious questions, and she wanted answers.

On the other hand, she couldn't afford to alienate them. *The best in the business.* Right now, they might be all that stood between her and public ignominy.

Well, Lucy Staveley might be sitting there nursing a sense of injustice, righteously indignant because she couldn't get her mendacious little yarn into print, but it was nothing against the grievance that she, Phyllis, felt. It might even have been a good thing if Lucy Staveley *had* rushed into print. Because she *was* wrong, and if she pushed that 'publish and be damned' button, like they sometimes did, Phyllis would make her suffer. Oh boy, yes. Making sure she never worked again would be only the beginning. You don't go round ruining people's lives without there being a price. And Lucy bloody Staveley and that scumbag Roger McGregor would pay it in full, every last penny. She'd utterly destroy them, however long it took. Even if she had to dedicate the rest of her life to it. Because let's face it, the rest of her life wouldn't be much good for anything else if they got their scummy way.

When she got out of the taxi, she almost slammed the door. She had no idea she was capable of feeling such rage. Hatred, really. She didn't even offer her usual tip. She wanted answers, and pronto.

The door to Carneghan Strake was three granite steps up from the street. It opened before she could reach the bell by the brass plaque. Inside: a grey-haired, straight backed man whose thin, straight nose and arched eyebrows made his face look longer than it probably was. He wore a suit. "Mrs Mordred," he said. "How nice to make your acquaintance."

She hadn't quite got used to hearing herself called that, especially accompanied by that idiosyncratic nineteenth century-type expression, but since it was her parents who'd hired him, she wouldn't demur. Apart from everything else, it was progress, Mum and Dad-wise.

"Pleased to meet you," she replied.

"Please follow me," he said, as he led her up a flight of stairs. "I'm Ian Batchelor, one of the partners. Sir Anthony's already here, plus one of the other partners, Dina Oforka-Jones. We're five in all. Partners, I mean. Dina and I will be dealing with *The Newbury Echo*. I hardly need tell you, we take this whole sordid business very, very seriously indeed. Right now, just to set your mind at rest, there's no chance of them going to press. None whatsoever."

"I didn't know Sir Anthony was coming."

"Oh, yes. He's very upset about the entire thing, naturally, and blames himself for part of it. However, I'm being indiscreet. I'm sure he'll tell you himself."

They'd arrived on a landing. Ian Batchelor opened a door for her, then stood by the frame, so she could precede him.

A large glass-topped desk filled one half of the room. A slim middle-aged black woman with hair in a bun came from behind it, offering a handshake. Sir Anthony Hartley-Brown, thin, balding with a moustache, dressed in a tweed jacket and grey trousers, stood to one side looking awkward. A disused fireplace occupied one wall. Framed black and white photographs of London monuments hung at precise horizontal intervals, exactly midway between the floor and the ceiling. The room was expensively carpeted and smelt of pot pourri and new furniture: two easy chairs and a sofa, all in beige leather.

"Hello, Mrs Mordred," the middle-aged woman said. "I'm Dina Oforka-Jones, one of the partners. You already know Sir Anthony, obviously."

"I can't say how sorry I am about all this Phyllis," Sir Anthony said. "I'm just on my way out, but I stayed to see you and apologise. Not that I know how they got hold of any of it, but it's my fault. I took a risk disseminating those minutes, and it backfired. Badly."

"You've nothing to apologise for," Phyllis told him. "You were only trying to be nice. And the minutes are part of a package, apparently. On its own, they're pretty meaningless."

"We'll put this right," he said. "I promise you. Thank you for being so understanding. You're in very good hands here." He turned to the lawyers. "Dina, Ian: keep in touch."

Ian Batchelor saw him downstairs. There was a roar of traffic as the front door opened and closed – it was apparently soundproofed in here. Then Ian Batchelor raced back up again. Meanwhile, Dina Oforka-Jones bade Phyllis sit down on one of the armchairs.

"Can I get you anything, Mrs Mordred?" she asked. "Tea, coffee?"

"I'm fine, thank you," Phyllis said. Ian Batchelor closed the door behind him and came to sit on another armchair. "And please call me Phyllis."

Dina Oforka-Jones picked up a wad of papers from the desk, and sat down on the sofa. "We'd better begin. We've told the police that, if they want to speak to you, they'll have to do it formally, with us present. They've decided not to bother."

Ian Batchelor crossed his legs, brushed a piece of imaginary fluff from his kneecap and nodded. "Which strongly suggests they were hoping to get you alone so they could trip you up; get you to say something indiscreet in the anxiety of the moment. Unfortunately, that's all too often how they work."

"Lesson one," Dina continued. "*Never trust the police*. They're not your friends and never will be. If they ever want to speak to you, and we're not there, then, however natural it might look – let's say you're both at the same scene, where something important's happening, or has happened – always say *no*."

"Not without us present. And we're only a phone call away."

"Understood," Phyllis replied.

"Good," Dina said. "Now, is it okay if we jump in at the deep end?"

Phyllis nodded.

Dina and Ian exchanged the briefest of solemn glances, as if they'd long since discussed which of them should shoot first, and Dina had drawn the short straw.

"One thing Lucy Staveley appears to have," Dina said, "is some kind of 'sex tape'. What can you tell us about that, if anything?"

Phyllis blinked slowly. So that was part of the package too. "When my husband and I arrived in our hotel room in Malta, we had sex. We're newly married. Then he noticed something that looked suspicious on the plant pot facing the Jacuzzi, in the *en suite*. It turned out to be a camera. We contacted the British High

Commission in Ta' Xbiex. They told us to come straight over. On the way, I contacted Aisling Baxter and Toby Mansfield, both friends of mine. Toby was at the airport. It later turned out his room was infested with cameras and microphones, just like ours. But he was forewarned. Aisling and Robert… well, they'd done what John and I had. I mean, they'd *had sex*. They were mortified, obviously. They joined us in Ta' Xbiex, along with Toby and his girlfriend, and Ted Taylor and his wife Millie, and we all spent a very uncomfortable night on an old-fashioned lounge suite while a couple of British IT technicians, flown in from abroad at very short notice, investigated our hotel rooms."

"It might be worth mentioning at this point," Dina said, "that, to our knowledge, the *Echo* only possesses a copy of Aisling Baxter and her husband having sex. There's no indication that she also possesses one of you and your husband."

"Although such a thing might turn up," Ian said.

"They might already have it, just not be saying," Dina told him. "I know this case better than you, Ian, and I know how hacks work. Contrary to the way they're usually presented in fiction and in films, they're not like scientists, bound to account for anomalies in their research. They're not even like detectives. They need a story and they need it fast. They'll look at the evidence in front of them, they'll hastily cook up a simplistic little narrative and they'll simply discard anything that doesn't fit. *Destroy the loose ends*, in other words: make as if they never existed. In doing so, they won't experience the slightest twang of conscience, because they're not committed to abstract notions of truth. They're committed to getting on in their careers, and there's no journalistic equivalent of the peer review system. No hack wants to spend weeks, months, years, assessing the relative virtues of different hypotheses. Well, maybe some, but they quickly discover they're not cut out for the job. They'll be overtaken by someone faster and less conscientious. If it sells papers, it's true. Because someone in the trade *makes* it true."

Ian gave an irritated frown. "So the *Echo* might actually have the two sex tapes – the one of Aisling Baxter and her husband and the one of Phyllis and her husband – and just not be saying anything about the latter?"

"Precisely," Dina said. "Because the story they want to tell is that Phyllis herself set up the cameras. She filmed Aisling Baxter so as to discredit her and ultimately replace her as Newbury's next MP. Obviously, Phyllis wouldn't film herself. The cameras in her room were put there by herself to make it look like she was equally a victim."

"But *I* told Aisling about the cameras!" Phyllis said. "It was *me* who alerted her! Without me, she'd probably never have known!"

"Can you prove that?" Ian asked.

"I – I don't know," Phyllis said. "I'd have to look at my phone, maybe."

"In any case, you can only have told her after she'd had sex with her husband," Dina said, "and you'd therefore 'got what you wanted'. I'm sorry, Phyllis. That's complete nonsense, obviously. I'm just trying to stretch the facts to fit the kind of outlandish story a couple of chancers like Lucy Staveley and Roger McGregor might fabricate."

"Or have," Ian said.

"Look, I think it's time we levelled with you, Phyllis," Dina said, "and in return, I'd like you to level with us. You need to tell us everything. This is how the *Echo* was hoping to spin it, although it knew it would have to be careful with its wording, and whether it alleged or merely implied, and if the latter, how strongly or weakly. You attended an interview a short time ago for the post of next Conservative candidate for the Parliamentary constituency of Newbury. You didn't get it. Aisling Baxter did. A short time afterwards, you and four other Conservative Party members, including Sir Anthony, met secretly on the first floor of The Red Lion in Westminster, where you hatched a plot to remove Aisling Baxter from the picture and re-run the selection process.

You subsequently went to work at Conservative Campaign HQ as a means of keeping an eye on the situation, and when Ted Taylor organised a trip to Malta with Aisling Baxter as one of the guests, you applied to an old friend of yours, Toby Mansfield, whom the database in Conservative Campaign Headquarters had told you was also on the guest-list, to get an invite. Your purpose originally was to film Aisling Baxter having sex with her husband and put it on YouTube. Simply to make her a laughing-stock, not to do her any serious harm. But she discovered the cameras, and you realised she might discover who was behind them. You therefore arranged to have her killed. Because the police accident report suggests it may not have been entirely an accident. She may have been forced off the road. At the time of her death, you were with Toby Mansfield in the LKX hotel, having received an invitation from Aisling Baxter earlier that evening. Only she never sent that invitation. You sent it to yourself, knowing she'd be out, and you also sent one to Toby Mansfield, so that he could provide an alibi. You were nowhere near her when her car ran into that boulder."

"That's the story we believe the *Echo* was hoping to go with," Ian Batchelor said after a long silence during which Phyllis's speechlessness spoke for itself.

"You can probably see why the police would like to talk to you," Dina said. "Only, eighty per cent of what I've said is invention. I've made it sound like a plausible story. But of course, in reality, it's simply a collection of facts, and you can connect facts to make any story you like."

Dina smiled. "What we do know is that Aisling Baxter went over there to investigate the online travel business. If there was foul play, that's a much more plausible source."

"Except it doesn't have the human interest value," Ian said. "It wouldn't make a BBC mini-series. It doesn't have the jealous rival determined to wreak revenge and take possession of what should have been hers by right."

"And naturally, it'd take months, possibly years, of work to establish," Dina said. "Lucy Staveley doesn't strike me as a grafter."

"How much do we know about what she's got?" Phyllis said.

"Virtually everything," Dina said. "We've got spies at the *Echo*. We looked at people who informed Sir Anthony of what was happening, and asked them who they'd got it from. We simply traced the thread back, in other words. Ultimately, we identified those people at the *Echo* who had mixed feelings about the Staveley-McGregor conspiracy, and we motivated them accordingly."

She and Ian Batchelor exchanged glances again. This time, it was Batchelor's turn to ask the awkward question.

"Talking about spies," he said. "Sorry to have to ask you this, Phyllis, but the *Echo* has documentation strongly suggesting you and your husband belong to MI6. That *must* be nonsense, mustn't it?"

"You need to be honest with us here, Phyllis," Dina said. "We're your friends."

Phyllis laughed. "I'm not sure where that could have come from. There's no truth in it whatsoever."

The silence lasted too long. They weren't just speculating from the 'evidence'. They knew.

"We used to," she said in a monotone. She felt a rosy glow of embarrassment filling her neck and face. *No truth in it whatsoever* was a falsehood. They'd told her they were her friends, then she'd lied. Admitting her duplicity a second later didn't necessarily make it any better.

But strangely, they did seem pleased.

Probably because from their point of view, it was progress. At least she'd admitted the connection.

Yet they still didn't believe her. They thought she still worked there.

"We know you're probably bound by the Official Secrets Act," Dina said quietly, "so we expected you to deny it. You're honourable. We respect that. But of course, it now means we have to ask you another question, possibly the most important one."

"We'll take it as given that you've now left MI6," Ian said, "but could it be that, when you were in Malta, you were still working for them? Because that would make sense of everything: the cameras and the killing. If killing is what it was."

"If you *were* employed by MI6," Dina said, "it would mean we could get the British government to approach the *Echo* on the grounds of national security."

"It would also be a narrative framework that would utterly trump Lucy Staveley's," Ian said, "and of course, it would mean that whatever happened in The Red Lion was totally irrelevant. Sir Anthony need never be named."

"I'd like to say yes," Phyllis said after another uncomfortable pause. "I almost wish we had been. But we left several weeks before the Malta trip. We left to get married."

"I see," Dina said. "That's a pity. Anyway, I'm sure we've given you lots of food for thought. We'll call it a day for today. Ian will show you out. If there are any developments, get straight in touch, any time of the day or night. And I know this probably goes without saying, but don't speak to *anyone* about it. Journalists sometimes disguise themselves as ordinary members of the public. They'll buy you a drink just to get you talking. You make a joke, or you say something ironic, and they'll print it as your solemn conviction. You did, after all, say it, and who were they to know you didn't mean it? And remember, everyone's a journalist nowadays. You get any hassle, even a whiff of it, get straight in touch with me."

"There is one other thing," Phyllis said.

Ian Batchelor had stood up. He sat down again, but he didn't look as if he thought it could conceivably be important.

"Anything at all," Dina said.

"There's been a man following me since we got back from Malta."

She noticed both of them jump, just infinitesimally. The sort of thing you wouldn't see unless you were looking for it. When they recovered – again, almost, but not quite instantaneously – they looked annoyed. Perhaps more with themselves than with her, like they knew they'd given something away.

"A man?" Dina said.

"'Following you' in what way?" Ian asked. "Where?"

Phyllis switched on her phone and showed them one of the photos. "A few days ago, I mentioned to my husband that I thought someone was shadowing me. We're trained to pick up on the signals, even if we can't immediately recognise their source. He came to have a look. This is one of his photos. There are others. Whoever this guy is, he's been on my tail almost continually."

"Have you told the police?" Dina asked.

"I'm not sure they'd believe me," Phyllis replied. "Even if they did, they probably wouldn't consider it worth investigating. With all the budgetary cuts they've suffered, and the moped crime, and the knife crime, they've enough on their plate. Besides, he hasn't actually done anything illegal. And they'd probably struggle to establish he *was* following me."

"Yes, of course," Dina said. "All good considerations."

"If it's been going on for a while," Ian said, "it's almost certainly got nothing to do with the *Echo*."

"Phyllis, I can't believe you didn't tell us about this *earlier!*" Dina said, finally letting her annoyance show. "We were about to show you out, and you mention this as an *afterthought?*"

"I've had a lot on my mind," Phyllis said. She felt stupid now. "I'm sorry."

"It must have occurred to you that someone's trying to *frame* you!" Dina went on. "*Someone* must have sent the Echo that material, and here's our first material lead, and you almost let it slip through our fingers, as a thing of virtually no account!"

"As I said, I'm really sorry."

Dina took a deep breath and let it out. "Apologies. I shouldn't have spoken to you like that. It was unprofessional. I'm sorry."

"It's fine," Phyllis said. She felt like a little girl who'd been scolded by the headmistress. As if she deserved it, and the apology was more than she had the right to expect. Humiliation mingled with gratitude.

"I need you to send me those pictures," Dina said. "We need to hire a private investigator or two. We need to find out who this guy is, and we need to talk to him. *Make* him talk, if he won't do it willingly."

"How will we do that?" Ian asked.

"I don't know," she said. "Not yet. Phyllis, thank you for your time. We really must call it a day now. I'm due in court soon and Ian's got another client to see."

Ian opened the door.

Phyllis still felt mortified. They'd set out to help her, and she'd fallen way short of their high hopes. She descended the stairs, and Ian let her out onto the street.

She noticed she was expected to make her own way home. No ride back. She didn't deserve one.

Any other time in her life, she'd have laughed. But she'd taken a lot of heavy knocks recently, and it was beginning to eat away at her sense of who she was. She didn't feel her usual confident self. She felt awful.

Then she noticed a man coming towards her on the other side of the road. Sharp facial features, serious expression, jet black hair retreating slightly from the front, long dark overcoat. Alec Cunningham. MI7 Alec. She beamed.

"Phyllis," he said, when he was in range.

"You can't believe how glad I am to see you," she said. "Sorry about the Ivy Grill. How did you know I'd be here?"

"Ruby Parker sent Kevin to watch your flat after Annabel called in. He followed your taxi here. Long story short: I've been asked to escort you back to Thames House. I mean, if you want to come. It's an invitation, not an order."

"Right now, I can't think of anything else I'd rather do," she said.

"Missed you," he said, as they began to walk.

She took his arm. "Missed you too. Missed everybody."

Ian Batchelor came upstairs, closed the door and sat down in the seat he'd just vacated.

"This could be bad," he said. "Very bad indeed. Have you ever seen that man before? The one in the photo?"

She ran her hands distractedly across her hair. "No. Never." She closed her eyes. "Why the hell didn't they speak to us first?"

"Academic, I suppose. What do you propose we do?"

"If they're planning to kill Phyllis Robinson, which seems probable, they'll want it to look as separate from Malta as possible. That's why they're biding their time. But in that case, Lucy bloody Staveley's got the potential to become their worst nightmare."

"In other words, we urgently need to get back the material we sent her. Did you believe Phyllis Robinson's claim that she's no longer working for MI6?"

Dina shrugged, then nodded. "Unless she's playing a very cunning game indeed, I'm sure she's telling the truth. She wouldn't have shown us the photo of the man who's following her otherwise. She'd have shown it at work, and they'd *know* who he was. One way or another, they'd probably have dealt with him by now. And the fact that she came haring over here at the drop of a hat. She must think she needs us. And that she hasn't got anyone else to fall back on."

"What about when she was holidaying in Malta? A spy then?"

"I bloody hope so. I don't dislike her. It'd be a shame for her to die for nothing. We mustn't have any more contact with her. If they find out we're seeing her, they'll want to know why. If she calls, we fob her off. If she comes knocking at the door, we don't answer it. I'm bloody glad I sent a car to pick her up now. It's unlikely they'll be following her that closely."

"What if they are?"

"Let's not get paranoid. Once we get that material back from Lucy Staveley, we can cut all ties with Phyllis Robinson. We'll have it done tonight. We won't bill her either. No money trail for anyone to follow. We'll be in the clear."

They sat in silence out of a kind of ersatz respect for the dead. Eventually, Dina shook her head. "They'll go after the travel agent too, in the end," she said sombrely, "Surely as night follows day."

Ian sighed. "Last of the loose ends."

"Then it'll be as if none of this nightmare ever happened."

"Amen to that."

Chapter 15: Adrian Fenech

Adrian Fenech, retired Malta police Sergeant Major 1, had been following Phyllis for over a week. He still didn't know who the hell her principal tail was. Obviously, she was in terrible danger. Whatever had happened to the deceased British couple on the coast road from Valletta – and the accident report wasn't clear: by the time he got to it, it looked a lot like a redaction – their deaths, followed by the appearance in Britain of a professional shadow attached to the second most prominent member of their party, didn't bode remotely well. Mrs Mordred was marked for elimination, and her condemners were using the passage of time to forestall a Maltese connection in the minds of subsequent investigators. In the meantime, they were determined not to lose sight of her.

Who 'they' were was the crucial question, and the one to which Fenech had dedicated the last two years of his life, long before he'd even heard of the Mordreds: ever since his estranged wife and daughter had been killed in a road accident almost identical to the one that – according to the official report - killed the Baxters. Sitting alone on his porch after the funeral, nursing a half-bottle of brandy and gazing at the sunset over the hills, a mixture of hard thought, bitterness and righteous indignation set him thinking about how the roads had become unusable because the guys at the top spent too much of what they raised in tax on themselves. Corrupt politicians attracted investigators, which the Baxters had probably been. And Phyllis Mordred probably was. Or had been, until she'd been scared off.

Not everyone agreed with him about the government. They said that to make potholes the pretext for a call to revolution was taking the business of road surfacing too seriously. But then he began to probe. Retirement gave him the time. And the more he found, the more he thought he was right. Among other things, he read Daphne Caruana Galizia's blog. The day she was killed by a car bomb, his convictions were finally set in concrete. He had a feeling he might be next.

When he heard a rumour that a soon-to-be British politician and her husband were coming to Malta to investigate something highly confidential, but probably focussed on Anglo-local legal misconduct, he looked for ways to make himself useful. After spy cameras were apparently found in their room, he succeeded in swinging a job at the LKX Hotel – their hastily rearranged accommodation – discreetly 'safeguarding their interests', a kind of bodyguard-at-a-distance, minder-the-client-needn't-know-about role. He used it to find out all about his charges, more than his employer, the hotel manager, strictly required. More than was probably legal.

His endeavours were propitious. When Aisling Baxter and her husband were killed – something he couldn't have prevented: with the best intention in the world, he could only be in one place at a time, and they'd taken off suddenly, under a veil of secrecy – he knew exactly where to find John and Phyllis Mordred after they'd left for Britain. Phyllis was pretty obviously Aisling Baxter's lieutenant because she'd been entrusted with an important document. And she couldn't be frightened of the crooks, otherwise why would she post its contents online? All in all, she was Adrian Fenech's kind of gal.

Thanks to the hotel register, he had her phone number too. And her husband's. He'd gleaned so much information about them, it seemed a pity to waste it. Which is what would happen if they went back to Britain and he stayed in Malta.

In short, God had given him an opportunity to hit back at the bad guys by becoming these guys' guardian angel, and he couldn't do that if they were separated by two thousand miles.

One problem: he didn't have the kind of money that would allow him to stay in Britain longer than about a fortnight. He could stay with his Aunt Julia, in the London district of Southall, but she was eighty, and although she'd be pleased to see him, fourteen days might be outstaying his welcome if he didn't make himself available for grocery errands and the like. Meaning less guardian angel time.

Still, if it was the right thing to do, you had to do it, no excuses. He flew to Britain, moved in for a short stay with Aunt Julia, and began to watch Phyllis Mordred.

And it was soon obvious his fears were real. She was being watched, and by someone he'd never seen before, an evil-looking son of a bitch. Whoever he was, after he'd finished tailing Phyllis, he repaired to a random London hotel: a different one each night. Somebody must be paying him an awful lot to stay off the radar. Fenech contacted an old colleague in Valletta, who unofficially ran the photos he'd taken of the mystery man past the various subsections of Investigations & Security. Nothing.

Which raised the obvious question: what next?

After ten days, the answer was obvious. He couldn't look after the Mordreds on his own, and carrying on the same would be useless. Tailing had turned up as much as it was ever going to, and if he didn't watch his step, he might even end up getting even more entangled. He certainly wasn't protecting anyone. He felt increasingly like a stalker. Sleazy and a little self-conscious.

And his cash was running out. And Aunt Julia was getting tired of him.

It was time to go home, wasn't it?

On the other hand, he couldn't just cut and run. All that good work would be wasted.

No, he had to tell at least one of them. If they refused to listen, he'd have done his moral duty. When he later read about Phyllis Mordred's death in the paper – if he ever did: it almost certainly wouldn't make the news in Malta – he'd have nothing to reprove himself for.

The main question was, how to approach them? He couldn't just turn up at their front door. That might spook them. And if they were being watched, and their flat was bugged, as it might easily be, he'd be putting them in more danger.

No, a phone call was his best bet.

There were all sorts of reasons why a respectable married woman wouldn't welcome the kind of message he intended to deliver. Her husband might be a little more receptive.

Then, an unexpected turn of events prompted a spur-of-the-moment change of plan. A morning in the Strand had ended unusually when Phyllis Mordred took off at speed. Fenech watched her shadow give up the chase, after which he ate indoors at Flamin' Hot Grill Guy on William IV Street and checked in to The Combermartie Hotel on Charing Cross Road. After an hour, during which he made no reappearance, Fenech had a brainwave. If he was quick, he could pay a visit to the Mordreds in Camden and speak to them in person. Way better than a phone call. True, he'd have to persuade them not to speak to him inside their flat – they'd almost certainly underestimated the possibility of bugs – but he could convince them he wasn't armed and dangerous. He could even take them to dinner – his funds were depleted but might just stretch to that – and show them he had their best interests at heart. Even if they thought he was crazy, at least they'd see he meant well.

He arrived outside their flat just in time to see Phyllis get into a taxi and disappear. She didn't turn in his direction.

Did this mean that her husband was alone?

Only one way to find out.

As always with these sorts of flats, it was in a semi-secure compound, fenced off by an imposing, brutal wooden gate with a keypad next to it. He buzzed their flat number.

"Hello?" came a man's voice. About the right age for John Mordred.

"My name is Adrian Fenech," he said, reciting what he'd rehearsed. "Ex-sergeant major 1 from the police force of the Republic of Malta, where you recently holidayed, and where Mrs and

Mrs Robert Baxter died in a tragic car accident that may or may not have been accidental, and I - "

"Stay where you are," the voice said. "I'll be down in a second."

Fenech straightened, unnerved not just by the firm instruction, by also by the tone of voice. Like he'd been expected.

What could it mean?

He hoped to God the Englishman wasn't humouring him. He might be calling the police. Mind you, his visa was in order, and -

The gate opened. John Mordred came out wearing a T-shirt beneath a suit jacket. He smiled suspiciously. "Let's go to the park," he said.

Chapter 16: Ted's in Nam

Alec and Phyllis took the tube to Westminster and walked to Thames House. He didn't seem to care if they were being followed. When he opened the door for her, and she strode into the lobby, Colin Bale stood behind his desk and beamed at her like she was the Prodigal Son and hang on, he was sure he had a fatted calf out the back somewhere. It was both like being home, and not, because he was being too creepily nice.

"Ruby Parker's waiting for you in her office," he said as she signed the register. "It's really lovely to see you again."

"Thank you," she said emotionally. "It's mutual." She hadn't expected to feel this way, as if all she'd ever wanted was to be a spy, and she'd had a short holiday which, apart from getting married and settling down with the man she loved, hadn't been nearly as enjoyable or rewarding as expected. She swallowed her sentiment and got into the lift with Alec. Of course, she wouldn't be allowed anywhere here unaccompanied from now on. Unless she reapplied for her job. And was successful, which wasn't a foregone conclusion.

Was *that* what this was about? Her being re-employed here? Actually, she had no idea. She'd just followed Alec in a kind of daze. After her interview at Carneghan Strake she'd probably have followed him, or Annabel, or Edna, or Ruby Parker, or even Suki, Ian or Victor, anywhere, without a single thought as to *where to* or *why*. She was fed up to the back teeth with thinking. Her fate wasn't good, Dina and Ian had impressed that much on her. She might as well let it wash over her and stop tormenting herself with counterfactuals.

The lift pinged - Basement 1 – and opened, revealing a corridor with a single door at the far end. They marched, knocked, and Phyllis entered in response to the command from within, while Alec closed himself outside from behind.

Ruby Parker, a late middle-aged black woman in a grey skirt suit, court shoes and stiff hair, stood before an unpretentious desk. Besides the desk – with its adjustable seat, PC, stationery holders, and trays marked 'In' and 'Out' - and the occupant, there was an empty chair for the visitor, a variety of house plants on different levels, and a portrait of the Queen hanging on the wall. As offices went, it was relatively Spartan.

"How nice to see you again, Phyllis," Ruby Parker said, with the warmth she probably reserved for guests. Normally, she was unreadable.

"Thank you for inviting me," Phyllis said. "It's nice to be back, albeit ever so briefly."

"How's John?"

"I think he's better."

She smiled indulgently. "I wouldn't be so sure. These things have a habit of coming and going. Sit down, please. I meant it when I said it was nice to see you again. We all miss both of you."

"John spoke to Annabel this morning," Phyllis said.

"I know. He's done some remarkable detective work. You both have."

"Thank you."

"At considerable risk to yourselves, I might add, which isn't anything I'd ever encourage. Be that as it may, what's done is done, and so far, you've remained safe."

"But I take it the prognosis isn't rosy."

"I'd probably have contacted you by now anyway. You're in danger, and you have been since the Baxters' supposed accident in Malta. I wouldn't have set Annabel to shadow you otherwise."

"*Was* it an accident?"

"Malta's a republic nowadays, and although the Baxters were British citizens and the Maltese police were very cooperative, I'm not so sure. Let's just say I have something like an intuition, without a shred of evidence to substantiate it."

"It feels suspicious," Phyllis said. "I agree. Did you know the man who helped organise the trip – Ted Taylor - has unofficially disappeared?"

"He's in Vietnam."

"*Vietnam?* What's he doing there?"

"He owns a villa in Phu Quoc. I would imagine the stress of staying in Newbury was becoming overwhelming. We've no reason to think he's done anything wrong. The fact that he didn't inform his daughter doesn't mean much. Apparently, they don't get on. She's going through the motions of looking concerned, because she's afraid that if he does get killed, she might be implicated. It's not a realistic fear. I assume you know why Ted Taylor and the Baxters were in Malta?"

"My understanding was: to investigate internet travel companies and the extent to which they might be engaging in unfair business practices, driving traditional travel agents out of the marketplace."

Ruby Parker nodded. "It must have struck you as very odd that you would be shadowed here in London for something like that. And yet that list of names that Aisling Baxter gave you: Edna followed it up, under her police alias, Detective Sergeant Leona Quarshie. Every person on the list was an ex-journalist, someone driven out of the profession after an editor caved in to legal pressure not to publish his or her investigative findings about internet travel companies."

Phyllis sighed. "'Legal pressure not to publish' sounds vaguely familiar."

"What do you mean?"

"Before I met Alec, about an hour ago, I was in a meeting with two senior partners in Carneghan Strake, a solicitors' firm on Cheapside. Which is probably highly ironic, although, to be fair, I've yet to see their bill."

Ruby Parker sat up as if someone had just prodded her. "Solicitors? Can I ask why?"

"A journalist called Lucy Staveley, working for *The Newbury Echo*, somehow came into possession of a cache of documents whose total effect – though it falls far short of proof, as of course it must – is to suggest that I arranged for Aisling Baxter to be murdered."

"My God. *You?*"

"Me."

"Sorry, I like to think we're fully abreast of matters here in MI7, but this is news to me. I knew nothing about it. And Carneghan Strake have prevented her going to press with it, presumably?"

"For the time being, yes."

"And how did *they* find out about it?"

"Sir Anthony Hartley-Brown's implicated. He and I and three other Conservatives had a meeting on the first floor of The Red Lion just after Aisling was selected. Lucy Staveley knows about that meeting, and what she's got may suggest that we hatched a plot to kill Aisling and put me on the throne, so to speak. I say 'may' because I don't know. I haven't seen what she's got. Carneghan Strake obtained some kind of injunction, and, as it stands, it's stalemate."

"You mean, Sir Anthony found out about it before it could go to print? Yes, that sounds plausible. Has anyone any idea where Lucy Staveley got this wad of so-called information?"

"I'm afraid not. An 'anonymous source', I believe. I know this sounds crazy, but I'm half-tempted to pick up the phone and ask to speak to her. The evidence *can't* point to me, however much it might seem to. Together, we might be able to work out who it does point to. However, I'm sensible enough to realise that would be a very bad idea. Carneghan Strake gave me strict instructions not to talk to anyone, under any circumstances. Technically, I shouldn't even be speaking to you, although obviously, that's absurd."

"You certainly *mustn't* call Lucy Staveley," Ruby Parker said. "Journalists want stories. Sometimes they want the truth as well, but not always. Err on the side of caution."

"That's what the solicitors said. Minus the 'sometimes they want the truth as well'. Have you any idea who's following me? When I think about it, that's what I came here to find out."

"It's all credit to you and John that we don't seem to be doing very well without you. I didn't know about Carneghan Strake, and none of us in this department knew that Marchus Grubfeld was being followed by anyone in addition to Annabel. Annabel didn't even know John was there, let alone a third player."

"'Marchus Grubfeld'? That's the name of the guy with the black hair and the lined face? Who is he?"

"Thanks to John pulling Annabel aside in the Strand, we've presently lost him. However, we expect to pick up the trail tomorrow morning, when he starts following you again. You probably won't be surprised to learn he's a contract killer, a gangster with delusions of grandeur. Unfortunately, the German police questioned and released him about a year ago. The consensus in Interpol is that there isn't enough evidence to bring him to trial. Innocent till proven guilty is the principle. In this case, I have serious reservations about it."

Phyllis sighed. "So we can't touch him."

"We can ensure he won't touch *you*. But he may not intend to."

"Oh?"

"If he's behind the death of the Baxters, he may be waiting before he strikes again, so that the British police are less likely to connect the two things. But another possibility is that he's hesitating. He's done a little research, or more likely, someone's done it for him: there aren't that many brains among 'international assassins', as they like to call themselves. He's found out you're a spy. He may not yet be certain you're an *ex*-spy. Which is why I asked Alec to pick you up today and bring you in. I don't know how you feel about coming back to work here, and I'm not going to ask you formally. Yet. What I am going to ask you to do, for your own safety, is to make a good *pretence* of working here, starting tomorrow."

"I'm not sure what you mean. Are you suggesting - "

"That every weekday morning, until we reach the end of this business, whatever it is, you come in to Thames House every morning at nine and you go home at five, just as you used to do. That should redouble whatever hesitancy he feels about killing you. It'll give us breathing space to decide what to do next. But, as I say, I'm not sure we'll need it."

"Why not?"

"As I've said, my gut instinct is that he and his bosses are prevaricating because they're not sure whether you work for MI7. I think they may already have decided that killing you is too risky, hence perhaps the parcel of 'information' sent to *The Newbury Echo*. It would constitute an alternative way of bringing you down."

"I still don't know why they'd want to."

"I would imagine because, against all the odds, Aisling Baxter was on the brink of discovering something damning. And, given sufficient time and freedom, it might conceivably occur to us in MI7 to set out on the same trail. We need to be kept busy, or eliminated. By 'we', I chiefly mean you."

Phyllis smiled. "I'm not sure how coming in here to work all day is going to stop Lucy Staveley."

"I agree with you that whatever she's got, we need to see. Which is why I'm going to send Annabel in, tonight."

"A burglary?"

"If Lucy Staveley and her editor are sensible, they'll have put it in a safety deposit box in their local bank. But my guess is they won't have got that far. It's worth a try."

"If they have, we're sunk."

"It's unlikely they'll anticipate anyone stealing it. They've had a call from a reputable firm of solicitors, not a string of menaces from the criminal underworld. They've almost certainly got a safe on the premises. It'll be there. Or in scanned files, on one or more of their computers, or in the cloud. Probably both. If we can get hold of those files, they need never know we've paid them a visit. We can't be sure of destroying what they've got, even if we remove it in its totality, because whoever sent it to them in the first place may just re-send it."

"Of course. What will I be doing while I'm 'working' here?"

"We can make good use of you. You know the ropes and you're still bound by the Official Secrets Act, so it's not as if anyone's got to cover up what they're doing every time you walk by. We still haven't found out who your second shadow is, by the way, the older man. As soon as we do, I'll let you know. We've checked with Interpol, though. He's not one of theirs, and not known to them."

"The mystery deepens."

"It can't deepen for ever."

"What about John? I mean, if I suddenly look off limits, might Marchus Grubfeld not just change tactics and go after him?"

"That's partly what we want to find out. If we take you both out of play, we might lose him altogether, and he might have other targets. John's intrinsically safer than you are. He works from home, and we can have him watched much more easily than we can follow you around London."

"Can I tell him?"

She smiled. "I'd strongly advise you to, yes. While we're on the subject of John, there's something we need to discuss."

"Oh?"

"Before he left, he gave me formal consent to broach his psychological evaluation with you, if I deemed it helpful. If you're not okay with that, we don't have to continue."

She relaxed a little. "If he's fine with it, so am I. But I probably won't keep it secret from him."

"I wouldn't expect you to. The point is, we missed something important. According to Doctor Chakladar, John has a 'subtle inferiority complex'. In short, he feels less capable than his colleagues. That may well have been at the root of his problems all along."

Phyllis smiled. "Sorry, I'm a bit of a psychology sceptic."

"So I've been told," Ruby Parker replied noncommittally. "Go on."

"I think it's useful for dealing with some mental disturbances, but only like exorcism once was. It's unhelpful to treat its diagnoses as objective analyses. Mumps and measles are real. They have causes and they have symptoms. Inferiority complexes and anxiety disorders aren't the same. They're all symptoms. John's a nice guy and he's self-effacing. Those two things go together. Too many people nowadays have no sense of their own limitations. I would imagine John 'suffers' from what used to be called the Christian virtue of humility."

"I agree with you… up to a point. The problem arises if virtues are relative to changing social conditions, which they probably are. What may have been one in the pre-modern age may not be one today. In any case, humility's a matter of degree. Too much, and it becomes harmful."

"Are you saying John's too humble?"

"Dr Chakladar is."

Phyllis sighed. "I wouldn't want John to turn into the kind of man a lot of men are."

"Agreed. I'm raising this simply because, in you and John, I lost two invaluable officers, and I might conceivably be able to offer you both a way back in. Assuming that's ever an attractive prospect, John would need to talk to Doctor Chakladar. A clean slate, since it was his slightly inadequate diagnosis. And do bear in mind that, in a discipline as fluid as you've claimed psychology is, it's difficult to see what might motivate a senior practitioner to rescind his own judgement. Since Doctor Chakladar has, we must assume he's a man of some integrity."

"I'm sure John will be flattered. I'll talk to him when I get in."

"As regards his returning here, we'd need to wait until this business with Marchus Grubfeld is over. At the moment, Grubfeld's uncertain whether you're in or out. That's sustaining his involvement and probably helping us. And I'd also want you both together. It wouldn't be good for your marriage, and hence for either of you as operatives, for one of you to work here and the other not." She came out from the desk and opened the door for Phyllis to leave. "Thank you for coming in. Alec will escort you home to Camden, and he'll follow you in to work tomorrow morning, at a discreet distance, in place of Annabel. We won't require you to be accompanied around the premises once you're here. You'll be on roughly the same footing as you were before, just not on any long-term projects."

Phyllis stood up. "Thank you."

Chapter 17: Adrian Fenech Part 2

John pulled the gate shut behind him. So this was 'Adrian Fenech', the guy who'd been following the guy who was following Phyllis. Up till this afternoon, it'd been difficult to work out his place in the scheme of things. Then things had become clearer.

Some journalist in Newbury had a dossier of false, or misleading, information, and she was threatening to go to press. Where had it come from? Well, sometimes an unlikely coincidence was your best clue. Lucy Staveley had been prevented from publishing by a prestigious law firm, then almost instantly, apparently out of the blue, 'Adrian Fenech' turned up, wanting a conversation.

On the other hand, it didn't pay to jump to conclusions. It was difficult to see how following Mr Wint around London could provide useful material for a set of documents designed to frame Phyllis. And obviously Mr Wint – *why the hell couldn't he stop thinking of him as Mr bloody Wint?* – was no friend of 'Adrian Fenech', otherwise they'd have been together. If Mr Wint, bloody hell, was a bad guy, it might suggest that Mr Kidd – 'Adrian Fenech', for God's sake – was a good guy.

Maybe best keep an open mind. At least for the moment.

They were walking along the pavement now, side by side, both with their hands in their pockets.

"Where are we going?" Adrian Fenech asked.

"Are you hungry?" John asked.

"Not really. I've just had a pie. A chicken and mushroom pie," he added unnecessarily, suggesting he was nervous.

John stopped to face him. "Have you ever heard of someone called Lucy Staveley?"

Adrian Fenech looked at him and shrugged. "Not that I recall."

John was trained to recognise a lie. Six of seven different 'micro-expressions' at least, none of which Adrian Fenech exhibited. They began walking again.

"We're going to the park," John said. "Oakley Square Gardens, where we can sit on a bench and talk about this. I'd have invited you into my flat, but I'm still not sure who you are, and anyway, it might be bugged. That might sound paranoid but - "

"Your hotel room in Malta was also bugged."

"Right. Tell me how you know that. And how you found my address. And what else you know. Before you do that, have a look at these."

He took out his phone and flipped through his pictures of Fenech.

They found a bench. Oakley Square Gardens was a narrow band of mown grass planted with trees, bordered by low hedges and roads, and surrounded by uninspiring buildings. Not the sort of place you'd notice unless you were actively looking for somewhere to sit down in.

"What can I say?" Adrian Fenech said. "They're me. Where did you get them?"

"I took them myself."

"You asked how I know who you are. I'm a retired Maltese police officer. Now I'm a private detective of sorts. One who works for himself and doesn't get paid. I'm a kind of social justice warrior. I - "

"Social justice warrior?"

"What's wrong with that?"

"It's a derogatory term used by alt-righters to poke fun at liberals, especially online petition signers and Facebook campaigners."

Adrian Fenech showed his empty palms. "I didn't realise."

"Sorry, it's irrelevant. You mean you act from a sense of civic duty rather than because someone's paid you."

"No one pays me."

"That's not very plausible," John said. "What are you doing in London?"

"I came to protect you and Phyllis."

"Right, so you know my wife's name as well. And no one's paid you, and we've never met before?"

"I know it sounds incredible, so I'm not going to waste too much of your time. As a matter of fact, I've run out of money now, so I'm going home to Malta in the next few days. I'm an anti-corruption, Maltese social justice fighter, yes, and I heard that your room had been bugged, so I arranged to get a job looking after you in Malta. The LKX hotel manager paid me. I looked up your details on the computer. I know I shouldn't have done, but I thought I might be able to help. Anyway, you came back to England. I thought someone might be after you. And they are."

"You just hopped on a plane and flew two thousand miles?"

"Yes. What else am I going to do?"

It was John's turn to shrug. "I don't know anything about your life, so I don't know."

"I don't *have* a life. I spend all day on the internet. I do *nothing*."

"I see. And this is better than that."

"If bad government goes on too long, but you've also got a kind of external assessment – in our case, it's the EU – it creates a kind of impenetrable shell around itself. Designed to keep the bad guys safe and stop the good from seeing in. Someone like me therefore needs a point of entry."

"And you think Phyllis and I can provide that?"

"Aisling Baxter knew something, otherwise she wouldn't have been killed."

John sighed. "I thought she died in an accident. A pothole in the road. And anyway, she was investigating internet travel agencies. I can't see what that's got to do with the government of Malta."

"Good try, John. Is it okay to call you John?"

"Not yet. Not that I can stop you. I still don't know whether Adrian Fenech's your real name."

Fenech took an EU passport from his inside pocket.

"Fair enough," John said after he'd flicked through it. "Okay, you can call me John. What do you mean, 'Good try'?"

"You know your wife's being followed by someone, and you've probably got photos of him, since you've got them of me. You obviously know he's no friend, otherwise you'd have approached him. You also know your room was bugged. Aisling Baxter's death occurred in between: after the bugging, before the shadowing. Can't you see that what you're looking at is like a poisoned sandwich? You work out that someone's deliberately infected the two slices of bread he's just given you, you're probably correct in thinking he's poisoned the filling too."

"Interesting metaphor. Doesn't quite work. I see what you mean, though."

"I don't believe Aisling Baxter was in Malta to investigate travel agents. She was there to look into corruption."

"And that's - what?" John asked. "Your hunch?"

"In a word, yes. Which is probably as good as it'll get, because I've reached the end of the line. There isn't going to be a breakthrough, not from me. One day the man that's following Phyllis will decide to strike. That's the only next thing that can happen now. It probably won't happen soon. Maybe within the next year. These people have an awful lot of money. I mean, a huge amount. They can afford to wait."

"An 'awful lot'? How do you know? I mean, yes, you put a contract killer on the streets for a few months, you'd need the cash to pay him. But he could be desperate. Maybe he's behind with his child support, or in debt to drug lords, or anything. Even if he isn't, the market must occasionally get lean, even for international assassins. He might have found himself with a lot of extra competition as cuts begin to bite in the British police force, and there aren't even the resources to fight knife crime or investigate household thefts. Or he might have agreed to do the job for a fixed fee, to prove himself. Or he might be working for new employers. A kind of introductory offer: *If you liked my last job.* Maybe he doesn't charge much because he simply likes the lifestyle. There's a whole range of possibilities."

Fenech smiled, like he was finally pulling ahead. "You're wrong. The people who are hiring this guy have an *awful lot of money.*" He reached into his inside pocket again and took out a scrap of paper. "I don't usually write this sort of thing down, in case I'm captured by the people I'm staking out. That's why it's in code."

"What's it mean?"

"It's a list of hotels Phyllis's shadow - "

"Let's call him Mr Wint. Just humour me. It's not his real name."

"Okay."

John folded his hands. "You were saying, it's a list of hotels…?"

"That 'Mr Wint' has - "

"And drop the inverted commas."

"Stayed in over the past week."

"So what's this first one? 'Oh What a Lovely War with Maggie Smith'?"

"That's The Judge's Court Premier Hotel, Bayswater."

"How the hell do you get that from 'Oh What a Lovely War with Maggie Smith'? What's this one: 'Goodbye Mr Chips with Petula Clark'?"

"The Amethyst Royale, Mayfair. He's stayed there twice."

John frowned. "Seriously?"

"It's about visual clues I pick up on location."

"That doesn't make sense."

"It works for me."

"But you must already know the name of the hotel if you can remember it like that. Why not just use the hotel frontage as your clue?"

"Do we really need to talk about this now?"

"Yes, because how do I know you're not making it up?"

"Because look at the last item on the list."

"What, 'My Fair Lady with Audrey Hepburn'?"

"I wrote that down about an hour ago. I'm certain it's where he still is now. Looking back, I wish I'd taken a photo of him going in."

"So do I, actually. That would be a much better system. If you were 'captured', it wouldn't matter, providing you stored your photos in the cloud, and your phone had a really strong access code number."

"The phone's always the first thing they go for. Then they torture you to get the pin. Whereas with a list of musicals, they just think you're crazy. If they think that, they're more likely to let you go. *Hey, what you writing down, motherfucker? Gimme. Whoa, it's a list of musicals. Hey, sorry, buddy, I thought you were looking at me.*"

"I see, yes. So where *is* 'My Fair Lady with Audrey Hepburn'?"

"The Combermartie Hotel on Charing Cross Road."

"Have you had an actual experience of something like that? Being tortured for your pin?"

"Not yet. It's about thinking ahead."

"So how about we go over to The Combermartie Hotel, if that's where he is? Then you can prove this is real."

Fenech smiled. "Actually, John, it doesn't matter to me whether you think it's real or not. I certainly don't have to prove it. As I said, I've reached the end of the line in terms of what I can do. I just came here today as a goodwill gesture, to tell you what I found out. But it turns out you already knew. Job done, fly me back to Malta, I'm leaving on a jet plane, fare thee well, all and sundry. If *you* want to go over to The Combermartie Hotel on Charing Cross Road, that's also fine with me. You definitely will see him there if you stake it out. I'm pretty certain he's staying there till tomorrow. You could even get creative and disguise yourself, book a room, scout around, sit in the lounge, see if he comes down to dinner, which I imagine he will, he's a big eater. Or you could set off the fire alarm and watch him come downstairs in his pyjamas, then rifle through his possessions. Not that he's got any, just the clothes he stands up in, as far as I can tell. Or you could dress up as a hotel employee, deliver something to his room."

"Okay, okay, I believe you."

"You probably wouldn't gain anything. There must be a reason why you haven't faced him down so far. You've got photos of him, so you could have. If you're not going to confront him on the streets, you're probably not going to confront him in his hotel. And it's not even useful to know he's there, because he swaps every night."

"Tomorrow, it'll be Mary Poppins with Julie Andrews."

"Funny. The point is, it's always a five star hotel. So don't tell me this guy isn't being backed by big money."

"Okay, you win."

"Have you thought about killing him?" Adrian asked.

"What?"

"Say you dressed up as a hotel employee, you'd deliver something to his room, he'd open the door, pop, straight through the left eyeball. That would certainly send a message to his employers. *Don't mess with the Mordreds.*"

John laughed. "He hasn't actually done anything yet. Besides, guns are difficult to come by in this country. With silencers, even harder."

"So you have thought about it?"

"No."

"Honestly? Because I would have."

"I promise, I haven't."

"Before I go, I wonder if *I* might ask *you* some questions."

"Fire away. If they're about 1960s musicals, I won't know the answers."

"One: who is 'Lucy Staveley'? Twenty minutes ago, you asked me if I knew her. It was almost the first thing you said, so it must be important. Two – and this may be personal, so just say if it's forbidden territory: why did Phyllis run away at such a speed when she was in The Strand earlier today? And where did she go in that taxi, before I arrived? As I say, tell me to mind my own business if you want to, but do remember: I may be able to help. I know I said I'm going back to Malta, but I can change my mind."

"I thought you said you'd run out of cash."

"You could lend me some. You could hire me."

"How much do you charge?"

"Bread and water, mainly. Expenses, too. Just enough for the odd emergency taxi. I don't need lodging. I'm staying with my Aunt, whose name and location must remain secret, in case you're captured."

"You've got a thing about being 'captured'. It's a reasonable fear, but the wrong word. It makes it sound like a World War Two movie."

Fenech sighed. "Tell me about Lucy Staveley."

"She's a journalist working for a newspaper called *The Newbury Echo,* in a town about sixty miles west of here. Someone passed her a wad of documents, apparently, whose sum effect is the impression that Phyllis ordered the murder of Aisling Baxter on the dark web. Unfortunately, Phyllis has a motive of sorts: a short while ago, she and Aisling were rivals for the post of Conservative candidate for Newbury, on the retirement of the current incumbent. Aisling got it, Phyllis didn't. It's more complicated than that, but the details aren't very interesting. The point is, another Conservative – a sitting MP – got wind of it and phoned the libel briefs. They weighed in with a gagging order, stopping the newspaper before it hit the stands. All this has only just happened. Phyllis was called in to talk to the lawyers."

"I see. And presumably, no one knows who sent Lucy Staveley these documents?"

"As I understand it, they were sent anonymously."

"Could it have been Mr Bint?"

"Wint," John said. "Maybe, but why would he still be following her? And when has he had the time to put something like that together?"

"Maybe it's what he does in the evenings."

"Then take it to Newbury? If it came to *The Echo* anonymously, it's likely to have been hand-delivered. Anyway, it seems too complicated: follow her every day *and* compile a dossier to discredit her? One or the other, surely? Not both."

"I see your point. Who are the solicitors?"

"Carneghan Strake, they're called."

Fenech's brow furrowed. He drew a deep breath and nodded. "I've heard of them. Presumably, they're in libel, and Malta's big on that. As I've already said, I used to be a police officer. I know libel would be civil rather than criminal law, but there's always overlap. Hang on." He took his phone out and tapped it intently for a few seconds. "Yes, they're active in Malta… Not in a good way."

"You think *they* could be behind the dossier?"

"As a hypothesis, it's a good starting point. Look, John, let's talk specifics. You strike me as an intelligent guy, and at no point today have I got the impression that you're stumped. The fact that you've got photos of me and Mr Wint shows you're proactive. You must have an idea about what to do next."

"True, but it's not a great one."

"One thing you are good at. Shadowing people and taking photos of them. We can use that."

"'We'?"

"You and me, working together."

"I couldn't presume. I'm short on money and - "

"I'm a social justice warrior. I won't charge upfront. I'll just give you modest receipts for taxis, Mars bars, cans of Fanta, and so on. Peanuts. Let me help you and Phyllis."

He ran his hand over his hair. "Okay. Thank you."

"So what's your idea? As to how to proceed next?"

"As I say," John said, "it's a poor one, but better than nothing. The list of journalists Aisling Baxter collected and Phyllis posted on all four corners of the earth. Before you called, I was trying to track them down. I thought I'd talk to them. Individually, they might not have much to say, but collectively – well, there might be common strands."

"You're a good detective. Now, I've a proposal."

"Go ahead."

"I want you to find out as much as you can about Carneghan Strake. I have a bad feeling about them. I want you to shadow its partners, take photos. We'll examine them together. If I do it and there is a strong Maltese connection, I might be recognised. You won't be. In exchange, I'll finish what you started: tracking down those journalists and talking to them. Deal?"

John smiled. "Deal. Let's exchange phone numbers."

Chapter 18: Never Go Out

John heard the front door open and close, then Phyllis's familiar, "Hi, honey, I'm home." She sounded as if Carneghan Strake might have eased her mind. Although, for all sorts of reasons, that seemed unlikely.

It had been two hours since his talk with Adrian Fenech in the park, and he felt good. He still wasn't sure how much to tell her about the plans they'd made. Hopefully, everything, but he'd play it by ear. She might not like him shadowing her solicitors, though. *Shadowed solicitors tend to get annoyed, then they stop defending you* would be a good argument. The question was, how far would she trust him to be extra careful? It had been different in the old days – the *old days* being three months ago. When Ruby Parker had ordered you to do something, the possibility of you being debarred because your nearest and dearest didn't trust you to be ultra cautious couldn't arise.

Oh, for the old days. Still, Annabel might have something in the pipeline.

He'd put a goat's cheese and fennel tart in the oven, boiled some potatoes and asparagus, made a cream cheese dip. Ten minutes till it was ready. Phyllis went into the kitchen, poured herself a glass of white wine and came to sit on the sofa next to him.

"Ask me anything you like," she said. "Guess what happened to me today?" she continued, before he could reply. "I went back to Thames House."

"Really? Wow. Let's start with the bad news, though. Lucy Staveley. How did you get on at Carneghan Strake?"

"They're confident they can knock it on the head. Have you done the usual sweep for bugs, by the way?"

"No one's watching us or listening in," he said. "Unless you count the usual Google folk and the Alexa."

"I think we should whisper anyway," she said.

"Haven't you always had this problem? I mean, I used to live in an MI7 approved compound. You've always had your own place."

"I never had the kind of friends I'd talk shop with before. Whisper, John. It's romantic, apart from being sensible."

"How did you get on with Carneghan Strake?" he whispered.

"In terms of what's in the dossier, it's not good. Lucy Staveley's got Aisling Baxter's sex tape. There's no reason to think she's got ours too, but no reason not to. Apparently, according to *The Echo*'s narrative, *I* was responsible for the filming. I wanted to bring Aisling down by any means possible, and when I failed to pin the sex tape on her, I plumped for murder. It's utterly insane. And vindictive."

"If you'd set up cameras to film Aisling Baxter having sex, and that's what the film shows, how the hell was that failure?"

"She 'discovered' the cameras. I don't know, John. I've no idea how Lucy Staveley thinks. Either she's got some sort of screw loose, which seems unlikely, because she's got a reasonable journalistic track record, or Carneghan Strake have got hold of the wrong end of the stick."

"Or Carneghan Strake are making it out to be ten times worse than it is, because that's how they operate. They scare you witless so you won't balk at the bill."

"I'm not discounting that possibility either. They asked if you and I were spies. Apparently, that's in the dossier too."

"Bloody hell. What did you tell them?"

"The truth. That we used to be, but now we aren't. The thing is, John, they already knew. And I'm not sure they believed me that we're out of it."

"Their problem. How did you end up at Thames House?"

"Alec was waiting for me outside Carneghan Strake's offices. Ruby Parker had sent him to come and get me."

"How did they know where to find you?"

"Apparently, Kevin followed me in his car."

"Kevin. The man who never speaks."

"Only to you. Or should I say, *not* to you. He's fine with the rest of us."

"So Alec took you to Thames House. Then what?"

"Two things. Annabel's going to burgle the Echo's offices tonight. Assuming she's successful, we get to see what's in that dossier, even though it's probably not irreplaceable."

"Good old Annabel. Second?"

"Ruby Parker wants me to pretend to work there for a while. Thames House. My old job, but with no prospects and a hundred per cent filing."

"Plus something you're not telling me about?" he asked. "Because it doesn't sound like much of an offer."

"Bit of background before I answer that. Marchus Grubfeld, which is Mr Wint's real name, is exactly what we always thought he was. Some kind of contract killer. He's coming after me, but waiting till Malta's faded in the juridical memory. When he's got me, he'll probably wait another long time, then kill you. It's all about creating the impression of isolated tragedies."

"Lovely. So what's that got to do with you getting your old job back with anti-perks?"

"If he thinks I'm an ex-spy, he's more likely to act sooner and recklessly. Give him the impression I'm still very much on Her Majesty's Secret Payroll – great title for a film, incidentally – and he's more liable to hold back. At least until Ruby Parker can decide what to do with him."

"Why not just give him a Chicago overcoat and feed him to the fishes?"

"Because, contrary to what you said, she's not Tony Soprano."

"So if he stops coming after you, what will he do then? Come after me?"

"Yep."

He turned to look at her. "I see from your face that you're not joking."

"Her idea is that you're cooped up in here all day, so what have you got to fear? Especially if the flat's also being watched by MI7 officers. Which it will be. You'll be as safe as houses."

"What if I go out?"

She shrugged. "Easy. Don't."

"What? Never?"

"You've got toilet facilities to hand, plus food and water."

"Never go out?"

"You've got an inferiority complex, by the way."

He took half a second to adjust. "How do you deduce that from me implicitly demanding to go out?"

"I don't. It's not my judgement. It's Doctor Chakladar's."

"You and Ruby Parker discussed my psychological evaluation?"

"You gave her formal permission, apparently."

He searched his memory banks and retrieved the relevant file. "Okay, yes I did. But Chacky never mentioned an inferiority complex. Not to me."

"That's because he's just found out about it."

"What? When I wasn't even there?"

"Apparently."

"So I'm actually more useful to him absent than I was two feet away on his couch?"

She chuckled. "Mine not to reason why."

"The real me's less important than the absent me?"

"Don't go on about it, John. It's not helping. I completely see your point."

"Bloody hell."

"Anyway, the good news is, if you want your old job back, all you've got to do - at least for starters - is go and have a few more sessions with 'Chacky'. Does he know you call him that?"

"No. Although who knows? Maybe the absent me told him."

"That would be so typical."

"To shoot the real me in the foot."

"Hang on, that's a bit unfair," she said. "The absent you's actually done you a favour. I mean, could the real you have pulled off the 'I've got an inferiority complex' scam?"

"No, because the real me's relatively useless."

"Attaboy. So did anything interesting happen to you today?"

"As a matter of fact," he said, "yes. The moment you left, someone buzzed at the front gate. To cut a long story short, it was Mr Kidd. I kid you not. Real name: Adrian Fenech, a Maltese ex-cop with a grudge against malefactors and a passion for justice. He had no idea who Mr Wint was either. Anyway, he reckons your solicitors might be involved, so, starting tomorrow, I'm going to tail them and take photos, which he's going to examine for Maltese connections. He's also going to look up the journalists on that list Aisling Baxter gave you, see if he can't get a few of them to talk. Right now, he's living with his Aunt, whose name and location must remain secret, in case I'm captured. So there we are: that was my day. You can tell Ruby Parker I'm not as 'cooped up' as she thinks. Thanks for the compliment, and a big hello from my non-self, the important one."

Phyllis was sitting upright. "Sorry, I missed everything after 'It was Mr Kidd'. Did you say *Mr Kidd came round?*"

"Then I made that excellent joke."

"Say it all again. Minus the joke."

"I think the goat's cheese and fennel tart may be burning."

"Forget the tart."

He repeated the information he'd already imparted, and added, "To be fair, I'll be a lot safer shadowing a few solicitors than I will Marchus Grubfeld. And I'll keep well out of sight."

She kissed him. "I don't actually like my solicitors very much anyway. And Ruby Parker didn't order me to make you stay in the flat. Marchus Grubfeld will probably attempt to follow you, but MI7 will have someone on him. And you can evade him. Let's live like we were meant to. Long live rock and roll."

Chapter 19: Into *The Echo*

Annabel Gould al-Banna was an expert at gaining access to locked compounds, buildings and safes. She knew how to disable all makes and models of alarms, and the best means to avoid, control or neutralise guard dogs without affecting their long-term welfare. She could burglarise the most impenetrable fortresses and the occupant would never even know she or anyone had been there. Until one day they discovered that, where their items used to be, there was now empty space.

She drove to Newbury at 3pm. With the traffic out of London, what should have been a ninety minute journey took her two and a half hours. She parked in the Cedar Tops housing estate, a mile from *The Echo*'s offices, put the hood on her sweatshirt up, and took a quick walk to her destination to get a sense of the lay of the land. She noted the positions of CCTV and other cameras, and passed through the industrial estate at a brisk pace, as if she had somewhere to go. She exited by a makeshift path at a slight acclivity through a narrow wood. She took out a pair of binoculars and scanned *The Echo's* premises. A red brick, single storey modular building, roughly 70 by 50 feet, on a much wider concrete base and surrounded by a galvanised welded mesh fence. Burglar alarm on the northern wall, ALVRO, monitored, probably the 2016 version. She made a series of assessments and decisions concerning points of entry, sites of vulnerability, transitions to personal safety. She identified probable makes of padlock, modes of ingress and egress, and what tools she'd need. Afterwards, she continued along the same path to a railway line bordered on both sides by green PVC-coated chain link fences, which she climbed over. This would be her approach tonight. When the track ended, she found herself, as expected, two streets away from where she'd parked her car earlier. She drove to

Newbury town centre, changed into a business suit in a public toilet, and checked into the hotel room she'd booked five minutes before leaving London.

Seven hours later, she breached the fence at the rear of *The Echo's* offices where it abutted the wood. She cleared the distance between that and the building at a sprint, without triggering the security lights. There were no dogs here, or anywhere on this industrial estate. Too expensive to maintain, probably. There might be a night watchman somewhere, but likely shared between all the units. Not someone *The Echo* could call their own. Statistically unlikely to find him here now.

Her first port of call was the burglar alarm. But she could already tell it wasn't working. Either someone had forgotten to turn it on, or...

Someone had preceded her. She was moving hyper-cautiously now. She removed a martial arts yawara stick from the inside pocket of her black tunic.

She reached the front door and saw a little light through a tiny gap in the venetian blinds. She checked no one was behind her - these people often worked in teams – and put her face on the glass.

A dimly illumined male face by one of four desks.

Another burglar.

Well, well, well.

She scanned the perimeter fence, looking for a hole of the kind she herself had just made. Too dark, and, in any case, any half-competent intruder would have come in the same way as her: at the rear, where the woods were.

She could see the front gates were locked. And there were no cars inside the compound. Anyone working late would have turned on all the lights. So it couldn't be anyone legitimate.

No, her initial instincts had been correct. She had a rival. But not much of one, because she had a black belt and the element of surprise.

She did a swift circuit of the building to confirm that whoever it was hadn't entered by a window, then checked the front door, bringing the handle down as slowly as she could and pushing it open just a millimetre, all she needed. This had been his point of entry. Let him do all the hard work in there – he'd already sorted the alarm - then pounce when he or she came out.

Two wheelie bins stood to one side of the entrance. She got down on her haunches beside them and became immobile. It was a still night, cloudy and moonless, but also silent. Every so often, she could dimly hear who was inside as a chair scraped or something fell over.

In the shock of finding she wasn't alone, and the mental re-adjustment, it hadn't occurred to her to ask who this guy was, or who'd sent him or her. Crouched by the bins, she realised it made a difference.

Was it Marchus Grubfeld, Phyllis's stalker? Or perhaps the other, older, guy John had identified? Grubfeld might prove a handful – better to assume he'd be formidable than be complacent – but she had the element of surprise, and that would probably clinch it. If it was the older guy, she'd better be equally careful, for different reasons. She didn't want a fatality on her hands.

Either one would be good, but the first – Grubfeld – would be Christmas Come Early. At the very least, it'd mean a complete reset for whoever was behind him tailing Phyllis.

But then, why should it be him? Most likely, he'd sent it to Lucy Staveley. He'd hardly come here to get it back.

But he might. Fill her hands with goodies then snatch them away when she was on the point of enjoying them. Infuriate her enough to make her do something rash.

He could do even better than that. Because, in disposing of the *actual* dossier – which was almost certainly full of distortions and downright lies – he might give life to the *remembered* dossier, which would quickly become the *mythical, unchallengeable* dossier.

She was thinking too much. John's malaise, it must be catching. She needed to concentrate on the here and now, empty her mind.

The front door opened. Here he came. She didn't believe in the British sense of fair play in this sort of situation, so when he emerged from the doorway and paused for a moment - as she anticipated he would, to reassess his surrounds before making a final dash - she simply kicked his chin in the air, then rammed his head against the window frame. Uncomplicated, clean, old school. He was unconscious before he knew anything had happened.

First things first. A middle aged man, by the looks. She removed his black balaclava and tied him up using the heavy-duty cable ties she always carried on this sort of mission. She didn't recognise him. She took a few photos for the team at Thames House, then looked in his haversack. She couldn't afford to make any assumptions here, and it suddenly struck her as odd that she'd assumed, all along, that he was after the same thing she was. Because he could be after anything at all.

But then, what else was there to steal in a place like this?

Here it was. A flick through told her yes, it was almost certainly what she'd come for. A wad of documents in a buff A4 wallet folder, helpfully separated into five sections with paper-clips. Minutes of an interview featuring Phyllis, a Maltese accident report, a letter written on Conservative Party notepaper, a collection of magazine clippings covering Phyllis's model days – my, someone was a fan: you didn't just happen on something like this when you decided you'd try a spot of blackmail – and a list of guests attached to 'Ted Taylor', the travel agent. Plus a USB pen.

She couldn't afford to leave anything to chance. There might still be material in the safe this guy had overlooked. She stepped over him and went inside.

She didn't have to search. She'd seen him peering into the safe when she was outside.

A glance satisfied her. In some ways, she couldn't have done a better job herself. Apart from knocking that chair over, and smashing someone's coffee mug, and leaving the safe door open. A solid six out of ten, because there was probably nothing here to identify him, and he'd got what he came for.

But *what he came for* wasn't enough. As far as she could tell – unless he'd switched them off some time ago - he'd completely overlooked the computers. Another thirty minutes of her time, at least, during which time he might wake up.

She removed a plastic bag marked 'sterile' from her inside pocket, tore it open, and removed a strong DNA-less fabric band, which she used to gag him. To be on the safe side, she took out a roll of tape, wiped it with a disinfected cloth and stuck it over his mouth.

Now she had all the time she needed to do what he hadn't: switch on the computers, upload the software that would allow Tariq, back in Thames House, to see which keys were being tapped and why, and finally – just as important – shut everything down again.

Someone in London would have to call Lucy Staveley early tomorrow morning. Get her out of bed and down here, before anyone at *The Echo* contacted her. That way, she'd fall gently into their hands.

Half an hour later, Annabel turned off the last computer, and stepped over her still unconscious predecessor on the way out. As she climbed back through the hole she'd cut in the perimeter fence, it struck her who he probably was. Obvious really. A rival newspaper, possibly one of the London tabloids, had heard about *The Echo*'s massive scoop. They'd done a quick calculation. They were richer, bolder, with access to better lawyers. They could afford, in every sense of the word, to hire an expert thief. Disturbingly, Phyllis Robinson supermodel, wasn't as completely forgotten as MI7 liked to think.

She took out her phone and called Thames House. Thirty seconds later, a man of about thirty, working in administration department, dialled 999 using a concealed number. "Police, please," he said. "I was passing the offices of *The Newbury Echo* in The Cedar Tops industrial estate. I'd like to report a burglary."

Chapter 20: Dina's Dismay

Dina Oforka-Jones arrived in Cheapside the day after her interview with Phyllis, ran upstairs to her office and looked at her landline phone. No flashing red light.

She sat down and put her head in her hands.

But Ian would be here in a moment. He might know something. Her best hope now was that the intermediary had lost both phone numbers she'd given him and gone straight to Ian. Because he had his number too.

On the face of it, no cause to worry. The actual burglar couldn't be traced back to either of them. They had networks and protocols for this sort of thing, and at no point was anyone in the firm allowed to deal directly with felons. Everything had to be third or fourth removed.

And when she thought about it, three times removed, which was what this was, *did* allow for contact details to go missing; might even make it forgivable. She wasn't particularly worried for herself – at least not that the police would arrive on her doorstep; there was no risk of that. But she might have to tell Angelo, and that would be excruciating.

As a last resort, she'd ring her contact. Risky in itself - it reduced the number of removes from three to two - but not overly. Two was still an acceptable distance. But if *her* contact had to call *his* contact, things could become traceable.

That would require a pretty dogged police officer, though, plus access to her phone, for which a warrant would be necessary.

Not going to happen, not in this lifetime.

But it wasn't pleasant that it had come to this. She was shaking slightly, the result of one coffee too many, perhaps. Loath to admit nerves.

Bloody Ian, where the hell was he?

Mind you, still only 8.55am. He probably believed everything was okay. He certainly wouldn't rush in to work.

Maybe she should call him.

Although that probably wouldn't achieve anything beyond letting him know how fazed she was. He'd be on his way now. The way London worked, once you got anywhere near the centre at this time in the morning, you found yourself part of a plodding mass of bodies with virtually no room for overtaking. Putting on a spurt wasn't an option. She mustn't look relieved to see him, either, when he finally did haul his useless backside through the front door. That would be a sign of weakness. In that case, he might even try to 'take charge', inviting more disaster.

If disaster it was. Half of her needed more caffeine, the other half knew she'd already overdosed. She went to her In tray, opened the top A4 folder.

But she didn't see it, not really. Her mind wouldn't focus. And Ian would be here in a moment. No point starting something important. She put it back.

She heard the front door open a floor below, then close. At last. He'd hang his coat up and ascend the stairs. He wouldn't go to his office first; he'd come in to see her, because he'd want to confirm last night passed off okay. He'd be expecting a quick nodded affirmative.

What was she thinking? A few seconds ago, all her hopes had rested on the thought that they might have contacted him. Maybe they had.

She needed to look strong for him. She couldn't appear un-concerned obviously, since they hadn't contacted her, but neither did she have to look frantic. If he'd got the confirmation, he'd gloat. Sometimes their contacts, increasingly lowlife the further down the chain you went, didn't like dealing with women.

That had to be it, yes! They'd contacted Ian because he was a man. Why hadn't it occurred to her before?

The expected knock. Ian put his head round the door. "Everything okay?" he asked.

"I'm assuming you received the phone call," she said as neutrally as she could.

"Me? I thought you were our representative."

Her mouth clicked open.

"*You* haven't?" he said.

She shook her head. My God, this really was bad. Nightmare to reality. She saw Ian's expression change too. Emotionally speaking, like looking in a mirror: a swift transition from insouciance to panic.

"Call them," he barked. "This is your problem, Dina. I told you at the outset bugging those rooms was a mistake, and it's got more and more outlandish ever since. We should have left it to Angelo. The way things are going, we may still have to get in touch with him, come clean."

"It won't come to that," she said, still not fully recovered. "Leave it to me. Go and do some work. Come back in thirty minutes' time."

"Or you come and see me."

Forty minutes later, she sat behind her desk. He sat on the sofa with a cup of tea.

"Our burglar was intercepted," she said, "at the point of exit. He's at the police station, claiming not to be a burglar at all. Just a concerned citizen who heard a disturbance, discovered a hole cut in the fence and decided he'd be a have-a-go hero. So far, the police haven't found any of his fingerprints, so, although his story looks suspicious, it's going to be hard to assemble a good prosecution. Obviously, his solicitors are pressing for his release, and it actually looks as if that might happen. Given how seriously he bungled, he may never work again. Especially for us."

"I very much imagine you're wrong," Ian said. "Those sorts of persons are horrendously difficult to replace."

"We'll see."

"In any event, this leaves us far from out of the woods. Depending on who's got that dossier now. You're saying we've no idea? What about CCTV? I mean, I can understand that our man would have disabled the on-site cameras, but there must be others in the locality."

"And none of them show anything. Which is a profoundly good thing."

He scoffed and sipped his tea. "I'm sorry, Dina, you're going to have to explain that to me. We've completely lost the very thing that twelve hours ago we considered it a matter of the utmost urgency to retrieve. It could be anywhere. How the hell can that conceivably be a *good* thing?"

"Think about it. There aren't that many possibilities to begin with. This wasn't an opportunist swoop. No valuables were taken. Whoever took that dossier came with the specific intention of taking it. To my mind, there are just two possibilities. One: a rival media outlet. But anyone like that would have left traces. They'd be on the CCTV footage somewhere, like you say. So I don't think that can be it. The second is that someone highly trained took it. A spy."

He smiled thinly. "Which 'spy' do you have in mind?"

"Come on, Ian, it's obvious. Phyllis Mordred's reputation's at stake here. Do you think her husband's going to take that lying down?"

He shrugged, apparently impressed. "Or I suppose it could have been Phyllis herself."

"Too obvious. She's the dossier's subject. She's got a huge motive for stealing it. If the police start asking about her whereabouts, and she can't account for them... Or let's say someone saw her boarding a train to Newbury. Whereas it's not likely to occur to them to ask about him. Remember, no one knows either of them are ex-spies. Just us."

"So you think John Mordred's got the dossier?"

"Or possibly someone from MI6, if they're keeping a benevolent eye on her, which they probably are. Either way, it means it'll probably never see the light of day."

"This is a best case scenario, right? Because I can think of at least two others. First, Lucy Staveley kept some sort of copy of the contents of the dossier. She'd have been extremely stupid not to, and we selected her – or you did – precisely on the grounds that she isn't 'extremely stupid'. That's the first fly in the ointment. The other is the possibility that our midnight gazumper is the man Phyllis told us about yesterday, the one who's been following her. If he's been shadowing her, it's not beyond the realms of credibility that he's tapped her phone."

"She's an ex-secret agent. She'd spot that sort of thing a mile off. She'd be expecting it, given that she knows she's being followed. She'd have taken precautions."

"We're speculating optimistically, of course. Which may not be sensible."

"I thought of both those things. They're connected. If the person that's following Phyllis has got it, it'll be because he doesn't want her exposed. He's presumably got other plans for her - "

"A nice, obscure death, no complications."

"Yes, possibly. And if that's the case, and Lucy Staveley starts rattling cages, he'll probably take care of her too."

Ian sighed. "I'll leave aside the fact that we're talking about people's lives here, and just concentrate on the technical problems, shall I? Because killing Lucy Staveley might not solve anything. It might simply – probably will – draw other journalists like flies to a honey pot. It's not even as if she's alone. Her editor's fully apprised. We couldn't have served that injunction on any other basis."

"I don't necessarily mean kill her, Ian. In fact, *we* could take care of her. Keep threatening her. Create a situation in which she's so worried about her own career, and even her personal prospects, that she wishes she'd never set eyes on the so-called Phyllis Mordred dossier. Meanwhile, we could throw other tasty titbits in her path, about some of the celebrities on our books – Stallone Laine, say, or Connie Glaser - to keep her occupied. This time next year, competently managed, she may have forgotten all about Phyllis Mordred."

"I think whatever happens today, you need to see Angelo, and confess everything. He is in London right now, and he did promise to look you up, so there's your ideal opportunity. It'll be no use waiting till he's gone back to Malta. Flashing your eyes at someone over Skype isn't half as effective. No, this is getting far too complicated, Dina. Between the two of you, you need to decide who's going to do what. Then *you* need to stick to it. No more Ms Clever Sides."

"Ian, you're wrong. And I'm not going to see Angelo."

"You're scared of him."

"I don't like looking a fool." She sighed. "And before you say it, yes, I know I *am* one. I just want a little more time to see if things will smooth themselves over."

"They won't. Look Dina, if *you* don't go and see him, *I* will. You've had your chance here. We're in trouble. It can still be contained with a bit of sincere grovelling and some sort of peace offering. Couldn't you take him to dinner? You two used to be more than close."

"Fifteen years ago, yes. In those days, we both had things the other wanted. I was young and supposedly beautiful; he had money and connections. Neither of us cares about the other anymore, except possibly for nostalgic reasons. There's very little of that on my side, I assure you."

The phone on her desk rang. She looked at it for a second as if it had no right to interrupt. Then her expression softened to anxiety, then fear.

Ian laughed incredulously. "Dina, *answer it*, for God's sake!"

She picked up. "Dina Oforka-Jones speaking. How can I help?" She listened. She visibly calmed down. She nodded. She took a ballpoint from the silver mug by the PC and wrote something on a pad. "I see," she said, then: "Thank you very much for calling, Mr Stevens. I really appreciate it, for both our sakes. I'll ensure it's taken care of. Thank you again, and if he makes any further contact, please do get in touch. Night or day. Goodbye."

"Going by your face," Ian said, "I take it we've yet more problems? Am I right in assuming that was *the* Mr Stevens? From Reading?"

She nodded. "One of the twenty-four names on the list that Phyllis Mordred tried to make viral, yes."

"So what's happened this time?" he asked.

"Someone got in touch with him. A man by the name of Lawrence Adami, claiming to be a Maltese journalist. But who called in person."

Ian frowned. "And who - unless he just happened to be in Reading, and he called on Mr Stevens on the off chance - must therefore think he's got hold of something important."

"I wasn't worried when that policewoman – what was her name? Leona Quarshie? – came looking. I expected that. But - "

"What's he look like, this 'Lawrence Adami'? Do we have a description?"

"Stocky, mid-sixties, grey moustache, an old-fashioned rimmed hat."

"I wouldn't worry. I suppose it was to be expected. Let's face it, it does look like the beginnings of an interesting story. British woman comes to Malta to investigate something, hands mysterious list of names to best friend just before dying in a car crash, best friend posts said list on the internet, meanwhile real list disappears in theft. I'm surprised Mr Stevens hasn't had more visitors, to be honest. As for 'Adami', he's probably a freelance. But you need to check with Angelo. He'll know. And let that be your wake up call, Dina. As I say, if you don't call him, I will. Now, if you'll excuse me, I've got actual work to be getting on with."

He stood up and calmly left the room, closing the door noiselessly behind him. She put her head in her hands again and emitted a loud 'yah!' meant to express her mingled frustration, anguish and gloom, then she picked up her phone, scrolled down the contacts till she reached Angelo and pressed call.

"Hello," a woman's voice said. "You have reached the voice-mail box for 00-356-5732-3671. I'm sorry, we cannot connect your call at the moment. If you would like to leave a message, please -"

She hung up and tried again. Stupid. Of course he wouldn't have switched it back on, or got off the line or whatever the reason was, in such a minute interval, but she was desperate. Suddenly, she needed to be through to him the *exact second* he became available again.

"Hello," came the woman's voice. "You have reached - "

She hung up and pressed redial.

"Hello, you have reached - "

She was on a kind of morbid roll now. Like gambling. The more you failed, the sweeter it'd be when you were finally successful, even though with each successive punt, the chances of that seemed to decrease. But you couldn't think of anything else. Strangely, she didn't even know what she'd say when he answered any more. She'd cross that bridge when she came to it. She'd become a zombie: redial, end call, redial, end call, redial –

She should try with her landline. Which she knew would make no difference, but she'd entered that strange mental dislodgement where certain objects might have magical power. The landline might be able to unlock parts of the universe the mobile couldn't.

She picked up the receiver, and keyed in the number as she read it on her mobile.

"Hello," came the woman's voice. "You have reached - "

She whimpered and banged it down so hard she was surprised it didn't break.

In the same moment, Ian put his head round the door.

Her anger redoubled, only now it was all directed at him. "*Knock* before you come in!" she exclaimed. "*I do it for you! It's common courtesy!*"

But there was something wrong. He flinched a little, but didn't look like he wasn't expecting it. He looked pale.

"Dina, something's happened," he said. "Go to a news channel – go to the BBC. It's – it's Angelo."

Three minutes later, they stood side by side behind her desk, arms folded in terrified silence, looking at her PC screen.

"… A vicious knife attack in Knightsbridge this morning," the announcer said. "The assailant apparently pulled the moped onto the pavement and stabbed his victim in the neck before escaping towards Central London. The victim has just been named as Angelo Bonnici, a seventy-six-year-old Maltese citizen who was in London on business. Police are provisionally treating the incident as a terrorist attack, and have appealed for witnesses. The suspect is still at large. Calls for the London mayor, Sadiq Khan, to do more about violent crime in the capital - "

Dina switched it off and slumped in her chair. "Oh my God," she said. Then she ran both hands over her hair and sat up. "We probably haven't heard the last of this. We'd better start ringing round, expressing our condolences."

Chapter 21: Thanks to Marchus Grubfeld

Fourteen hours earlier, Marchus Grubfeld lay on his bed in The Combermartie Hotel on Charing Cross Road. Number 89 was identical to virtually every other room. A wardrobe, a dressing table and a ceiling so low you didn't even have to stretch to touch it. A shared bathroom lay along the corridor.

He'd eaten fish and chips downstairs about two hours ago, in the most basic of restaurants, and come back for a sleep before the night's excursion. Pretty soon, he'd have to kill John and Phyllis Mordred, whom, as far as he could tell, were good people. Good enough to require some sort of advance atonement. You didn't remove two such individuals from the world without eradicating at least four bad. If tonight passed off well, it'd redress the balance. Yet in itself it was merely the means to an end. His advancement. Which would come early tomorrow morning, in Knightsbridge.

He'd done a lot of walking around London after dark recently, seeking examples of the city's famous two-wheeled muggers. He hadn't yet seen a theft, but he had stumbled across a group of four men in Islington whose former pizza-delivery moped was kept locked up and under tarpaulin during the daytime. Three nights in a row they went out excited and, two hours later, came back bearing a collection of goods – phones, he guessed - in a sack. They wore hoods and tied scarves over their faces, and obviously thought highly of themselves. He suspected that, once on the streets, they pulled on rubber masks. At the moment, they were just thieves, but no probable future involved them vastly improving. They'd almost certainly continue to spread misery till they died. So best for everyone if that happened as soon as possible.

He put together a change of clothing – shorts, T-shirt, sunglasses, trainers, baseball cap – and wrapped them, together with a small can of lighter fluid, in a plastic bag, which he sealed with sticky tape. He checked out of The Combermartie at 10pm and caught a bus to Knightsbridge. He walked into a side street he'd identified several days earlier and climbed over a high wrought-iron gate into a tall, nondescript building which, as far as he'd been able to discover, was always open in the daytime. He taped the change of clothing to the bottom of its lowest stairwell, so snug that not even the most punctilious cleaner would notice it.

He left the building by its front entrance, scaled another gate and caught the bus to Islington. When he arrived at the men's block, he checked the gun in his bag to make sure the silencer was fitted. He walked upstairs to their flat and knocked on their door. After a few seconds, it opened slightly. He kicked it and thrust a knife into the chest of the answerer as he tried to recover. Another man emerged from the living room and froze. He shot him. The final two men were in the living room, yelping, and scrabbling for anything that might facilitate a response. He shot them.

He closed and bolted the front door.

It smelt a little in here. He put the kettle on, found a jar of coffee and some milk, and then the moped keys for later use. He laid the corpses one on top of the other behind the sofa, so they'd be out of the way before rigor mortis set in. He found a thick wad of twenty pound notes in a can marked 'teabags' in the kitchen. Probably just over two thousand pounds, all told.

He took off his clothes. As he'd shot his second victim, he noticed a washing machine and dryer in the kitchen. The instructions were in the drawer by the cooker. He set the cycle to number 2, made himself a mug of coffee, and went in the shower.

Ten minutes later, he toasted a teacake, buttered it, made a second coffee, and put the TV on. They had iPlayer, so he watched *Socrates: Genius of the Ancient World*. Afterwards, he washed his cup and plate and put them back in the cupboard. He went into the bedroom, got into bed and switched out the light. It had been a good day's work, all in all. Six or seven probably decent people had been set to lose their phones tonight; possibly their short-term peace of mind too. Now, they'd be okay. Thanks to Marchus Grubfeld, the world had just become a slightly better place.

Within five minutes, he was asleep.

He awoke at eight the next morning. The men were starting to smell now. Unusual for four guys to be living alone, but it was almost certainly a pre-furnished flat, they probably had the money, and they needed a base of operations, so maybe it wasn't too outlandish.

Someone might come and call for one of them early on – a workmate or a lift somewhere - so he needed to be ready for a knock at the door. Whoever came would go away when there was no answer. They definitely wouldn't call the police, even if it was the landlord. The landlord probably had some idea what they were up to. It'd be one of those setups where the tenants pay over the odds by direct debit and, in return, the owner gives them full latitude.

He fished his clothes from the dryer, ironed them, made himself a pot of tea, had a bowl of cornflakes, and then went around the flat cleaning away fingerprints. It wasn't possible to erase DNA, not entirely, and he was on the Interpol database, but the police in this country wouldn't bother with that. They were underfunded and apathetic. And they weren't going to spend that year's budget probing the deaths of four big-time delinquents. They'd chalk it up to 'London's increasing gang violence', and leave it there. Even the media probably wouldn't care much. It'd be news for a day. The alternative was to torch the flat, but that would be overkill, and it would spread. There were probably lots of nice people living in this block. Mothers with kids, struggling to get by. A conflagration was the last thing they needed.

At ten o'clock, he donned a hoodie from the wardrobe and pulled up the hood. He put on one of the full-face motorcycle helmets from the kitchen. He grabbed the ignition keys, thrust the wad of twenties into his pocket, left the flat and descended the stairs to the moped. He removed its tarpaulin, got on and drove out of the courtyard. He turned right at the junction.

Ten minutes later, he was in Knightsbridge. Just in time to see an elderly man briskly approaching the traffic lights on the same side of the road. Angelo Bonnici. Perfect.

He was looking down at his phone.

Talk about good luck! He did a sharp left and pulled his moped on to the pavement.

Everyone in the vicinity froze. They'd all seen something like this on the news and in their nightmares. The only consolation was that this time, it wasn't going to be them.

He snatched the phone from the old man's grasp and thrust it into his own pocket.

In a robbery, that would have been the end. The moped would have turned and accelerated in the optimal direction for escape. But this particular thief wasn't finished. He took out a large knife, grabbed the man's ear with one hand and dragged the blade hard across his jugular with the other.

The victim gasped. He still hadn't registered quite what was happening, even in the process of dying. Around him, people screamed. Someone yelled.

The rider turned his vehicle and raced away. Half a mile on, he entered a side street. He disembarked, abandoned the moped and proceeded on foot.

It had all gone like a dream. Which was odd, considering there was no God to thank.

He chuckled and almost skipped for sheer pleasure. A perfect plan perfectly executed.

Chapter 22: Lucy Gets Really, Really Angry

Lucy Staveley was disturbed at eight o'clock that morning by a text message. For years she'd acclimatised to her phone pinging at all times of the day and the night. As her teenage friends gradually began to move out of Newbury, or widen their circle of acquaintances, the frequency reduced. And as she got older, she'd learned to ignore it more. But 8am was an interesting time. It would have to be someone on their way to work with something important to say – otherwise why not wait?

Or it could be a mistake. Someone hitting 'send', but to the wrong person. She turned reluctantly over, picked her phone up from the bedside table and accessed it.

A text. *Editor. Roger.*

She sat up, instinctively aware that this wasn't a drill. Something had happened.

It read: *Lucy, I need you at the office, asap. The police are here. DON'T TRY TO CALL OR TEXT ME BACK.*

Shit!

Okay, she was awake now. She threw the bedclothes off, thrust her glasses on and ran to the bathroom.

Locked. Bloody hell.

"I'm getting ready!" her dad called from inside. "Just give me five minutes!"

"It's me," Lucy said pleadingly, as if the fact that it wasn't her mum – which he'd probably assumed it was - and she sounded desperate might make him think twice.

"It doesn't matter who it is," he replied. "I'm *getting ready!* Just five minutes! What are you doing up at this time anyway?"

She clicked her tongue and ran downstairs. Why didn't they have two bathrooms, like normal people?

She needed to go to the toilet, that's all. A wash could wait. She'd been in the shower last night, and Roger had made it sound urgent.

She should get something to eat, help her concentrate. She might need it.

"*You're* in a hurry," her mum said when she entered the kitchen. She was sitting at the table with tea, toast and her phone. "What's going on?"

"I've had a call from Roger. Is there anything to eat? I've got to go, now."

"There's one of those granola bars in the cereal cupboard, next to the Alpen. What's so urgent?"

"I don't know. He didn't say."

"Be careful. It's out of the way, that industrial estate. Lots of garage mechanics, always hanging about with nothing to do."

For reasons Lucy had never understood, her mum saw all garage mechanics as potential sex offenders. She didn't seem to suspect any other category of workers in the same way. Which was *super annoying*. For a start, it assumed that all garage mechanics were men, which might have been true in the nineteen seventies, but –

"I'm out!" her dad called from upstairs. "It's all yours!"

All systems go. She grabbed the granola bar, ran upstairs, used the toilet, washed her hands, brushed her teeth, combed her hair and went back into her bedroom. She was shaking now. She got dressed – grey York University T-shirt, jeans, beanie - put her phone in her bag, checked she had her purse and ran down the stairs, uttering a loud 'Bye!' as she passed through the front door.

The queue for the bus was already nine people long. She didn't get up this early, usually, but neither was her coming down here at this time completely unknown territory. It always surprised her that the bus could fit so many people in. Most times before, it had always looked full when it got here.

Which it was this time. A double-decker with 'Town Centre' on the front. She paid her three pounds sixty – exorbitant, really:

how much profit were they making? There must be a story there somewhere! – and sat in the middle row on the bottom deck, next to the central aisle. The most boring seat in the entire vehicle, when you thought about it. Nothing to look at except weary-looking commuters, depressed schoolkids, a glassy-eyed mother and her sleeping baby, and the everlasting grey suburbs outside. She took her phone out and joined everyone else in looking into a screen.

As usual, it took forever to get anywhere. The way buses worked in this country, they had to visit every conceivable stop between here and their destination, even if it meant travelling to Utah, Buenos Aires and Bangladesh. You'd think it would fill up, and the driver could just change the 'Town Centre' notice to 'No Vacancies', but in practice, that never happened because, spitefully, people kept getting off. Not just getting off, but getting off in the middle of nowhere, or dinging the bell for the driver to pull in somewhere that wasn't even marked as an official stop.

After a zillion hours, they arrived at Cedar Tops. The housing development. Amazing that they weren't nearer the industrial estate. They'd taken in just about everywhere else on the planet, yet it was still nearly a mile away. She looked at her phone again as if she hadn't been looking at it every ten seconds since they set off.

No messages. She took a tissue out and blew her nose.

But it must be serious for him to tell her not to call him. Serious enough for her to call for a taxi? Maybe he wasn't with the police at all. Maybe it was an armed gang, sent in by Phyllis Mordred to retrieve the documents. Perhaps Roger had disturbed them in the act.

Although, no, because if they could actual perform a burglary, they'd do it at night.

But perhaps they weren't safecrackers. Maybe their *modus operandi* was to wait till someone arrived – Roger, in this case - then make him open the safe with menaces. Then get him to call the person initially responsible for collecting the evidence – her, in this case – so they could put the fear of God into her.

The police being there wouldn't give you any reason to write, 'Don't call or text me back'. So it *did* look suspicious. And scary.

On the other hand, neither would a gang of menacers. They'd try to use their hostage as a source of reassurance. *Call me back if you get delayed on your way here, Lucy,* that sort of thing.

But she couldn't afford to take any chances. She went to her contacts and called a taxi.

"I'll be walking along to the industrial estate," she told the woman who answered. "Along Wilson Road on the Cedar Tops estate."

"We'll be as quick as we can," the woman replied. "It's a busy time of day, with the school runs and people trying to get to work. Could we say… about ten minutes?"

"I'll leave it," Lucy said. "Thank you." She hung up. She knew enough about taxis to know that ten minutes meant twenty. She'd be there by then, even at this pace.

She entered the industrial estate twelve minutes later, slightly out of breath, and picked up her pace to a jog. She was panicking now.

When she reached *The Echo's* compound, her fears evaporated. A police car stood outside the front door, and Charlotte, the middle-aged receptionist, was actually talking to a policeman.

Then a completely new set of fears grabbed her. What *was* going on?

Charlotte caught sight of her as she entered the gates. She made her excuses to the policeman and walked over. "Hi," she said sombrely. "I see you've heard."

"Roger texted me. What's happened?"

"Someone broke in last night. Or rather two people. Like, in competition with each other, apparently. To cut a long story short, one of them's in police custody, the other got away. Whoever it was, took that stuff you and Roger put in the safe yesterday."

Lucy's jaw plummeted and her mouth fell open. "You're kidding!" she said, just for something to say.

But it didn't remotely capture what she was feeling. Because she felt angry. Furious, in fact. This easily topped yesterday's outrage, when she'd had an excellent story all ready to go – the kind you might well wait a lifetime for under normal circumstances – and somehow Phyllis Mordred had been ahead of her. And Carneghan bloody Strake had spiked it at the last minute.

Which was fair enough, in a way. That was what you expected sometimes. Part and parcel of being a good investigative journalist. You had to be patient.

But sending a burglar in to steal it – and that's what it was: *stealing* – was beyond the pale. No part of that was fair in love *or* war.

She suddenly had an idea. She'd get bloody Phyllis Mordred now. She'd let her know her big heist hadn't worked. Wherever she was – sipping a cocktail at the Ritz, probably – her day would be ruined.

"Are you okay?" Charlotte said as she walked away.

"Fine," Lucy shot back.

She went into the building. The police forensic team had fenced the bit around the safe off, but she didn't need to be there. She just needed a computer. Any one would do.

She found one next to the window, where she wouldn't be interrupted. They probably had questions they wanted to ask her, but that could wait.

Thirty seconds and it had loaded up, ready to access. She entered her username and password, and went straight to her cloud storage.

It was there, just where she'd left it. All the documents she'd been sent, scanned, in order, all sensibly labelled. You had to get up bloody early in the morning to catch Lucy Staveley out. And they hadn't. Not early enough.

Right: here it was. Phyllis Mordred's mobile number. She grabbed a post-it notepad and wrote it down.

She wasn't even scared. And she knew it wasn't very sensible, *The Echo's* lawyers would have a major go at her, but didn't they always, these people?

"Hi," a posh voice said. "This is the voicemail for Phyllis Mordred. If you'd like to leave a message, please speak after the tone."

"Hi, this is Lucy Staveley, your arch-nemesis. I don't suppose you can *possibly* have been behind last night's theft" – keep it ambiguous, so the solicitors wouldn't have *too* hard a time extricating you – "but just in case you ever find out who was, you might like to know that I spent several hours photographing everything in that folder, and I've got it safe and sound on the cloud. Have a great day!"

Her adrenalin was pumping. Maybe she should check whether Phyllis Mordred had another phone, a landline, say.

But no, that would be overkill. It would make her look spiteful rather than sophisticated.

Even so… Nothing ventured, nothing gained.

When she turned back to look at the screen, there was an empty space where the folder had been.

It took a second for her to realise what she was seeing.

Emptiness.

Which wasn't a thing. It was a *no*-thing. Nothing.

Then another second for the significance to sink in. The folder – it couldn't have got lost, could it? That didn't happen.

But - it wasn't *there*.

But it *couldn't* have gone! It *had* to be there!

One the one hand: the fact that it had apparently gone missing; on the other: that folders didn't just 'go missing'.

The first alternative contained the word 'apparently'. Which is what it must be: a mistake. It must have got transferred lock, stock and barrel to another folder somehow. That sometimes happened.

She accessed her other folders. She went to the search bar and typed in some of the names of the files.

Nothing.

Oh my God. *Oh my God.*

She logged out of the cloud, then back in again. Nothing.

She logged out of the computer. Then logged back in. Then into her cloud account. Nothing.

It had gone. There was no other explanation for it. But even now, she didn't believe it. Give it five, ten minutes, look again.

She took out her tissue and blew her nose. Then she realised she was crying. She wiped her eyes. Pride came before a fall. She'd taken it upon herself to call Phyllis Mordred and taunt her. And God had punished her.

Roger suddenly appeared from behind two of the metal cupboards the police had moved. Fifty-ish, swept-across straight hair, blue corduroy jacket, massive hairy hands, beige slip-on shoes. "What are you doing here?" he asked.

"You *told* me to come in," she said self-pityingly, trying to swallow her tears.

"You okay? Listen, don't forget, you backed it all up in the cloud. This changes nothing. Er, wait a minute. Point of order. Did you just say *I* told you to come in? When?"

Waste of time arguing, although something weird was definitely going on. She picked up her phone and went to messages, intending to show him.

But it was gone. Nothing.

Just like the folder.

Suddenly, she saw. Phyllis Robinson, *spy*. A chill ran down her spine, so visceral it was like a tropical snake, endlessly long, intelligent and lethal.

She picked up her phone and pressed re-dial. She was shaking hard. "I know exactly what you've done, you bloody bitch," she said when the polite invitation to leave a message had terminated. "I want you to know that this isn't over. Someone out there *wants* me to know what I know, and they want me to be able to prove it. I'm like the hydra. Have you ever heard of the hydra? Eh? *Have you? Chop off one of its heads and two more grow back!*"

She hung up and blew a sigh. She was about to cry again.

"Who were you talking to?" Roger asked nervously, trying to make like he didn't already know.

"My mum," she replied.

Chapter 23: Bruce and Jonathan

Phyllis awoke at 6.15am, just as she used to in the 'old days', a few weeks ago, when she and John had worked at Thames House. She set off exactly as she always had, knowing that Alec was somewhere in the background, and possibly alongside another pair of friendly eyes. She boarded the tube at Mornington Crescent, changed at Embankment, disembarked at Westminster, picked up a *Metro* and ran up the final flight of steps between the underground and Bridge Street. She hardly had time to look at the scaffolding around Big Ben before being swept right by the mechanical throngs of fellow commuters under the brown fog of a summer dawn. The sudden, universal sense of a countdown to 9am. She crossed the road to Abingdon Street. After a few moments, she fell to wondering whether Annabel actually had burgled *The Echo's* offices last night, or whether it had been called off or postponed. She'd find out soon enough. In any case, it might not solve anything. There were many ways Lucy Staveley could have copied those files, and any number of places she could have stored them. She entered Millbank. Two minutes later, she mounted the steps to Thames House.

"Good to see you back… again," Colin said as she signed in. The mid-sentence pause was clearly meant to signal sincerity, but it also revealed that he wasn't quite sure it would come across that way, and that he'd already agonised over the question of when, given that she could be here indefinitely, it would be okay to stop expressing pleasure at her return.

"Great to be back… again," she replied.

"If you could wait here till Alec arrives, he'll brief you on your responsibilities for the day."

She sat on one of the chairs by the doorway, switched off her phone, opened her copy of the *Metro* and flicked through it till she arrived at the fashion pages. Alec came through the door three minutes later. He looked around the lobby till he found her sitting almost beside him. She closed the newspaper and stood up with a smile.

"Good to see you again," he said.

"Great to be back again," she replied.

She registered Colin's disapproving expression out of the corner of her eye. Alec liked to advertise himself as a man's man, and over the years had created many deluded victims, of whom Colin – despite his well-known contempt for macho culture - was one, and she wasn't. Right now, Alec's manly status was confirmed not only by his complete disregard for the mid-sentence pause, but by his affecting Phyllis so powerfully that she also omitted it. She could almost read Colin's thoughts. *Now he's mesmerising poor Phyllis as well.*

Alec led her upstairs and through the open-plan communal office. She noticed someone sitting at her desk: a balding middle-aged man in a blue suit with skinny trousers. He didn't look up as she passed. John's desk was occupied by another middle-aged man, who looked disgruntled.

"I'm sure you've clocked two guys where you and John used to be," Alec said. "I've told them you used to work here. They're doing carousels, I'm afraid, and you've been deputed to help them. Also, set them straight if they seem to be taking short cuts or making errors. I don't suppose you'll be doing this every day, but you're familiar with it, and they're new, so they could definitely use some assistance from time to time. You get your own computer, of course. Just over there," he said, indicating- a workstation almost equidistant from the two men, and slightly behind them.

"Okay," she replied. Disappointing, really. She hoped she'd be working with one of her old friends. Ideally Edna, but Suki, Victor or Ian would have been more than okay. Even Alec, though he did tend to get a bit dogmatic if you differed from him. Even

Annabel, despite her single-minded dedication to all things *The Realm*.

"What are their names?" Phyllis asked. "Are you going to introduce us?"

"Before I do that," he said, "I should just point out that I didn't notice anyone shadowing you on your way in this morning, nor did Suki. Don't misinterpret that. I know Grubfeld exists, we all do: we've got Annabel's exhaustive reports to prove it. But I'm pretty sure he wasn't there today."

"I wasn't following my normal routine, obviously," Phyllis replied.

"I expect he was getting a little complacent, and he waited for you in one of his usual spots, and so missed you. Tomorrow will probably be different. Don't worry, anyway. We've got your back. *Bruce, Jonathan*," he called. "Come and meet your temporary supervisor!"

Two hours later, her brain was beginning to melt. Carousels were the closest thing to thumbscrews that were both (a) still prevalent in the modern world and (b) formally compatible with the Human Rights Act 1998. She needed a cup of strong tea, and she'd worked long enough to be entitled to a short breather. Bruce and Jonathan were progressing well, and even seemed to be enjoying themselves, although that was probably affected.

She was wondering whether to tell them she was taking a break, and if so how to do it without implying they should join her, when a message flashed at the top of the screen.

Ruby Parker. *Please come to my office at your earliest convenience. It won't take long.*

She logged off, called the men over and told them she had a meeting, and that afterwards, she was going for refreshments in the canteen. They were also entitled to a break.

"Not for me," Bruce said. "I've got a bottle of water." He held it up, apparently so she could confirm it.

"I'll work through," Jonathan said. "I'm really enjoying it. Thank you for all your help."

"Sorry, I should have said that too," Bruce said. "Thank you. You've been really constructive. I wouldn't say it's the most enjoyable thing I've ever done, but it's definitely better than *any* job in local radio."

"You betcha," Jonathan said darkly. They shared a chuckle then resumed work.

Three minutes later, she knocked on Ruby Parker's door. She heard the word 'Enter'. A seat had been reserved for her.

"This should be a very quick meeting," Ruby Parker said. "I thought you'd like to know that Annabel's burglary last night was a complete success. We've got the supposedly incriminating dossier, and I'm surprised her editor thought it was worth printing. If it had gone anywhere near publication, your solicitor really could have demolished both him and Lucy Staveley and *The Echo* without even breaking stride. Carneghan Strake are probably wishing they'd held back with their threats to desist now."

"Maybe it wasn't actually at the imminent publication phase," Phyllis said. "Maybe Sir Anthony heard a rumour and overreacted."

"Anyway, you're not out of the woods yet. We've deleted Lucy Staveley's virtual copy – which we believe is her only one - but there's still the vexatious question of who sent her it, and whether they'll try again."

"Obviously, I'll let you know if I hear anything."

"If you'd like to see what we retrieved, have a word with Annabel, but I can't imagine it's worth your troubling over. It's patent nonsense."

"I'm just pleased it's out of circulation. However temporarily."

"I understand from Alec that you weren't followed this morning. But we'll remain vigilant. There is one other thing I wanted to ask you about. Have you ever heard of Angelo Bonnici?"

"The Knightsbridge murder victim? Only on the news. There wasn't much about it on TV. As I understand, the police began by treating it as a terrorist incident, then decided it wasn't. After which, it started to fade into the background."

"The victim was Maltese. I'm not saying there's any connection at all, but we've got to look at every possibility. And the man who attacked him was roughly Marchus Grubfeld's height and build. Which again, may be sheer coincidence."

"I'm pretty sure I never heard anyone mention Angelo Bonnici when we were in Malta. John might remember differently, but I don't think so. He'd have mentioned it last night."

"I'm probably clutching at straws. We'll keep an eye on it, anyway."

Ten minutes later, Phyllis sat alone in the canteen, next to the window, with a cup of tea and a cracker biscuit. Beyond the trees, the Thames was its usual grey, and because the trees were in full leaf, the opposite bank was obscured. Apart from the heavy traffic on Lambeth Bridge, and the uniformity of the foliage, she could be in the countryside.

She felt depressed. When she'd arrived this morning, she'd hoped to bump into some of her old friends, at least for a few moments. Now, she was glad she hadn't. She couldn't put her finger on it – it wasn't the hackneyed feeling that things had moved on here, because they hadn't – but something was definitely getting her down. It wasn't loneliness either. It wasn't Bruce and Jonathan. It wasn't even the carousels.

Then she realised. She'd changed her footing. Previously, she'd been one of the knights, forever ready to ride out into the world across a lowered drawbridge. Now, she was someone the knights were here to protect. She was here 'for her own safety'. *We've got your back,* as Alec had put it. Effectively, she was hiding. In a sense, Marchus Grubfeld had won. She'd been forced to acknowledge that he was stronger than her.

But she wasn't used to being passive. She was used to taking the fight to the enemy, returning blow for blow. She certainly didn't want to be cosseted, which was what was going on now. They weren't even briefing her fully on things that directly concerned her. Ruby Parker, for example, had made no mention of her 'second shadow', the man who'd now revealed himself as Adrian Fenech.

What would she, Phyllis, have said, if she had? *Oh, John met him. They're working together now*? Because that probably wouldn't have gone down very well. And how would John have felt, when she told him? Would he be okay with it? Or did he want to keep Adrian Fenech a secret?

She was already getting torn in terms of loyalties. And if she felt this way on the first day, how would she feel in a week, or a month? For all she knew, she might get used to it, becoming ever more dependent on Thames House, and, at the same time, as part of the same process, more and more jumpy. If so, she was set to end up a wreck.

She had to do something. Break free.

But how? She was trapped by the very people who were most solicitous for her welfare.

God, she really needed to speak to someone on the outside. Her husband, yes, good idea. That was the point of getting married, after all: someone to share your problems with from time to time, so they'd be as depressed as you were. Or maybe, just very rarely - but enough to make the whole thing worthwhile - they'd have a solution.

She switched her phone on.

Two voicemails from 'Unknown'. Great. Had she been mis-sold PPI? She couldn't wait to find out.

She sipped her tea and went to the first message. She immediately sat up.

"This is Lucy Staveley, your arch-nemesis. I don't suppose you can *possibly* have been behind last night's theft, but just in case you ever find out who was, you might like to know that I spent several hours photographing everything in that folder, and I've got it safe and sound on the cloud. Have a great day!"

Phyllis chuckled. She could already guess what the second message was about. Turn the anger up a few notches.

"I know exactly what you've done, you bloody bitch. I want you to know that this isn't over. Someone out there *wants* me to know what I know, and they want me to be able to prove it. I'm like the hydra. Have you ever heard of the hydra? Eh? *Have you? Chop off one of its heads and two more grow back!*"

A bit like listening to an arch-criminal in a superhero film. *You haven't heard the last of me, Jessica Jones!* Groovy, as John would say.

Then she had an idea. My God, she could use this. It was her way out of the protective fortress/prison!

She waited till she was on her way home. Alec would be following her, but she had a few minutes between Thames House and Westminster, and she could walk slowly. She took a deep breath and pressed 'Call'.

"Hello?" came Lucy Staveley's voice.

"You called me this morning and left two messages," Phyllis said.

Pause. "Is this...? Sorry, it's not...?"

"Phyllis Mordred *née* Robinson, the woman you were on the cusp of unjustly vilifying in print."

"Er, what do you want?" There was nothing of the arch-criminal in her tone now. On the contrary, she sounded scared, like she knew she'd gone too far and the headmaster had just appeared round the corner and that, should he choose to chop one of her heads off, that'd be more than fair, no hydra shenanigans, promise.

"Look, you must have had a talk with your editor at some point," Phyllis continued. "You must know you haven't got enough evidence to start making public accusations. I can guess what you were doing – putting the information out there in the form of a vague rumour to see if you could attract anything else, anything that might complete the picture you thought you had, so you could go to press."

"Maybe, yeah, but we had eighty per cent."

"At best, you had sixty per cent of what you *thought* you had - "

"Seventy."

"If the missing section can only be supplied in fictional form, it's irrelevant whether it's sixty, seventy or eighty. I had nothing to do with Aisling Baxter's death. Someone's trying to frame me."

"What do you want *me* to do about it?" Lucy Staveley asked.

"Aren't you interested to know who?"

"If you're so innocent, and you're so convinced there's nothing in that folder, why did you send someone to pinch it?"

"I didn't send anyone. It wasn't me."

"Yeah, pull the other one."

"Okay, put it like this. Your voicemails made it clear you're not holding any cards any more. You've got nothing. Zilch. Why would I be contacting you if I was guilty? Let's face it, whoever sent you that dossier isn't going to resend it, not to you. You've proved yourself inadequate. If they try again, it'll be with some other journalist. You're far from the only campaigning journalist in this country, even in Berkshire, and this is a national issue. So you tell me: why am I calling?"

"To, er, make fun of me?"

"Does that sound like what this is?"

"Okay, no. So why *are* you calling?"

"Because I'd dearly like to find out who's trying to frame me, and I need the help of someone who knows the territory."

"Me?"

"Lucy, if Carneghan Strake knew I was calling you, they'd have me publicly flayed. I'm taking a big risk here. I'm doing it because I believe you're a good investigative journalist, and you're already familiar with the background. And I'm offering you the opportunity to claim victory from the jaws of defeat. Get to the bottom of this, and you really *have* got a story."

A long pause. Finally: "Yeah, okay, that sounds good, I suppose. But what specifically are you suggesting?"

"First, we need to meet. I'd like you to come to my flat in London. For dinner. I promise I won't bite."

More silence.

"If you'd prefer to meet in a restaurant," Phyllis went on, "somewhere public, that'd be equally fine. You could choose the venue. I'd pay."

"No… no, that's okay. I'll come to your flat. We don't want anyone overhearing. And you're supposed to take risks in this job. And you've got to know when people are being kosher, which I think you are now. Okay, done. I'll bring a bottle of wine. When?"

"As soon as possible. Tonight, ideally."

"Tonight?"

"Hey, that's journalism. It's the early bird that catches the worm."

"I'm a vegan. I mean, dinner-wise. If that's a problem - "

"My husband's a vegetarian."

"I know. It said in the dossier."

"He does most of the cooking. I realise it's not the same. No eggs, dairy, etcetera, but he'll have a recipe, believe me. About eight-ish? Can you be in London by then?"

"Sure. I've already got your address. One of the few things I made a hard copy of."

Chapter 24: The Dinner Party

At seven o'clock that evening, John and Phyllis were still alone. They'd dressed for a small dinner party, because as well as Lucy Staveley, they expected Adrian Fenech and his Aunt Julia. Mordred wore an Aran jumper and blue cords; Phyllis wore a beige flared dress and pearls. They felt like an advertisement for middle-class one-upmanship. It didn't help that Phyllis had put a Bach concerto on. Maybe they should have played Stormzy. But that would be down-with-the-kids middle-class one-upmanship, which was the worst of all the fifty subtly different types of middle-class one-upmanship. So Bach it had to be.

"How did you get on following Dina Oforka-Jones?" Phyllis asked, as she dispensed five wineglasses from a box.

"I drew a blank," John replied from the kitchen. "Two meetings, one in Oxford Street, the other in Canary Wharf. Nothing suspicious that I could see. And I sent the pictures to Adrian. He didn't recognise anyone. She seems to spend a huge amount of time in her office in Cheapside. Strange, given how close that is to the official Carneghan Strake HQ. I'll shadow her again tomorrow, see how that goes. It's a trip out."

"Ruby Parker asked me if I knew Angelo Bonnici today."

"The Maltese guy who was killed in Knightsbridge? Yes, I'd thought of that. The very word 'Malta' makes me sit up now."

"She said his murderer was roughly Marchus Grubfeld's height and build."

"True. What's she intend to do about it?"

"What *can* she do? She said she'd keep an eye on it."

"She'll be sending a few detectives to the funeral. I'd dearly like to go myself, but it'll almost certainly be in Malta."

"She didn't say any more about Adrian Fenech. I wasn't sure what to make of that. Whether she's worked out who he is yet, or not."

"I doubt it. She'd have to send a wide probe to pick up someone so low in the official pecking order: small island-stroke-archipelago, retired. If there's something going on in Malta which we need to know about, and the authorities there get to hear we've sent a general alert about Adrian Fenech, it'll be tantamount to giving them a heads-up. She's probably waiting to see if he reappears on your tail, grab him that way."

"And how's he getting on with that list of journalists?"

"They're not very keen to talk to him. Same sort of reaction Edna got."

She laughed. "So all in all, things are going fabulously. We're really making progress. If Ruby Parker asks about Adrian Fenech, am I allowed to tell her?"

"You should probably have told her today. The longer you leave it, the more it'll look like we're hiding something. And if we do go back and work there someday, it'll make trust difficult."

Phyllis came and leaned against the door jamb. "I really wish you hadn't said that. Think about it: if I tell her about Adrian Fenech, I'll have to tell her about Lucy Staveley. Then she'll know I've been going behind her back. It's all a big tangle of lies, and it'll start to unravel."

"No one's lied to her."

"We've just been unfaithful, that's all. We've used her to protect me, whilst concocting our own little schemes behind her back."

He reached for the black pepper, ground some into the pan and stirred it. There's a simple solution. You tell her the truth about me and Adrian, but tell her I didn't tell you until today. You also tell her I contacted Lucy Staveley, and the first you knew about it was when she turned up at our front door brandishing a bottle of Prosecco."

"Blame you for everything?"

"I'm not getting Thames House official protection. I can do what I like. And isn't that what marriage is for?"

"Having someone to blame? I'd never thought of it like that."

"I'm not saying that's its *only* benefit."

"So first thing tomorrow morning, I go and tell her …?"

"As much or as little as you like. For all she need know, I'm scheming behind your back and putting my dastardly plans into operation while you're out."

"Okay. I can't help thinking it might blow up in our faces, though."

"We've got Marchus Grubfeld to worry about. Let's credit danger where it actually lurks. And don't forget, you called Lucy Staveley because you felt trapped. If you turn up tomorrow morning and just spill every single bean in the can, won't that put you back where you started? Worse, because you'll have reinforced your sense of dependency by voluntarily handing over the things you created specifically to keep you independent."

"So it's qualified honestly and surrendering my new-found independence versus the prolonged guilt of implicit deception."

"That's right. Welcome to the crazy world of overthinking."

She laughed and put her arms round him. "Thanks. I knew I'd get there in the end."

Two hours later, five people sat around the dinner table, having just finished a red lentil curry, and drunk, between them, two bottles of wine. At the 'head' of the table, and at ninety degrees to everyone else, sat Adrian Fenech in a suit. Side-by-side in front of the curtains, were John and Phyllis. Opposite them, Lucy Staveley and Adrian Fenech's Aunt Julia.

Aunt Julia wore a blue jumper, and a matching cardigan and skirt, and she had a hairstyle like a rococo sculpture. When she stood up, she stooped so much that she only seemed four feet tall. Upright she'd have been ten inches taller. Minus her hair, only four. She hardly spoke, except to say how lovely everything was.

When the meal was over, she walked alone to the sofa, switched the TV on, and watched *Flights from Hell: Caught on Camera*.

With the small talk over and Aunt Julia safely out of the way, it was time to begin. John and Adrian sat back to allow Phyllis to question Lucy, which was what the three had agreed before she arrived.

Lucy kicked off. "I get what you want from me," she said. She wore what were probably her work clothes: pullover, black baggy trousers, high-heel platforms. She reclined slightly.

Phyllis smiled. "Go on."

"If the rumour's spread that *The Echo*'s got a case against you, and that I'm behind trying to make it stick, people who have a grudge against you might find their way to me, and we might find out who sent the dossier. It might be someone who knows someone. Or it might be the original sender. Either way they'd speak to me for the exact same reason they definitely wouldn't speak to you."

"Except that you don't have to wait for them to come to you," Phyllis said. "If you've got that reputation – and since Sir Anthony Hartley-Brown heard about you, others must have – there's nothing to stop you being proactive. Sometimes people need a little nudge before they're prepared to talk."

Lucy Staveley took another sip of her wine. "But it's only fair to warn you that I'm keeping an open mind. You've been nice, and I'm sorry I left those voicemails – it was highly unprofessional of me – but I've got to go where the evidence leads. You said I might have sixty per cent of a lawyer-proof story. Okay, fine, but if I find the other forty per cent – assuming it does exist, after all – I *will* write it up, and I probably won't tell you beforehand."

"I won't lose any sleep over that possibility," Phyllis replied.

Lucy Staveley grinned. "Well, now that we've cleared the air, you might be surprised to hear that I've already got a lead."

"Already?"

"Like you said, it's the early bird that catches the worm. On the way here, I rang Aisling Baxter's parents. Guess what? They actually want to speak to me. They wouldn't say what about, except that it's important. The day after tomorrow. They're in London, unfortunately, staying with some relative, so I'll have to come back."

"You could stay here, if you want. I mean, you're staying overnight. What difference will one more day make? Or one and a half more days? You could ring home, just tell your, er - "

"I live with my parents. Yeah, I know, but so does everyone under thirty nowadays. Unless they're loaded. I wrote an article about it. 'Living in the Vault of the Bank of Mum and Dad'. Short-listed for the New Voice in Journalism Award, 2016. Seems like a long time ago now."

"Right. Well, ring your parents, tell them you're staying here till the day after tomorrow, and you can go home then. You don't have to stay indoors. I've got a spare key, and I can tell you the gate number. You can come and go as you please."

"Wow, that sounds great!"

"We're agreed then. And we'll make you another vegan meal tomorrow night. Just one other thing. If anyone asks who contacted you this afternoon, could you tell them it was John? Not me?"

"Sure. Why?"

"Because if it gets back to Carneghan Strake that I contacted you, they'll probably sue me for disregarding strict instructions. You know how lawyers can be."

She laughed. "Tell me about it. No, that's fine, Phyllis. Consider it done."

Chapter 25: Conference at the Italian

After Marchus Grubfeld abandoned the moped, he ducked into the building he'd entered last night and retrieved his T-shirt, shorts, sunglasses, trainers and baseball cap. He squirted the motorcycle helmet with lighter fluid, put the gloves in, and set everything aflame. He changed, then put Angelo Bonnici's phone and his old clothes into the plastic bag. He left the building by its front entrance. Ten minutes later, he was in Oxford Street, using the crowds as cover and ducking the CCTV. He bought a second change of clothing and ditched the first, then a third, and ditched the second. Something like this, you could never be too careful. Half an hour later, he sat on a bed in the Moore Intercontinental Hotel in Knightsbridge, on the grounds that it was always best to hide in plain sight.

It took him half an hour to access the phone. He transferred the data to his own, then set to examining it.

Five calls in four minutes from 'Dina Oforka-Jones'.

He tapped on Bonnici's Contacts.

She worked for Carneghan Strake, the legal firm, here in London.

He went to Google images. Then to the photographs he'd taken at Bonnici's party in Malta.

And there she was.

It all fitted together now. This morning's killing had paid off quicker than expected.

He switched the TV on. Crucial to keep an eye on the police in this sort of situation.

The worst was over, though; and he'd got what he came to London for. Incredible, Angelo Bonnici actually walking towards him like that with his phone; and being so easy to kill, like he knew his time was up.

Anyone remotely paranoid would have seen the spectral arm of a hostile conspiracy in there. But not Marchus Grubfeld. That's the way the universe went, sometimes. You were incredibly lucky. It didn't even mean you'd have to pay for it later.

On the other hand, complacency was a luxury no one could afford. To guard against it, he needed to compress his timetable so he could leave the country at the earliest opportunity. With everything at the police's disposal nowadays – DNA recovery, forensic podiatry, dactyloscopy, video analysis, device forensics, all the miserable rest of it - he could find himself in trouble even faster than Bonnici had. John and Phyllis Mordred would have to die quickly now.

No point in rushing Dina Oforka-Jones, though. She'd have heard about Angelo and she was probably panicking. Let her terror mount, then visit her tomorrow. Pointless calling ahead. She'd run a mile. Just turn up and offer her reassurance. Pretty soon, she'd be willing to embrace anything.

The next day, he rang the doorbell next to the brass plaque of her office in Cheapside. He assumed she'd be in. From what he'd learned on the internet, this was her lair and refuge, and if she was busy at all at the moment – which she probably would be: she'd be using work as a means of distracting herself from the ominous demise of her partner in crime – she'd be here.

No answer, though.

He waited a full minute before ringing again, depressing the button longer this time.

The door opened suddenly. A livid-looking grey-haired man with a long face opened the door just wide enough to confirm that the caller wasn't welcome. His eyes darted about, as if he was looking for someone on the opposite pavement. "What do you want?" he hissed.

"Angelo told me - "

"Take this and go away!" He thrust a piece of paper at him, still scouring the vicinity with his eyes. "You're being *followed! Go away!*"

The door slammed. Marchus turned around slowly, pretending he was a cold caller who'd been given his marching orders. But he was rattled. *Followed?* By who?

The grey haired man was bluffing. Of course he was.

He pretended to put the piece of paper in the bin, walked twice around the block and pulled into a side street and read it.

Ginello's, 47 Graham Stark Road, Hackney. 10pm tonight. BE CAREFUL.

Several hours later, he sat opposite Dina Oforka-Jones and her colleague, the grey-haired man, Ian Batchelor, at a corner table in the small Italian restaurant one or other of them had specified on their missive. Presumably one of Carneghan Strake's rendezvous points for solicitor-client meetings of a sensitive nature, somewhere the waiters' discretion could be relied on. They'd begun by frisking each other for listening devices. Then they'd switched off their phones and put them screen-up on the table.

Both lawyers looked pale, as if Marchus Grubfeld had recently popped out of a grave with *d. 1769* on the headstone. He reclined in his seat with his mineral water. He hadn't expected it to this extent, but he was clearly in charge here. And so far, they'd exchanged barely a word.

"Angelo told me that if anything happened to him, I was to make my way straight over here and report to you," he told them.

"Who are you again?" Dina said.

"Marchus."

Ian shook his head as if the question had been pointless given that it wasn't going to elicit a truth. He reached into the briefcase next to him and pulled out a wad of photos. "Look, 'Marchus', we already know who you are in one sense, and so does Phyllis Mordred. This is a collection of pictures her husband took of you."

Marchus sat up. He'd assumed they were lying about that. "How did you, er, get hold of them?" He immediately regretted the 'er', and sat doubly straight as if to annul it.

"Phyllis Mordred came to see us," Ian said. "Someone tried to blackmail her using a dossier of highly redacted materials designed to produce the impression that she engineered Aisling Baxter's death. We were called in to make sure the story never made the newspapers."

"And that's when she gave you these?" Marchus asked.

"She wanted to know if we had any idea who you were," Dina replied. "Of course, we truthfully answered no. Neither of us had clapped eyes on you till this afternoon."

"How do you know that dossier was 'highly redacted'?" Marchus asked.

Dina and Ian exchanged looks. "Because we produced it," she said as if it was a confession she knew she'd have to make sooner or later. "To put Phyllis Mordred in our power. We knew she'd find out about it and that sooner or later, she'd find her way to our door. She's a spy – or was – and we needed to know what was going on behind the scenes vis-à-vis Aisling Baxter's 'unfortunate' death and those cameras and microphones."

"Which turned out to be: nothing," Ian said. "Nothing whatsoever's going on. She's not even a spy any more. Not that it matters, I suppose," he added, seeing Dina's look. "We can't be too careful."

"When she showed us the photos of you, Marchus," Dina went on, "we realised you must be Angelo's man. So we sent someone in to recover the dossier on the grounds that, if you killed her, it would have the effect of linking her death to Malta. The opposite of what we all want."

"And was that recovery successful?" Marchus asked.

"Completely," Dina said, before Ian could speak. "Look, 'Marchus', I don't know about you, but I'm beginning to wonder whether we might have overestimated John and Phyllis Mordred. I mean, in terms of the precise level of threat they represent.

They're thinking about Malta more than they should be at the moment because you're following them, and, well, what *else* could something like that be related to, given their singular experiences while they were over there? But my feeling is that if you were to just… *disappear*? … they'd probably forget all about that list. I certainly don't think there's any need to kill them, really. Not anymore. Time and forgetfulness have worked most of their familiar magic already. Leave Mr and Mrs M in peace and it'll all be all right."

Marchus returned the photos to Ian. "It's not about the list any more, as you rightly say."

"So what *is* it about?" Dina asked tetchily.

"Angelo wasn't my only paymaster. The other people bank-rolling me recognised Phyllis and John Mordred as ex-spies. Why they've left the employ of MI7, we don't know. On paper, they're both huge assets, meaning, of course, that they're massive thorns in the side of its rivals."

"In your 'paymasters' sides," Ian said.

Marchus nodded. "The decision's been taken to kill them while they're still off the leash. Before the inevitable happens, and MI7 re-recruits them. It's simpler that way. More 'honourable', believe it or not."

"How do you intend to… kill them?" Ian asked.

Marchus grinned. "From your point of view, it really doesn't matter. But since you've asked, I'll probably shoot them. Bang."

Ian rolled his eyes contemptuously. "Great."

Dina held her hand up. She smiled. "No, you're wrong, Ian. I see what Marchus is saying. Make it look as much like spy killing spy as possible. What could be more natural? And who'd think to trace it back to Malta? It's just some unknown hostile power liquidating two individuals who've threatened it in the past, and could conceivably do so again. No reason to link it to us, or Aisling Baxter, or the list."

"And what's the catch?" Ian asked wearily.

"There isn't one," Marchus replied. "I'm here because Angelo asked me to report to you."

Dina smiled. "There must be more to it than that. What do you want?"

"An unnecessarily brutal way of putting it," Marchus said. "At this point, it's about what I can offer you.

Dina sighed. "Let's hear your sales pitch then."

"Angelo told me all about you," he lied. "So I know how risky your operation is and how high the stakes are. You'll *need* someone like me from time to time if you're to keep afloat. Sadly, Angelo's gone now, but I'm equally discreet, and we can deal directly. I can break and enter, blackmail, shadow, crack safes, forge new identities, infiltrate all types and levels of gatherings, kill, and a whole list of other helpful things you probably wouldn't find in the London Business Directory. I don't come cheap, but I'm good, and I'm one hundred per cent reliable. And I certainly won't talk in the highly unlikely event that I'm arrested or captured. I can endure torture."

"You certainly sound like an asset," Dina said. "I admit, I'm tempted. But at the moment, I'm not sure we're desperately in need any of those things. And as for paying you … well, money's always traceable."

"You may need me more than you think," Marchus said. "Like I said, my other paymasters are keen to get rid of John and Phyllis Mordred. Their worry is, once they're gone, MI7 might launch a full-scale inquiry. And they'd probably find out who – I mean, which country - was responsible for their deaths."

"How does that affect us?" Ian asked.

"It's the outcome my employers are keen to avoid at all possible costs. So they're thinking of throwing MI7 a large bone in the form of your Malta operation. If what I've heard on the grapevine's anything to go by, you may be on the brink of being framed, big time." He beamed. "A huge irony, given that fake dossier you told me about, a moment ago. Carneghan Strake stands to lose everything."

Dina and Ian sat frozen.

"So you see," Marchus went on, "that when I said, a moment ago, it would be a good idea to have someone like me on your books, I wasn't exaggerating. We're at a crossroads now. I believe my bosses are about to order me to kill the Mordreds in a looks-like-an-accident kind of way. That would set the scene for a little judicious framing. A leaked document about you and Angelo, for example, linking you both to Aisling Baxter. Suddenly, a lid appears to be blown, leading all the way back to that badly-maintained road from Valletta. MI7 gets to work – and with you in its sights. Before you know it, you're both looking at a lengthy spell in prison."

"Okay," Ian said hoarsely. "What's the alternative?"

Marchus nodded sagely as if the deal was as good as done. "That I act as soon as possible, before anyone has a chance to modify my instructions. I make it look as messy and brutal as possible: an obvious targeted assassination by a hostile foreign power. And I can add elements of my own to augment that impression. It'll be too late to frame you then."

Dina smiled. "I take it there's a price."

"Three-quarters of a million," Marchus said. "Sterling, not euros or dollars. Paid in Ethereum via the dark web. Completely untraceable."

Dina took a sharp breath. "Of course, given this afternoon, you could already have led John Mordred to us. We may be in Shit Street right now."

"All the more reason to get rid of him quickly," Marchus said. "And from what Angelo told me, you'd like him dead anyway, quite apart from that."

Dina chuckled. "Don't take this the wrong way, Marchus, but John Mordred's had his eyes on you for a long time. For all I know, he might be watching you right now. That does kind of indicate that you might not be as good as you think you are."

"And anyway, how do we know you're telling the truth about any of this?" Ian added. "I mean, about what your 'paymasters' supposedly want, and how they're ready to throw us to the wolves?"

Marchus stood up. "If that's how you feel, I'll be on my way."

Dina grabbed his hand. "Sit down. Let's not be too hasty. No one's out to humiliate you. Both Ian and I have made good points. It's up to you to answer them. Please."

"As regards sabotaging your Malta operation," Marchus said, sitting down again, "it's already under way. Why do you think Angelo's dead? The thief got his phone. He didn't need to murder him too. What he *did* need to do was begin a chain of killings, the next of which are those of John and Phyllis Mordred, with the word 'Malta' emblazoned all over them. Then the authorities start raising questions about that list, and one or two other things get thrown into the mix, and it's all starting to look very bad for Carneghan Strake. It'll happen faster than you can possibly imagine."

"Yet my point about John Mordred being one up on you still stands," Dina said. "We'll give you two hundred thousand."

Marchus made a show of frowning. "Five."

"Three," Dina replied. "And we'll set it up for you. Save you hours of hard work, and make it so you can walk onto a plane and get out of the country before anyone even knows what's happened."

"Four," Marchus said. "And I'll kill any two members of that list Phyllis Mordred published for you. The ones you consider the weakest links, those most likely to talk. And I'll make both killings look accidental."

"Within what sort of time frame?" Dina asked.

"Six months."

"Five hundred K," she said, "if you make it four on the list within three months."

Marchus shrugged. "That'll be much more difficult."

"Excuse me, but we're doing a lot of your work for you here," Dina replied. "John and Phyllis Mordred are the hardest part. We've said we'll take care of that. You're getting a hell of a lot of bang for your half a million bucks."

Marchus smiled. "And you've an awful lot to lose if I walk away."

"I'm losing track here," Ian interposed. "Summarise, if you would, please, 'Marchus': exactly what are you offering, and how much are you asking?"

Marchus drew a deep breath. He grinned again, and leaned back. "Okay, look," he said wearily, "I want to show you how good I am and what an asset I can be. You set up the Mordreds, I'll eliminate them, I'll then strip any four individuals from that list of yours, and we'll call it four-fifty. All within three months. Deal?"

Dina accepted his handshake. "Assuming it all goes to plan," she said, "we'll definitely keep you in mind afterwards."

He stood, and picked up his phone. "I'll send you the payment details by post."

He could tell Ian Batchelor was still sceptical, but it didn't matter: he was under Dina Oforka-Jones's thumb. He wouldn't cause any trouble.

He left the restaurant by the back door and walked along a dark side-street until he came to the main road. He'd get a bus back into the city, find a hotel somewhere and have a few drinks before turning in.

He'd concealed it well, but he was still rattled. The thought that he'd been followed all the time he was watching Phyllis Mordred had left him feeling angry and humiliated. Had Dina decided to turn the knife, she could easily have turned his discomfiture up to boiling point. But she'd been wise enough to recognise it wasn't in her interests.

Until now, he'd felt nothing for the Mordreds. They were simply targets. Now, suddenly, he hated them. Part of it, he knew, was the strong suggestion that they were better than him. All the time he'd thought he was in control, yet in reality he'd been under observation. And of course, when that happened, it was touch and go as to whether your observer was relatively benign. This time, he'd been lucky. But it had served to show him he wasn't as clever as he thought. Not a happy revelation.

He stopped for a moment on the pavement and turned to look into the road and around. Behind him, a high fence, but in front, a cinema, several people in a kebab shop, a three-person queue at a bus stop, four unlit side-streets, a multi-storey car park the interiors of whose topmost tiers receded into darkness. Was John Mordred watching him now?

He didn't know.

That made it ten times worse. He might have followed him to *Ginello's*. He might be following him this very moment.

My God, his future was by no means assured! In pledging to kill the Mordreds, he might have signed his own death warrant!

If they were that good.

But no. If John Mordred really was that omnipresent, he'd know that it was he, Marchus, who'd killed those four crooks and Angelo. And he'd have alerted the authorities. And Grubfeld's Interpol mug shot would be all over the news. Which it wasn't.

What had probably happened was that Phyllis Mordred had sensed being followed – spies and even ex-spies sometimes had such abilities – and she'd set her husband to work finding out if she was right. Once she went home in the evening, so too would he. He'd have no idea where to look for her shadow the next day unless the shadowing resumed. Which it hadn't.

So he was safe for the time being. All he had to do was stay calm and carry on.

Chapter 26: Lucy Gets an Invitation

Lucy Staveley never enjoyed sleeping on a sofa, but this time it was worth it. She didn't get to come to London much. The rent she paid to her parents wasn't exorbitant, but being freelance didn't pay well either, and most weeks she had barely enough for a Friday night beer and a vape. Even if it had been affordable, a trip to the capital for anything other than work would have left her feeling dispirited and guilty, given that her mum and dad hardly ever went. She got enough self-reproach in Newbury.

The beauty this time, though, was that it was work. And what's more, productive: it stood a good chance of turning something really important up. Aisling Baxter's parents obviously thought they had information worth the telling. Even better: she'd made it absolutely clear to Phyllis that her sole loyalty was to the truth. So what could go wrong?

The day after her arrival in London was a waiting period: she wasn't due to conduct her interview till tomorrow. Nevertheless, she got up at 6.30am. Not good to get in anyone's way and especially bad to be found lying on the Mordreds' sofa in her underwear. After all, they'd have to come into the living room at some point. She showered quickly, dressed and pulled her shoes on. She didn't see John, but then he was probably sleeping in: he worked from home.

Phyllis emerged from her bedroom as she was on her way out. "Hi," she said. "You're up early. Did you sleep okay?"

"Absolutely," Lucy said. "It was much more comfortable than I expected."

"Had any breakfast?"

"I always carry a granola bar."

"If you want to come back here any time for any reason, just let yourself in. Otherwise, we'll see you again this evening."

"Thank you. Have a good day at work."

Phyllis laughed. "Thank you, I won't."

Lucy took the bus into Central London. She'd been lying about the granola bar, but she bought four hash browns in McDonald's at Marble Arch. Then she decided she needed fortifying since it was London, so she ordered oats made with water instead of milk, and topped with strawberry jam. Afterwards, she realised she'd eaten too much. She sat on a bench in Hyde Park and read a *Metro* she'd picked up at Mornington Crescent tube station. Homeless people wandered up and down, distinguishable not only by their clothes and defeated looks, but also by not apparently accelerating whilst holding a disposable branded coffee cup or gazing at a mobile phone. Compared with the commuters, they somehow looked human and, for the first time in her life, she felt truly sorry for them. The pigeons also looked real. It said something that you weren't allowed to feed them here. Like a science-fiction thing, the robots in charge.

She'd maybe work for the *Metro* someday.

She cried a little. She didn't know why. She called her mum, just to check in home. They said they loved each other. The wind built up. It threatened rain for ten minutes, then the sky cleared, the sun came out, and she felt gloriously optimistic. She had no idea what she was going to do today.

She spent the next six hours wandering as if she was homeless. By mid-afternoon, she felt exhausted and depressed. She couldn't believe London was so big. A bit like Sainsbury's or Tesco: when you went inside, it looked like the freezer-section was a reasonable walk away, but it wasn't: no, they'd deliberately constructed the whole thing as an optical illusion. Try walking to the freezers without going anywhere else first, and you'd immediately appreciate its devious nature. Likewise, on her phone, and even on the official Underground map, Marble Arch looked close to Oxford Circus. But it wasn't. It was a million miles away. London was a megalopolis, like in *Blade Runner* or something. Not that she'd ever seen *Blade Runner*, but she'd heard about it.

At midday, she sat in Trafalgar Square with a cauliflower pie. She'd been on the move for nearly four hours now, and she'd hardly seen anything. She walked up the steps to the Tate and took four photos of Nelson's Column, but Nelson came out so small, you could hardly see him.

She'd had enough.

Mind you, there was nothing to stop her sitting here all day. No law against it.

But that would be a complete waste. She went into the museum and looked at pictures for an hour, then she went to a pub in Westminster and made a pint of beer last an hour.

When would it be okay to go back to the Mordreds'? She hated London now. It was big and unfriendly and boring. If only there was somewhere you could check into for a few hours and go to sleep. Somewhere free. Like in Japan, those pods.

She bought a potato pasty and sat on the Thames embankment with the London Eye in front of her. The best that could be said for today was that it wasn't raining. She was already homesick for Newbury.

She went back to Camden at six o'clock. John let her in. He'd been out somewhere all day he said. "What have you been doing?" he asked.

She laughed. "Wandering about like an idiot. I'm absolutely bushed. To be honest, I just want somewhere to sleep right now."

"Dinner will be ready in an hour. Go and curl up on the sofa for a while. I'll let you know when it's ready."

She hadn't noticed before – she'd been too focussed on Phyllis – but John was quite hot. Mind you, so was Phyllis. They both were; in a way that she, Lucy, wasn't. She felt even more homesick now. The Mordreds were being so nice to her, and that wouldn't have been so bad, had niceness not been one of the major attributes of perfection. And they also possessed all the other attributes. It wasn't fair. And London wasn't fair either. She'd begun the day wanting to like it, and all it had done was set her tramping about like the vagrants she'd seen in the park. Like it was eager to underline her uselessness.

She sat on the sofa and fell asleep watching *Celebrity Eggheads*. John woke her up at seven. Phyllis was in. They ate maple mustard tofu burgers and talked vaguely about their day. Afterwards, they watched TV. John and Phyllis went to bed at nine, and she showered and followed suit. As she fell asleep, she wondered what she should ask the Baxters tomorrow. Best not to plan. Let them do the talking.

She awoke at 6.30 again and followed her routine of the previous day, with the difference that this time she felt a lot more frazzled. She was out of the flat at seven. She wasn't due to meet Aisling's parents until one o'clock, so she still had several hours to kill.

For some reason, probably because she was in Hell, she found herself doing exactly what she had the previous day. She ate in McDonald's and went to sit in Hyde Park. She cried and this time, she knew why: because she felt lonely and superfluous, like she could die right here and no one would even notice. She rang her mum, and when she told her she loved her, she had to control her voice. It seemed too good to be true that she'd be home in nine hours' time at the outside.

Then a fresh surge of misery. She'd forgotten to give Phyllis her key back, which meant another trip to Camden before she could get on the train home.

Maybe she should go now to the Mordreds', get it over with. Bloody hell.

But that would be a waste of a day.

Why was she still *thinking* like that? *This* was a waste, sitting on this bench!

But actually, she could do anything she liked. She was free. She could go to a pub, have ten pints, blow all her savings on a turn on the Eye, go to a matinee performance of The Tina Turner Musical, anything.

Only she didn't want to.

She'd bitterly regret it when she got back to Newbury. She'd wonder what had come over her, and she'd despise herself.

Which she kind of did already.

Her phone rang. *Unknown*, so not either of her parents, not Roger, nor Mrs Baxter, and not any one of her diminishing circle of friends.

"Hello?" she said.

"Is this Lucy Staveley?" a woman's voice asked. Upper class, probably middle-aged, definitely not Phyllis.

"Speaking."

"This is Dina Oforka-Jones, one of the senior partners at Carneghan Strake. I understand *The Echo* was burgled the other night. I wonder if we might meet. I may have something for you. We'd pay your expenses to London, of course."

"Meet? Us?"

"As I say, it could be in your interests. That is, if you're still chasing that particular story."

"As a matter of fact, I am," Lucy said. "I don't give up that easily."

"Good. So I take it you're not categorically opposed to us meeting?"

"When?"

"No time like the present. How soon can you be in London?"

"I'm here now. I'm in Trafalgar Square."

Slight pause. "I won't ask what you're doing here, since you probably won't tell me and it's none of my business anyway."

"I'd probably have published that stuff if it hadn't been for you. I'd be hot property right now."

Dina Oforka-Jones chuckled. "Not after we'd sued *The Echo*. And if we hadn't, some other law firm would. You'd have become a pariah overnight. We saved you. Thanks to us, your career in journalism's still intact."

"What do you want to talk about?"

"Why don't you come to my office in Cheapside and find out? Say, forty minutes' time?"

An hour later, Lucy sat in an easy chair opposite Dina Oforka-Jones's glass-topped desk. She'd signed a non-disclosure form about what they were going to discuss, and a grey-haired man, presumably from elsewhere in the building, witnessed it, then brought in a tea set with two cups. "No milk for me, please," Lucy said. "Two sugars, though."

Dina waited till Ian had served the beverages. He let himself out.

"Nice office you've got here," Lucy said. She was obviously nervous.

"You should see our place round the corner. Twelve floors above the City. All glass, chrome and neon. Very Stern, Lockhart and Gardner. Are you a fan of *The Good Wife?*"

"Not really."

"I prefer it here. It's cosier. And I'm not really into razzmatazz."

"What did you want to talk about?" Lucy asked.

"Okay. To business. You did well to get hold of that dossier, although, from what I understand, it contained nothing conclusive. Since it disappeared, however, I have come into possession of a tranche of *new* evidence – at least, it claims to be new - that suggests Phyllis Mordred may just be guilty after all. Remember that non-disclosure agreement you just signed. It's absolutely imperative that none of this goes outside these four walls."

"Of course."

"I don't want to labour this, but given that you lost the last batch of evidence you received - "

"I didn't lose it. It was stolen. We were burgled."

Dina smiled solicitously. "I meant the word 'lost' in the legal, technical sense, Lucy, not in its colloquial signification; not as an expression of reproach."

"Oh. Okay."

"Since it was taken from you, whoever sent it to you in the first place may have decided you're not to be trusted with a facsimile of that evidence. I don't mean to be brutal. I'm just stating the facts. It's unlikely you'll be given a second chance."

Lucy shrugged. "I guess. But that doesn't mean I have to give up."

"Which is highly commendable. And I would imagine that's exactly what you're in London for. What if I was to tell you that whoever sent you that dossier – and I don't know his or her identity – has now sent *me* a copy of it, plus some new, rather more incriminating material?"

"I'd say, 'What do you want from me?'"

Dina smiled jadedly. "In a moment. It's likely that whoever sent said material to me has also sent it to another journalist. In the next twenty-four hours, I fully expect to get *another* set of instructions from Phyllis Mordred to the effect that I halt a *second* publication. Now, this is where you come in. You see, when we were dealing with *The Echo*, I felt pretty confident that Phyllis Mordred must be innocent, although the question of why anyone would want to frame her still hasn't been satisfactorily answered, in my view."

"But now you're *not* so sure she's innocent?"

"Precisely. The thing is, you see, I don't like defending *actual criminals*. I'm a litigation lawyer. I defend people with poor reputations, not murderers. I'm willing to take a heavy load on my conscience from time to time, but I draw the line at getting a killer off the hook. And I'd like to know whether that's a prospect. As soon as possible."

"And I suppose that's where I come in?"

"I think if you were to call on Phyllis Mordred at home, and beg to speak to her, be persistent, she'd probably be willing to grant you an interview. You could look contrite, ask for her side of the story. If she gets wind of this new parcel of damning evidence, she's going to need all the friends she can get. Especially where you both live, in Newbury. I'm pretty sure that will swing it."

"So I go and interview her. Then what?"

"I want you to see if you can photograph her front door key."

"What?"

"Regard it as a challenge. Look, I just want access to her flat. It's a pity you're not a fan of *The Good Wife*, because you'd know that Stern, Lockhart and Gardner have an in-house private detective called Kalinda. All big firms have them. We've got one. If she can access the Mordred's flat while they're out, she can probably discover whether or not they're guilty of the murder of Aisling Baxter, which – without giving too much away about the new evidence I've received - I personally believe they *may* be. She's very good at her job: the Mordreds will never know she's been in. And of course, if we get enough to suggest guilt, we'll probably have to pass everything to the police. But you can have the scoop. We'll stop anyone else getting there first."

"What if you *can't* ascertain their guilt?"

"In that case, Phyllis Mordred is still our client, and you can't touch her. For your own good. And, if that sounds harsh, it isn't: because neither can anyone else. But I can offer you a massive consolation prize as a way of saying thank you for your help. Access to one or two of our highest profile clients. You've presumably heard of Stallone Laine? We could get you an exclusive interview with him. And what about Connie Glaser? She doesn't give interviews very much, but she's highly sought-after, and I'm confident I can get you a toehold. And occasionally, we need journalists to divert the public's attention with snippets of information. Say there's going to be a minor scandal around Beth Corea. Well, we put out some kind of exclusive about Stallone. The resulting noise from the latter drowns out the former. Naturally, though, you'd have to give up working in Newbury if you were to become our go-to journalist in that sense. You'd need to work in London for one of the national dailies."

"And you want me to – what? – photograph the Mordreds' front door key?"

"From both sides. That's it. Nothing more. We've got a software program that can convert photographs into 3D printer files, so you can relax and let us do the rest. Even if they do find out there's been an intruder, which is highly unlikely, they'll never know how he or she got in. None of their keys will ever have gone missing."

"Let's say I got you those photos, how do I know you'd fulfil your end of the bargain?"

"How about if I gave you ten thousand pounds, right now? Cash? I don't mean to say that would be a cast-iron guarantee, but it's the best I can do, and you could regard it as surety. Pay it back when you've got what we agreed. Or not. You could keep it, even after we've got you all those scoops." She reached into her desk, took out a fat, sealed envelope and pushed it across the desk. "All I need is to make sure the Mordreds aren't murderers, Lucy. That's easily worth ten thousand pounds to Carneghan Strake, and of course, it's also *the right thing to do*. If they're innocent, which I hope they are, no one will be happier than me. And if they're guilty, you'll have helped prevent them getting away with it and possibly killing again. I just want a clear conscience, that's all. And so, I'm sure, do you. Take it out and count it, if you like. Just keep tight hold of it when you get out of here, that's all."

Lucy reached over and put it in her bag as casually as if she was helping herself to another cup of tea. "You're right. If they are murderers, they should pay the penalty. And if they're not, I want to help them, and – *ta da!*"

She held up a front door key.

"Oh, my goodness," Dina said, "is that what I think it is?" She pulled her phone out. "Hold it up, that's right, so the light's on it. Now turn it round. That's it. Two more, just to be on the safe side, and we'll do one from the top and bottom."

"Hang on, you're getting my fingers in."

"That's okay, we'll crop them out before we put them in the printer. We have to eliminate everything extraneous, otherwise it impairs the program. Don't worry."

"They've got an outside gate too. The code's 6739."

"Thank you. That's very helpful."

Two minutes later, it was over. Lucy returned the key to her bag. Dina put her phone back in her desk drawer. Both cast their eyes downwards as if what had happened was shameful, best never mentioned again.

"I'll be off then," Lucy said, standing up.

"We'll be in touch," Dina told her. "Probably within the next few days. I called you earlier, so you've got my number on your phone now. Let me know if you need anything."

Lucy brightened a little at this. "Thank you," she said.

Dina held the door for her and watched her descend the stairs and let herself out of the front door.

Chapter 27: Kevin Speaks

On Lucy's first full day in London – the day she ate a cauliflower pie in Trafalgar Square and later fell asleep in front of Celebrity Eggheads – John awoke at 4am, changed into a sweat shirt and jeans, packed a pair of trousers and an oxford shirt into a shoulder bag, and left the flat at five. Fifteen minutes later, he stood in front of Dina Oforka-Jones's four bedroom detached house in Greenwich. She emerged at eight, the same time as yesterday, and walked to the tube station talking on her phone. He joined her on the train. They changed at London Bridge and got off at Bank. She walked briskly to her office on Cheapside, let herself in with a key, and disappeared from view. If this was anything like yesterday, she'd stay there all day. He didn't think she'd be watching him from the window. Nothing about her body language suggested she thought she was being followed.

From now on, it was a case of keeping an eye on her front door for as long as possible from as great a distance as possible. Yesterday, he'd found a pillared recess in a vacant to-let office block building eight doors down. But a permanent watch wasn't possible. Occasionally, you needed to visit the toilet, or move on to avoid suspicious glances. Then you were best advised to change your outfit. Which again took time, and required an appropriate location.

He'd long since accustomed himself to the boredom. He emptied his mind and focussed on his breathing, counting ten exhalations at a time. He tried to keep still, allowing himself as much awareness of his body as was consistent with watchfulness. The first time he tried all this, he'd worried about missing something he'd been put there to discover, but he quickly realised that, weirdly, it actually increased his concentration on the task.

Ian Batchelor arrived. He walked past John without seeing him and crossed the road. He let himself in through the office front door in exactly the same way Dina had earlier.

Cars tooted, buses roared, the smoggy smell intensified and the commuter swarms gradually thinned and were replaced by tourists and shoppers. Nothing about Carneghan Strake's front door indicated that anyone was in there. If today was a repeat of the previous day, they wouldn't even come out for lunch. God knows what they ate, because no one arrived with sandwiches or their equivalent, and neither Dina nor Ian seemed to be carrying anything much when they arrived.

John withdrew into a meditative vigil, and thought of nothing but his surroundings.

Then Marchus Grubfeld walked past him.

He had to look twice to confirm it. But it was no mistake. Suddenly his thoughts were racing, trying to calculate possibilities. On one level, it wasn't a surprise. It was, after all, roughly the reason he was staking Dina Oforka-Jones out. Only he hadn't expected it to yield fruit so quickly.

Unless it was a monstrous coincidence.

But no. Grubfeld crossed the road at the exact spot Ian Batchelor had earlier. He mounted the three granite steps up to Carneghan Strake's front door and rang the doorbell.

He waited. No answer. John had registered the spyhole in the door yesterday. There was a good probability Dina and Ian were looking at Grubfeld now. And he probably knew it. The fact that he didn't try to avoid it indicated that maybe he didn't expect a rebuttal.

On the other hand, maybe the doorbell batteries were dud. Hardly anyone ever seemed to call, so it was a possibility. In a minute, he might try knocking.

He stood without turning or even moving for nearly a minute, then rang again, holding his finger in for longer this time.

Suddenly, the door opened a few inches. Ian Batchelor poked his head out. Mordred could see everything from here, and he could lip-read. He took out his phone and went to Camera. *What do you want?* Batchelor said. Grubfeld apparently began to explain – his back was slightly to John, so his words were lost - but Batchelor thrust something at him, said, *You're being followed. Go away*, and slammed the door in his face.

Grubfeld backed up and looked about himself warily. He descended the steps and walked away. After a few paces, it became obvious he'd considered Ian Batchelor's warning and didn't believe it. He relaxed.

John's chest thumped. A bit like being struck by a mild bolt of lightning. Ian Batchelor knew who Marchus Grubfeld was, and he'd told him he was being followed!

… Okay. Which he'd got from Phyllis, obviously.

But despite the hostile tone in which it had been issued, 'You're being followed' was clearly intended as a charitable warning, not the sort of thing you'd say to a categorically unwelcome cold caller.

And that - thing he'd thrust at him. A scribbled note? Likely the time and place of a rendezvous, somewhere discreet, sometime soon.

John pulled on a baseball cap and took off in the opposite direction to Grubfeld, hoping against hope that they'd both describe a circle from opposite ends, and complete it at Bank tube station. The alternative - following him just after he'd been warned - was just a risk too far.

Yet there was a roughly 66.6% chance that Grubfeld would head for either St Paul's or Mansion House tube station. John's margin for error increased if you took buses into account. Anyway, the universe had been so kind to him already, he wasn't sure he deserved any more. As Ruby Parker would have put it in the old days: this case was finally beginning to open up.

And he could see what was going through Grubfeld's mind: that Ian Batchelor was an over-cautious fuddy-duddy who'd decided to scare him in order to gain some sort of psychological advantage, and/ or the edge in whatever pending negotiations were imminent at their rendezvous. He definitely *wasn't* being followed. It was the sort of thing an amateur like Batchelor might say to spook him, the debased linguistic coinage of low quality genre fiction. *You're being followed, Marchus, take my advice, let me help you.* Yeah, yeah.

God was very good, as the Muslims said. Grubfeld appeared at Bank station exactly on cue, just in front of the Royal Exchange, and descended the steps to the underground. John watched from the entrance opposite Mansion House. As Grubfeld disappeared, he went after him. They reconnoitred ten metres apart at the turnstiles.

An hour later, Grubfeld checked in to The Noveauehotler Marlinburger hotel in Barnet. John pretended to be a homeless person, sitting on the ground in a side street several blocks up the road where he could keep an eye on the entrance. This was it. He was close to a breakthrough. He didn't need Ruby Parker. He could do it on his own. He was elated and depressed in equal measure. He'd killed his mum and married his dad. Now all he had to do was poke his own eyes out with a brooch.

He stood for two hours and counted his breaths. Then a car screeched to a halt in front of him.

Bloody hell. Kevin. Alec stepped out from the back seat. "Ruby Parker wants a word," he said.

John ground his teeth. The only chance he now had of Grubfeld not looking out of his window and making him was to comply. He sighed bitterly and got onto the back seat.

Alec slid in next to him, and the car pulled away with a screech.

"Hi, John," Kevin said, from the driver's seat. "Long time, no see. How's life on the outside? We've missed you. Not everybody. I don't know about the others. I have."

John suddenly forgot about Marchus Grubfeld. This was *Kevin, the guy who never spoke.* At least to him. And he'd just spoken. To him. What was going on? It was worthy of an out of body experience, yet just when you needed one, it wouldn't come.

"Um, fine," John blurted out. "Thank you."

"Sorry for never speaking to you before, buddy," Kevin continued. "A joke that went too far. Once it got started, I couldn't stop it. I felt bad when you'd gone and I hadn't explained."

Was this a dream? Kevin had one hand on the wheel, both eyes on the road, yet he reached behind to offer a handshake. John accepted it. Suddenly, Marchus Grubfeld didn't matter anymore, nor Ruby Parker, nor anyone. His eyes involuntarily gathered water to spew in all directions like in a celebration. Stupid, stupid. And yet – so absolutely *not*.

On Lucy's first full day in London – the day she ate a cauliflower pie in Trafalgar Square and later fell asleep in front of *Celebrity Eggheads* – Phyllis awoke at 7am. John was long gone. When she came into the hallway, Lucy wasn't only fully dressed but obviously on her way out.

"Hi," Phyllis said. "You're up early. Did you sleep okay?"

"Absolutely," Lucy replied. "It was much more comfortable than I expected."

"Had any breakfast?"

"I always carry a granola bar."

"If you want to come back here any time for any reason, just let yourself in. Otherwise, we'll see you again this evening."

"Thank you. Have a good day at work."

Phyllis laughed. "Thank you, I won't."

She showered, dressed and set off for Thames House, just like in the old days but with superadded guilt. *You should probably have told Ruby Parker today. The longer you leave it, the more it'll look like we're hiding something.*

John was quite insightful, she had to hand it to him. On the other hand, maybe that was marriage. Maybe she was just slipping into the implicit woman-she-not-so-clever, man-he-oh-so-wise division of imagined labour always lurking behind the world's oldest contract.

Thankfully (in a way), it was her own insight she was unable to shake off. *It's qualified honesty and surrendering my new-found independence versus the prolonged guilt of implicit deception.* Not much of a consolation, though, because of what it was. It was *qualified honesty and surrendering her new-found independence versus the prolonged guilt of implicit deception.* Exactly what it said on the tin.

On the tube from Mornington Crescent she already knew she'd have to arrange an urgent interview with Ruby Parker once she got in. The question wasn't whether she would spill the beans anymore; it was how many, and over what precise square meterage. Definitely, not the whole can, and not very messily. John was right: she could plausibly blame him for a lot. He was beyond Ruby Parker's power to reprehend now. And it's what marriage was for.

One thing, anyway.

She arrived at Thames House at ten to nine, signed in without making eye-contact with Colin – she sensed he'd resolved on the same dumb solution to the threatened infinity of their shared *welcome back, lovely to see you again* dilemma – and went straight to her phoney desk behind hyper-congenial Bruce and Jonathan. She logged on and emailed Ruby Parker with a request for a meeting.

She swallowed and her stomach jumped to where her heart ought to be. Too late to turn back now and she still hadn't thought it through properly.

I have an engagement in ten minutes' time, came the reply almost immediately. *The earliest I can see you is 2pm. Is it something Alec or Annabel could deal with?*

I'll wait, she emailed back. *Thank you.*

At 1.55, she knocked on Ruby Parker's door, heard the 'Enter' she'd received a hundred times before and went in. She'd never really noticed before, but there were always exactly the right number of chairs for the number of interviewees, never more nor less. Yet there were no spares in here. Who brought them in and took them away? And when? And from where? She sat down.

"You asked to see me," Ruby Parker said. She wore a beige jacket over a cashmere sweater and pearls, and wrote on a pad. She looked as if she'd already lived through exactly what was about to transpire and re-living it was merely an irksome formality for the sake of some unspecifiable higher purpose.

"John's made contact with a Maltese detective called Adrian Fenech," Phyllis said. "The man who's been following Marchus Grubfeld, alongside Annabel. Fenech claims to be a retired Maltese detective, and John believes he's genuine. He's been investigating Maltese political corruption for quite some time on an amateur basis. He heard about us when we were in Malta, and followed us to England. He found John, not the other way round, although obviously, John knew him by sight in advance. The upshot is, after a long talk in a park in Camden, he and John have agreed to work together. Fenech's going to re-examine the journalists Edna looked at; John's now following Dina Oforka-Jones, my principal solicitor. He's following her because Fenech recognised the name 'Carneghan Strake' from his time in the police. Together, he and John have decided to treat the possibility that Lucy Staveley's dossier came from Carneghan Strake as a working hypothesis. They think there may be a link there to Marchus Grubfeld, in other words. Last night, on my way home, I rang Lucy Staveley. Lucy came to dinner with John and I last night. She's on my side now, provisionally. Aisling Baxter's parents have new information. Lucy's going to meet them tomorrow. We expect to make progress."

Ruby Parker had put her pen down. Her eyebrows rose. Her mouth opened and closed. She folded her hands. Her eyebrows lowered.

"My God," she said. She blew a short, sharp breath. "You've taken what we're doing here and you've replicated it in a shed at the bottom of an ordinary suburban garden." She paused as if mentally reviewing this assessment, then approving it as fit for general release. "Two hundred grams of high grade explosive in a test tube and you're not even wearing safety goggles. You do realise how much danger you're putting yourselves in?"

"We're used to danger," Phyllis replied, not knowing whether to feel proud or ashamed. "And given that Marchus Grubfeld's probably got something against me, and we don't know for certain that my checking in here every morning will help, and John's not even been offered the same level of protection – for very good reasons, I admit – I think we're justified in being a little proactive."

Ruby Parker laughed humourlessly. "Is that what you call it? 'A little'?"

"Okay, a lot."

"I did anticipate that you might end up feeling trapped. I hadn't expected it would occur this quickly. Where's John?"

"Now?"

"Right this moment. This needs to stop, for the good of you both. We need to pool our efforts."

Phyllis smiled. She'd taken a step back and now her confession was out of the way, she was thinking clearly again. "I'm not sure he'll be pleased to be called back," she said. "Especially with me. He told me to pretend that he rang Lucy Staveley."

"How noble of him. The point is, neither of you knows how deep this goes. None of us does. Put it another way: what do you ultimately hope to achieve?"

"I suppose John's looking to find out who's behind Grubfeld, and… I don't know, discover something incriminating."

"Something you can go to the police with? You'll have a hard time convincing the Met you've been shadowed by a hired assassin, and that he's in cahoots with one or more senior partners in one of London's most prestigious law firms. I don't mean any disrespect to the police, but it's not the sort of story that normally falls within their purview."

"I suppose not."

Actually, Ruby Parker was right. How exactly *were* they hoping all this would end? They might well find 'the truth', although even that was far from given. But without the power to do anything about it, how would they benefit?

Ruby Parker said nothing. But it was more than that. Like she'd deliberately imposed a rigid silence.

Phyllis felt awkward. She knew she was expected to think, and although for a moment her intense self-consciousness prevented her, suddenly she had full clarity. She saw the only endgame there could be. Neither John nor she had fully envisioned it, but had someone sat down and calmly explained it to them – rather like Ruby Parker was now, except with words – they'd both have recognised it as the only plausible outcome and themselves as idiots for not having seen it.

"Okay," Phyllis said, nodding. "You're right. We've been looking for a case to present to *you*. MI7's the only organisation capable of dealing with whatever we discover."

"Good, we're making progress. Now, I'm going to save you the tortuous step of having to persuade me you're not just two amiable eccentrics with a persecution complex, so that should simplify and accelerate matters. We'll pick John up now, and we'll see if we can join forces."

"What about Adrian Fenech and Lucy Staveley?"

"Since you've co-opted them, we'll watch their backs. But I draw the line at anything more than that. You're both trained, and potentially very useful to us. They're not."

"Would you like me to phone John?"

"Yes please, and tell him to come here. Do whatever you can to persuade him. You don't have to do it here, in front of me. Go up to the canteen. Apart from anything else, there's a much better signal up there. If you can't contact him for any reason, go and see Tariq, tell him I want a fix on John's present location, and I'll send Kevin and Alec to pick him up."

Phyllis got up. As too often after a confession, she felt small and a little foolish.

"And Phyllis?" Ruby Parker said as she was halfway through the door.

"Yes?"

"It would have been easy for you to lay the blame for contacting at John's door, but you didn't. I appreciate that."

John arrived at Thames House an hour later. Colin directed him to Ruby Parker's office. Annabel and Phyllis were waiting outside. Annabel gave him a 'hi' and a little wave, as if he'd never been away. Phyllis proffered a guilty smile and blushed slightly. "I'm sorry," she whispered.

"Don't be," he said. "I was beginning to wonder where we were going with all this anyway."

"Now you're here, is it okay for me to knock?" Annabel asked.

John grinned. "How long have you been waiting here?"

Annabel ignored him and knocked. They heard 'Enter', and walked in to find three chairs. John sat in the middle. He got the strange impression that something important had been decided before his arrival.

"Welcome back, John," Ruby Parker said. "Phyllis has been telling me about your joint exploits."

"Thank you," he replied. "Kevin spoke to me."

Ruby Parker ignored him. "Annabel, I'm considering sending you in to Carneghan Strake's Cheapside offices tonight, to see what we can find. We've examined the dossier you recovered from *The Echo's* offices, and there are reasons to believe – not watertight reasons, but strong enough – that it may indeed have been the work of Carneghan Strake. John and Phyllis, I believe you've been proceeding on the same hypothesis."

"Correct," John said. "Why am I here? No one's really explained yet."

"Partly to keep you out of danger," Ruby Parker replied.

"Do we get our old jobs back?" he went on. "I mean, is that what you're offering? Because I've been doing roughly my old job, and I'm quite enjoying it."

"Do you actually *want* your old jobs back?" Ruby Parker asked.

Silence.

"I think so," Phyllis said. She turned to John. "But we'd have to talk about it together. In a different setting. It's a big decision. I love it here. I didn't realise how much till I came back yesterday. But I also know you've got to make decisions based on what's right in the long-term. You can't just say, 'I'm homesick, I want to go back', and act exclusively on that."

"Let's work together on this one case," Ruby Parker said, "and you can make a decision one way or the other once it's over."

"Sounds good to me," John said.

"Phyllis tells me you've been following Dina Oforka-Jones," Ruby Parker said. "How is that going?"

"Have a look at your Inbox," John told her. "I sent you a few pictures five minutes ago. I anticipated our coming to it sooner or later and I thought you'd appreciate it better on a bigger screen."

"'It' being what?" Annabel said.

"Marchus Grubfeld knocking on Carneghan Strake's Cheapside office door, and Ian Batchelor telling him to go away because he's being followed. It's not video footage. I picked up the words myself. Ian Batchelor also gave him what I believe was a note. Marchus Grubfeld then got on a train at Bank, and went to The Noveauehotler Marlinburger hotel in Barnet, where I was staking him out. Then Kevin arrived, and I got in the car because I thought being uncooperative might cause a commotion and cause Grubfeld to bolt. Thanks to my cool professionalism, he's probably still there now. If you send two agents over, you stand a good chance of finding out where he's headed next. Did I mention that Kevin spoke to me?"

"You're not being funny, John," Annabel said.

Ruby Parker was looking at her screen. "You've done a good job," she said. "Given that Grubfeld's known to Interpol, this could mean the difference between our launching a burglary and our getting a warrant to search Carneghan Strake's premises." She flicked through a few more pictures. "On the other hand, he was never charged, so perhaps we shouldn't build our hopes up."

"So I may not be needed after all?" Annabel said.

"I don't know," Ruby Parker said. "Safest to assume the worst, so expect to be sent in at some point. Meanwhile, I'll get two agents over to The Noveauehotler Marlinburger, as you suggested, John, and I'll consult with one or two of our legal experts about that warrant."

"What do you want Phyllis and I to do now?" John asked.

"This is officially a major investigation now," she replied, "and you and Phyllis are integral to its success. You've got the same clearance you had before you left, so do whatever you think is useful."

"No more Bruce and Jonathan?" Phyllis said. "Although, now I'm no longer half on the outside, maybe their passionate dedication to duty won't seem so irksome."

"I like them," Annabel said. "They've got potential."

"When do I get to meet them?" John said. "Sorry," he added after a few seconds. "I realise I may be slightly overdoing the 'I'm no longer depressed' thing."

"Just a little," Ruby Parker said drily. "I think it's time to declare this meeting closed."

Chapter 28: Mr and Mrs Baxter

When Lucy Staveley left Cheapside, she rushed across London to Fortnum & Mason, the only place in London she was certain she'd find free, high quality toilets. Still an hour till she was due to meet the Baxters and this wouldn't wait. She climbed the staircase, found the ladies and slipped inside one of the cubicles. She did a pee, since she might as well, she was here, and she was excited. Then she took the package out of her bag, took a deep breath, and opened it.

Ten pound notes, a huge wad of them. It didn't look much, but she counted through twenty, and realised the overall thickness was easily right.

Ten thousand pounds!

Really!

TEN THOUSAND POUNDS! My GOD!

She shook. What if she was mugged? That'd be just her luck.

She needed to stop thinking about it. Maybe use some cash to buy a really *secure* bag, here in Fortnum's. Thinking about it, this was probably the one place in London you were unlikely to encounter a mugger. Maybe she could get something like a body wallet – did such things exist? - to wear under her clothes.

She took out two hundred pounds, thrust it in her pocket and left the cubicle.

She caught sight of herself in the mirror above the hand basins. In her slept-in pullover and creased trousers, she didn't exactly look well-dressed, and carrying two hundred pounds in cash, any respectable shop assistant might think *she herself* was a mugger, come to spend her ill-gotten gains. Who carried two hundred pounds in cash nowadays?

She needed to stop worrying. Guilt, that's what it was. She felt guilty about betraying Phyllis – even though she knew rationally that she'd done absolutely nothing wrong – and it was manifesting itself as a lack of self-confidence. As, in fact, it always did, whenever she felt guilty about anything at all.

She had to stop thinking full stop. She had ten thousand pounds.

She'd have to put it in the bank when she got home, keep it safe.

But how suspicious would *that* look?

In small instalments then. But what if her parents found it, under the bed? They'd think she was a dealer.

An elderly woman came in. She looked suspiciously at Lucy, walked into one of the cubicles and bolted the door loudly.

Time to go. Aisling Baxter's parents wouldn't appreciate her being late. They were her priority now.

Thirty minutes later, she sat in a low-ceilinged hotel room in Bayswater. Two chairs, a sofa on one side of the room; on the other, a double bed with an old-fashioned bedspread and a pair of plumped up pillows for each head. A large window looked out on other tall buildings, but a thick net curtain gave them a ghostly appearance.

The Baxters sat opposite Lucy Staveley on the sofa. Mrs Baxter – Glenda - was small with a grey bob and wire-rimmed glasses. She wore a dark dress and lace-up shoes. Her husband, Alfred, was muscular and bald. He wore a navy blue V-neck jumper and an oxford shirt and tie. Both had the kind of trampled demeanour you'd expect in a couple who had recently lost a daughter. They looked to be in their mid-seventies.

Lucy Staveley sat on one of the chairs. She switched on her digital voice recorder and put it face up on the desk. It wasn't as good as the one in her phone, but she knew from experience that old people didn't like you using your phone on them. They thought you were doing more than you admitted.

She recited the date, stated her location, then listed the room's three occupants - a little as if she was doing a police interrogation - then said: "Mr and Mrs Baxter, you invited me over to talk about your daughter, Aisling?"

"This shouldn't take long," Alfred said. "We called you here largely because we've discovered some new information."

"We wanted to help poor Phyllis," Glenda said. "We heard, from some of our friends, roughly what you were intending to say about her. We're not blaming you, of course. You've a job to do, and you've got to go with the evidence you've got. Thank goodness it never got to print, though, because it would have been a complete travesty of justice."

"Neither of us has ever met Phyllis to our knowledge," Alfred said, "although our paths might have crossed in the past without either of us being aware of it. Newbury's not that big a place, and the Conservative Association's even smaller."

Glenda nodded. "What I can tell you, though, is that Aisling … well, she … I don't quite know how to put this … she *hero-worshipped* Phyllis. From afar. It only began after she beat her in that interview."

"We didn't find any of this out till a few days ago," Alfred continued. "You don't look at your daughter's emails, obviously you don't. Especially not when she's older, independent, married. But then, when she's passed away, and you've had the funeral, it's a different matter."

"You want to find out everything you can about her," Glenda added tearfully. "Especially if she's died in a tragic situation that some people might say was suspicious."

"Suspicious how?" Lucy put in.

"Let's just say we think you already know the answer to that," Alfred said. "That's not meant to sound confrontational either. As my wife just said, you've got a job to do, and you're just doing it."

"From what we heard," Glenda said, "you were intending to suggest that Phyllis may have murdered Aisling to take over from her as the next Conservative candidate for Newbury, and ultimately get into Parliament."

"Which is absurd," Alfred said.

"I don't mean to argue," Lucy said, "But you just said you'd never met Phyllis. How do you know it's absurd?"

"Because of what we discovered in Aisling's emails," Alfred said. "Let's get back to what we were saying earlier. My wife said that Aisling's death might appear suspicious to some people. She was out there investigating something. Internet travel companies, we were told - "

"Told by *her*," Glenda interposed. "It's what *she* told, us. Aisling."

"And then she's coming back fast somewhere late at night, and suddenly her car careers off the road and she's killed? Sounds very dodgy, even without that thing you were intending to print."

"It sounds very Mafioso," Glenda said. "Which fits a little bit with what we've found out about Malta. You've got a quite decent bunch of people who mainly live in the north, people who care about the rule of law, and then you've got a much more relaxed attitude elsewhere. The sort of people who don't care who's in power, or how they behave, so long as, at the end of the day, they bring home the bacon."

Alfred shrugged. "A lot of people in Malta didn't bat an eyelid when Daphne Galizia embarrassed their Prime Minister. He called a general election, knowing the majority would vote him back in. And they did."

"Shame on them," Glenda said.

"Excuse me for asking," Lucy said, "but what's this got to do with Aisling's death?"

"A lot," Alfred replied. "You see, Phyllis had a 'big idea', apparently. That's what everyone said about her. How she was going to push reforms of various different types once she got the job that Aisling got and made it into Parliament. Aisling didn't have that. She's just a local farmer. She's never been an intellectual whizz kid. But she envied Phyllis that. She wanted to be like her. As my wife said a moment ago, she came to idolise her. I don't think that's too strong a term."

"Is that what she says in her emails?" Lucy asked, as a way of bringing the interview back to what she considered the most important thing.

"It turns out she and Ted Taylor were working together," Alfred said. "Ted suggested internet travel companies initially, but they soon got past that. It wasn't big enough for her. Turns out Ted had a massive villa in Malta. And she'd heard about how a lot of British legal firms were doing business in Malta. Things they really shouldn't have been doing morally, given that they're all based in a democratic country, but which were legal, and incredibly profitable. Helping highly shady characters get EU citizenship – apparently it's for sale in Malta – and then facilitating their money laundering somehow."

"It may *seem* legal," Glenda said, "but Aisling wasn't convinced that it was. And she was committed to stopping it. We're not going to be part of the EU for much longer, but some of the things I've heard about these supposedly 'reputable' legal outfits, well, it makes you ashamed to be British."

"We wanted to tell you you're looking in the wrong place, Lucy," Alfred said. "You've got the wrong story. Someone's trying to frame Phyllis Mordred, and I'm pretty sure Aisling's death wasn't an accident."

"I can report that," Lucy said. "But it's still speculative. What I had before wasn't much cop, truth be told. *The Echo* made it out to be more than it was in the hope that other people would come forward. Sometimes, that's how papers work. But it was a bluff, and Phyllis's lawyers called it. No one will come forward for this, because we're talking about a bunch of mobsters several thousand miles away."

Alfred and Glenda looked significantly at each other.

"You're a good investigative journalist, Lucy," Alfred said. "We read your articles on that sports centre. Then again about the council and that rugby club. If anyone can get to the bottom of this, it's you."

"Sorry, I'd have to go to Malta," Lucy replied. "I mean, thank you for the compliment and everything. You've been really nice and I'm sorry for your loss - "

"We're offering you *two hundred thousand pounds*," Glenda said. "That's after expenses: accommodation, food, etcetera. We'd put you and a colleague up in Malta for six months, see what you can uncover."

"You would need to go with a colleague, though," Alfred said. "We couldn't have you going alone. It's too dangerous."

"Don't say anything now," Glenda said. "If you decide to accept, we'll give you personally *ten thousand pounds*. Up front."

Lucy swallowed. "I'll have to talk to my editor, Roger," she said after a pause. "But if he's okay with it – and I'm fairly certain he will be: we've developed a big interest in this Malta thing since we were stopped from going to press – I'll be more than happy to accept." She could see that, with this affirmation, the interview was over. She picked up the digital recorder and put it in her bag. "I'll get back to you tomorrow, or the day after at the latest."

They all stood up. Handshakes were exchanged. "We look forward to working with you, Lucy," Glenda said.

She rang her mum on her way out of the hotel, but she didn't tell her about the ten – twenty, now! – thousand pounds. She told her she'd be in for dinner.

"I'm at work, obviously," her mum said drily. "But I've got your favourite planned. Sausage, burger, egg, chips and beans."

"Can I have two veggie sausages?"

"And a Quorn burger, I know. And go light on the beans."

"Maybe a bit of bread. Like one of those buns with seeds on the top."

"I don't want you being late, and me having to put it in the oven for God knows how long. Where are you now?"

"London."

"And you're on your way to the station, right? Because if you're not, you probably won't be home in time. You might as well get some kind of lettuce wrap thing at Vegan Heaven."

"There's no such place."

"You know what I mean. I'm not making a slap-up meal for you if you're not guaranteed to be here to eat it."

"Right ho. I'm on my way to the station right now. Bye."

She'd had enough of London, anyway. It had yielded up its precious wealth to her, and she was sated. She wanted to go home.

As if to continue her good luck, the train was about to leave when she reached Paddington. She went to the self-service ticket machine and boarded the carriage with thirty seconds to spare. It began to move just as she found a seat. Next to the window. Another stroke of unbelievable luck, although maybe not, because it wasn't rush hour yet. Maybe it was just normal at this time of the day.

All the time she'd been walking from the hotel, she'd felt uneasy, like there was something she had to do. She put it down to the fact that London had been so good to her, it was hard to leave, but she simply had to. She had money enough in her bag to *pay*, if she wanted to, for veggie sausages, a Quorn burger, chips, an egg and baked beans at somewhere like Claridge's. But she wasn't going to blow it. She was going to use it as the deposit for a flat, like a sensible girl.

It wasn't until she was sitting down by the window that she finally realised.

Bloody hell, she'd forgotten to give Phyllis her key back.

Shit shitty *shit balloon!*

And oh my God, what if they discovered Dina Oforka-Jones's private detective/ burglar? They'd assume it was her, Lucy, that had given her a key!

Which yes it was, but that was beside the point.

Things were getting complicated. She needed to really show the Mordreds she was on their side, so they couldn't suspect her duplicity. She took her phone out and scrolled down to *Phyllis*.

"Hi, you've reached the voicemail box for 07865497456," a woman's voice said. "Please leave your message after the tone."

"Lucy here. I'd just like to say thank you for everything. I'm on the train now and I forgot to return your key. But don't worry because I'm coming back to London tomorrow. I thought we could meet because what I got from the Baxters was pretty important. It turns out Aisling wasn't there investigating travel agents. She was looking into British legal firms and their dodgy doings in Malta. They're big fans of yours. They'll be happy to talk to you. And they want me to go to Malta to investigate, so I was hoping you might be able to give me a few pointers."

As she put the phone down, she had another unpleasant realisation, much worse than the one of a few moments ago about forgetting to hand back the key. The act of speaking to Phyllis's voicemail box had made something explicit which so far she hadn't even noticed. It was like a giant set of dots had suddenly been joined, and what they depicted was an axe about to bury itself in her skull. *Aisling wasn't there investigating travel agents. She was looking into British legal firms and their dodgy doings in Malta.*

British legal firms.

Like Carneghan Strake?

What if it was Dina Oforka-Jones that was trying to frame Phyllis?

But then – why would she have stopped *The Echo* going to press?

It didn't make sense. But something wasn't right. She needed to get that key back to Phyllis and perhaps even confess to her in person.

But she couldn't.

She suddenly realised she had literally *no idea* what was going on. She'd believed she was in charge, but the truth was, she'd probably been played. She felt horrible. She'd definitely

have to go back to London tomorrow, and she wasn't even sure
she was up to her mum's special meal any more.

Chapter 29: Away/ Home

In a major city nearly six thousand miles from London, an old Englishman, tanned, dressed in a cream suit and crocodile-skin loafers, made his way alone through the crowded streets, resting heavily on his walking stick. He'd come a long way for this, and it wasn't easy. None of the street names in this country made sense – he'd never learned to speak the language – but he had Google Maps, and each time he took his phone out, he could see he was getting closer to his destination.

Eventually, he found it. A tall off-white building, modern but efficient looking, with large glass windows. He wasn't optimistic. He'd read too many comments about it on the internet. *It's not an embassy for UK citizens, it's a business model overcharging and extracting money from vulnerable UK citizens, Absolutely hopeless* and *They provide absolutely zero service to British citizens.* Maybe he'd have better luck, but he wasn't confident. No smoke without fire.

He showed his passport to the man on the door and went in. He told the receptionist – a young woman in a blue suit, with a Yorkshire accent – exactly what he'd come for. He might as well be direct, given that the likely alternative was waiting God knows how long while some chinless wonder out back got his arse in gear. She went pale, stood up, and said she was going to find someone.

Ten minutes later, a man appeared. Tall, with combed-across straight black hair. Yes, he had a chin, but maybe that was just an effect of his incredibly stiff shirt collar. He didn't look pleased, but neither did he look angry. Obviously, not anyone connected to law enforcement then. Maybe embarrassment was the chief emotion written on his face.

"If you'd like to follow me, please," he said.

They walked to a small office with a gilt-framed picture of the London Eye on the wall. They sat down like they were about to begin a job interview.

"We probably don't have anyone in the building at the moment who's qualified to deal with something like this," the chinless man said. "But I can take a rough 'statement', if that's acceptable, and you can sign it. You'll probably be asked to make another, more formal version later. I can't get you a solicitor, and you'll have to sign to the effect that you were aware of that at the start. Is that okay?"

"Sounds pukka to me," the old man said.

"So just go at whatever speed suits you. I'm doing shorthand, but I've also got a digital recorder here."

The old man cleared his throat. "An acquaintance of mine – a Mrs Aisling Baxter, from Newbury in Britain – was killed in a car crash in Malta. The official report described it as an accident, but I can state categorically that she was murdered. I know that, because I'm ashamed to say I was party to it. My name's Ted Taylor. I'm a retired travel agent ..."

Annabel Gould al-Banna arrived at the Carneghan Strake office in Cheapside at 6am. She got out of her taxi and gave the driver a big tip. She wore an overcoat and a trouser suit and carried a clipboard. Today, she was the senior manager of what looked like a cleaning consortium, but was really a front, heavily contracted to the security services for the purpose of infiltrating specific buildings. Cambridge Office Hygiene was 'on call', highly affordable, and always happy to step into the breach when a *bona fide* cleaning company experienced unforeseen difficulties on any particular day. Which, when MI7 wanted access somewhere, it always did.

The 'cleaners' were hard at work when she arrived. The legal team at Thames house had briefed her in advance about roughly what to look for. She let herself into Dina Oforka-Jones's office, rifled through the filing cabinets and photographed everything that looked relevant. No one kept much in the way of hard copies any more, but she couldn't afford to be complacent, especially since the computers were almost certainly secure and the files encrypted. Luckily, lawyers generally still dealt in masses of paperwork, and since some of it was under lock and key – no barrier to her – it stood a reasonable chance of yielding something crucial. The search warrant was still pending, and Ruby Parker believed it would probably be denied, so this might be their best and only chance.

When she'd finished in Dina's room, she went into Ian Batchelor's office and conducted the same meticulous process of flicking through foolscap suspension files, scanning documents for key terms and photographing them for later inspection. By 8am, she was finished. She had nearly two hundred pictures. Enough to be getting on with.

She called for a taxi. She left the building to wait a few yards along the road in front of St Mary-le-Bow. The 'cleaners' locked up behind her, having done an exemplary job, and faded into the London morning.

Chapter 30: John Gets Sent Home Early

Phyllis and John got up at 6.55am. They ate breakfast together at the table by the window: two Weetabix for him and a bowl of muesli for her. Afterwards, he'd wash up and clean the kitchen; she'd go in the shower. They'd listen to Radio 4's *Today* in the bedroom while she put her make-up on. They would only meet properly again, in their suits, on their way out of the flat.

"What are we doing about Lucy Staveley?" he asked.

"I told her to let herself in. She's to remain here until I get back. If she's got new information, we need to know what it is. And she needs somewhere safe to stay."

"Why can't she just tell you on the phone?"

"She's has to bring the key back, so we might as well have a proper discussion. Phone meetings are usually rubbish. That's why they invented Skype and videoconferencing. Anyway, she's probably a bit paranoid after *The Echo* was burgled."

"And you're sure her taking the key was an accident?"

Phyllis bobbed her head slightly to the side. "Reasonably. I can see how she might have forgotten to give it back in the excitement of getting important new information. And she did call me from the train, so that's fairly considerate. But you're right, I'm taking nothing for granted. Although it's difficult to see what she might gain by taking it and bringing it back the next day. If she wanted a copy – let's say she was planning to break in sometime – she'd simply have had it made somewhere in London."

"If you've got to meet her, won't you need to leave work at some point?" he asked. "She probably won't want to wait around till clocking off plus getting home time."

"I've already put a request in to Ruby Parker to leave as soon as I hear from her. I'm coming home early, in other words. I'll try and get rid of her once we've talked – I shouldn't think she'll want to stay anyway – and I'll cook tonight. How does that sound for a fabulous treat?"

"Groovy."

"How's Adrian getting on, by the way?"

"I haven't heard from him."

"Not at all? Aren't you worried?"

"He's got his own way of doing things, and I get the impression he likes to work alone. I'll hear from him when he's got something to report: I think that's the deal. In any case, he's got his phone turned off a lot of the time."

"And that's not sinister?" she asked.

"I don't know for certain. I do know he's not very good with technology, because he told me. In his world, turning it off is a lot simpler than putting it to silent."

"My parents are a bit like that. Putting it to silent's like solving Hilbert's thirteenth problem."

"How are they, by the way?"

"So-so. They've still got Buster. A dog never lets you down." She stood up with her empty bowl and kissed his hair. "See you."

He finished his Weetabix and took the dishes into the kitchen. Maybe they should re-do their wedding, a kind of reconstruction of what it *should* have been in the eyes of Phyllis's mum and dad. Just for the sake of burying the hatchet. The forty day cooling off period had passed some time ago.

But Phyllis would never agree to that. And his own parents would be livid. They'd accepted the new status quo like it was just another episode in *The Zany Life of John*. Similar things had happened before. They'd happen again. They'd keep happening. Get over them.

Maybe he should call Phyllis's mum – she was obviously the chief power in their house - and try to apologise/ explain.

He'd already had the same thought a million times. But Phyllis would be up in arms. This was between her and them. It had nothing to do with him.

He picked up a bottle of eco-friendly disinfectant plus a cloth to wipe the units, and mentally changed the subject. There'd been talk yesterday of Annabel getting into the Carneghan Strake offices in Cheapside. If she had, a new mound of evidence would need itemising and interpreting, and today would be mainly reading and thinking. A breakthrough might be in the offing. The fact that someone had Phyllis in the metaphorical threads of a gun scope was paramount. It trumped her parents' sulk a million times over.

Apparently, Grubfeld had gone when Ruby Parker's two agents reached the Noveauehotler Marlinburger hotel, and since then, he'd been completely off the radar. He could be anywhere. It wasn't a nice feeling.

They arrived at work together an hour later and went to their workstations. A glance at their monitors showed Annabel had been in to Carneghan Strake this morning and hadn't even had to break stride. However, there would be no poring over piles of evidence for indications of wrongdoing – at least, not yet - because everything was written in legalese and required the attention of experts.

"So what are we supposed to do while we're waiting?" John asked.

"I guess there will be work on here somewhere," Phyllis replied, indicating her monitor. "Normal schedules. Meet in the canteen in an hour's time. Me drink tea, you eat Wagon Wheel. Go back to our computers. Do a few carousels. Wait for the briefs to finish. Have a meeting. I bet they don't find anything. Dina Oforka-Jones and her team are too crafty to commit anything to writing. And if you're doing anything illegal, you probably don't keep it in a filing cabinet."

"Because that's the first place anyone would look?"

"Obviously."

"So they probably wouldn't look there, because it's too obvious. So it might be a good hiding place, after all."

"You only double bluff when you're expecting an incursion," she said, "and you're up against the clock."

Of course, she was right. If you had to hide something and you weren't in a rush, you wouldn't put it in a filing cabinet. You'd encrypt it and bury it on Tor, or put in a numbered security box in Zurich.

Alec came over. He wore a blue cardigan and a wide smile. "Welcome back. You are coming back, yes? 'For real', as the Americans say?"

"Depends whether we pass our probation," John said.

"You're already some way towards that," Alec replied. "From what I've heard – and I don't know how anyone knows this, but it's being circulated as true – Ruby Parker feels pretty cut up - "

"As the Americans say," John interrupted. You scored a point if you got in the transatlantic attribution before the speaker.

Phyllis sighed. She knew of the game's existence but, as far as they knew, didn't rate it. She preferred actual conversations.

"What's Ruby Parker 'cut up' about?" she asked, silently daring either to add, 'As the Americans say'.

A long pause. John and Alec exchanged glances. She'd neutered them.

"As the Americans say," she said, apparently taking pity on them. "Boy, this is fun."

"Okay," Alec said. "She's upset because, in sending me and Kevin to get John, outside The Noveauehotler Marlinburger, she apparently alerted Marchus Grubfeld. If she'd left you alone, John, we'd still be in charge of him."

"She wasn't to know that," Phyllis said.

Alec smiled. "True, but she's a bit like Annabel in that regard. A perfectionist. Even about the things she can't control. And you know how that is. It gets worse as you get older."

John's computer pinged. He swivelled leisurely on his chair to look at the screen.

Internal email from Ruby Parker: *Please could you and Phyllis come and see me at your earliest convenience?*

Nice how, unless it was a national emergency, she rarely commanded anyone. As if she knew her team had things to be getting on with. Although they never did. A bit like getting a personal summons from Queen Victoria might have been, a hundred and fifty years ago. You'd drop everything and get the first boat out of Bombay.

"Meeting with the boss," he announced.

"Me too," Phyllis said.

"Play her discomfiture to your advantage," Alec said. "I'm only one of a million employees who want you both back here. You wouldn't believe how everyone's missed you. You're the only ones with a sense of humour. We need you to come back and save us from ourselves."

They went to the lift, descended two floors and strode to her office. They knocked. They heard 'Enter'. They went in. They sat down on the chairs. She wore a brown suit and didn't look up as they came in. She was writing.

"Firstly," she said when she'd finished, "I want to apologise for losing Marchus Grubfeld. In hindsight, I shouldn't have sent Alec to bring you in, John. We must have alerted him."

"We simply need to keep following Dina Oforka-Jones and Ian Batchelor," John said. "They're up to something. Even if Annabel's haul comes to nothing, if we keep a close enough eye on them from now on, they'll slip up. Whatever they're up to, we've got them, just by virtue of the fact that they're now in our sights. Grubfeld's just a symptom. The actual disease is deeper."

He felt Phyllis turn to look at him. She wasn't used to hearing him employ such melodramatic terms. She'd thank him later. He was trying to put Ruby Parker at her ease.

But Ruby Parker ignored him and turned to Phyllis. "I understand you want time off for a meeting with Lucy Staveley," she said. "Which I'm not going to grant. I'm sending John. As far as we know, you're still Marchus Grubfeld's prime target."

"John was in Malta too," Phyllis said. "And I don't think Grubfeld's going to wait outside Thames House all day on the off chance that I might leave unexpectedly."

"My feeling is that he's not working alone," Ruby Parker replied. "I know John going is a poor alternative, but he can leave by our Pimlico exit, two thirds of a mile away. There'll be little chance of anyone seeing him there. And given his ability to decipher the nuances of body language, I think he's better equipped than you to anticipate danger from unlikely sources."

"I'm not arguing," Phyllis said. "But I think she's expecting me. She might not open up to John in the same way."

"As far as she knows," Ruby Parker said, "she, you, John and Adrian Fenech are a team. Her main purpose in coming to London is to return a key. The meeting's just a bonus."

"Okay," Phyllis said, finally mollified.

"I'll go straight home," John said, "get the key from her, hear her out, send her packing, then come back here. By that time, the lawyers might have finished going through The Selected Works of Dina Oforka-Jones. The two things – Lucy Staveley's revelations, and their report – might prove mutually illuminating."

"Thank you," Ruby Parker said, indicating that the interview was at an end.

An hour later, they sat opposite each other in the canteen. Outside, dark storm clouds hung low and it rained hard. She stirred her tea and put the teaspoon on the saucer. He wasn't hungry or even thirsty. Somehow, he had a bad feeling about going to meet Lucy Staveley. He couldn't say why. Maybe the weather. So as not to betray it, he'd bought his usual Wagon Wheel, plus a cup of cocoa in which to dip it. To his surprise, Phyllis wasn't put out by being grounded. He'd expected her to be a little more indignant.

"Be careful," she said.

"It's just a trip home and back."

"This may not have occurred to you, but since Marchus Grubfeld knows you were watching him outside that hotel - "

"We don't know that. It's Ruby Parker's guilty conscience speaking. It's equally possible he was summoned to meet Dina Oforka-Jones and Ian Batchelor in between me leaving and our two agents arriving."

"Since he knows you were watching him outside that hotel, he may have decided to advance his itinerary."

"Or he may have thought, 'Well, I've been made. The game's up. I might as well bow out and go home.' *Home* being somewhere abroad."

"Fat chance. That's not how these guys think. As far as they're concerned, they're 'international assassins', not losers with an empty space where their conscience should be and an un-shakeable self-belief born of easy access to guns and a willingness to kill innocent people."

"You mean, international assassins don't normally go home."

"Not until they've wasted someone - as the Americans say. We probably shouldn't even be calling him Marchus Grubfeld. He probably thinks of himself as The Scorpion or The Tarantula or The Spectre, or something equally naff."

Her phone rang. She looked at the screen, showed it to him – *Lucy S* – and answered. "Hi Lucy, are you in London? ... I can't get out of work today, unfortunately. Something important's come up and I'm needed here ... John, if that's okay ... Well, he's in the area, so I can call him now, and he could meet you at the flat. You could let yourself in. You know the gate number. Just make yourself at home till he gets there. Make yourself some tea or coffee ... Yes, no problem. I quite understand. Bye."

She put her phone back in her bag and turned back to John. "She can't stay long. She's going to sit tight till you get there. Which should be about thirty minutes, I told her. You'd better get going if you're going to leave via Pimlico."

He kissed her on the lips and went downstairs to board the high-speed shuttle to the secret exit within the tube station. His phone rang. *Fenech.*

Things were looking up. For a start, Adrian was alive. Probably.

He picked up. "Hello?"

"I'm in trouble, John," the old man said. "I'm in London, and I don't know where to go. They're after me, and they've already killed some of the guys on that list. They're eliminating them, one by one. Not in obvious ways. Car accident, one; 'suicide', another; fall down a flight of stairs, a third. Five in all, but still counting. And I'm high on their kill list. I can't go back to my Aunt Julia's – I don't want to lead them to her - and I can't go back to Malta. I definitely wouldn't be safe there. To make things worse, I'm starving. I haven't eaten since we last met. And I don't even know why I'm telling you that, except that I'm delirious."

"Go to mine in Camden. You know where it is. Let yourself in through the gate – the code's 6739 – and just wait. I'm meeting Lucy there. I'll get a company car to come and pick us up afterwards; after you've had something to eat and I've debriefed her. I'm getting on the train at Pimlico any minute, so I won't be long. Where are you now?"

"I daren't say in case someone's listening. I'm in a bad way, John. Forgive me sounding sorry for myself. I can be there in about thirty minutes." He hung up.

Could it be some sort of trap? What if he'd been wrong about Adrian Fenech all along?

But that was stupid. As Ruby Parker said, he could read people. He'd read Adrian Fenech, and he'd found him to be what he claimed. And if you were going to dupe someone, you wouldn't trail that sort of an Aunt Julia. Your Aunt Julia would be more like a thinly disguised Rosa Klebb.

No, he was genuine. And in trouble.

Three hours earlier, Marchus Grubfeld stood in the recess of a third-floor landing in the block of flats on the opposite side of the road to the Mordreds' flat. He had a bucket of soapy water, and a mop which he pushed up and down for the benefit of passing residents, all of whom were on their way out of the building, on their way to work. He might have been invisible for all the notice anyone took of him. He wore a thick jumper, jeans and a pair of cheap trainers.

He saw the Mordreds exit the front gate of their block of flats. He waited ten minutes to be sure they weren't coming back, then emptied the bucket in the sink in the downstairs cupboard, and wiped it and the mop clean of fingerprints, before putting them away for good.

He crossed the road at a brisk pace, keyed the code into the Mordreds' gate, ascended the stairs to their flat, let himself in, sat down on a chair in the living room, and took out his gun. It would probably be at least six hours till they returned. If they came in together, that would be ideal. If not, he could kill them separately. He poured himself a glass of orange from the fridge and ate an apple from the fruit bowl on the table beside the window. Then he settled in for the vigil.

About an hour later, he was startled to hear a key in the lock.

My God, they – did they have a cleaner? Or had one of them come back for something?

He took up position opposite the living room door. Getting blood anywhere in the hallway would be a major mistake. It would alert the next entrant.

"Yoo-hoo!" a woman called. "It's just me, Lucy! Is anyone home?" He heard her groan in response to the silence.

He shot her as soon as she appeared in the living room doorway. A small woman, very long hair, thick framed glasses and a woolly jumper. Someone he'd never seen before. She looked a little surprised as the first bullet went in, but by the second, she'd ceased to think or feel anything at all. She lurched lifelessly backwards and lay prone on the floor.

He'd been too quick. In his compassionate desire to give her a quick death, he'd done exactly what he'd told himself not to. Not only was there blood on the floor and the walls, but there were two bullet marks.

Shit, shit, *shit!*

But stay calm, it was still early. He probably had time to clean up.

But who *was* she? Was it possible he'd been given the key to the wrong flat? That Dina Oforka-Jones and Ian Batchelor were setting him up?

The police might be on their way. He needed to think, *think!*

He knew the Mordreds lived in this block, because he'd seen them leave. But this might not be their flat. He hadn't actually checked for tokens of ownership when he'd come in. For all he knew, it might not be their place at all, and not even Dina Oforka-Jones and Ian Batchelor might know that.

But of *course* they would! Phyllis Mordred was their *client!* They'd know *exactly* where she lived!

Suddenly, that was his main concern. He forgot all about the corpse and feverishly opened drawers and cupboards looking for anything to confirm the identity of the residents.

He soon found what he was looking for. Three utility bills and a bank statement. Two family photos in the bedroom. Enough. He could afford to relax.

Or not. The body of the dead woman had now soaked the hallway. As he'd had occasion to notice many times in the past, that old cliché about not realising just how much blood the human body contained until it spilled out in front of you was all too true.

What to do?

He had a choice. Stay here and finish what he came for, or leave and somehow orchestrate a new assassination attempt sometime in the future.

But who was he fooling? Once the police saw this, there wouldn't be a second opportunity. They'd hunt him with everything they'd got. And he'd have failed.

No, here, today was his best chance to do what he'd been paid for, and he still had the element of surprise. By the time they opened the front door, it would be too late. It would take them a second or so to register what they were seeing, but that was all he needed. He only needed make one slight modification to his plan. Stand waiting in the hallway instead of the living room.

He'd put his gun down in the frantic search for proof that the Mordreds lived here. He couldn't even remember where. He laughed at himself. Non-problem. It would take him ten seconds to find it, and he still had several hours to wait.

But he felt rattled. He still had no idea who he'd killed. For all he knew, she might have several successors through the front door before the Mordreds came back.

But – supply of bullets allowing - he could kill them all, *and* them. He just needed to keep his nerve. Now where was that *damn gun?*

Suddenly, the front door opened again.

Chapter 31: Adrian Fenech Part 3

John got off the train at Camden Town, the station after Morning-ton Crescent, just in case his movements might appear too pre-dictable. In terms of distance from home, there wasn't much to choose between them, but anyone waiting for him at his usual stop would be disappointed. As he ascended the escalator, running on the left past the late-morning shoppers, he was struck by a thought. Something he really ought to run past Ruby Parker right now.

As he reached the surface, his phone rang in his pocket. He took it out. *Ruby Parker*. Amazing. How often had the exact same thing happened in the past?

"John Mordred," he said. "I was just about to call you."

"Ted Taylor's just checked in at the British Embassy in Saigon," she said. "We're getting someone over there to process the details, but he claims to have been party to Aisling Baxter's murder. He also says he put cameras and listening devices in your room, but that someone else also did. Someone unknown to him. And that they also put the same equipment into his room."

"Bloody hell, that's some confession. What was his motive?"

"He claims to be working with the Russians principally, but also the Azerbaijanis."

"Their governments, or just particular citizens of those na-tionalities?"

"The former, although that's one of the things we're eager to substantiate. He may be mistaken about the deeper facts. From what I've read so far, whatever he's doing, he's a pretty minor player, so he may think he knows more than he does."

"Does he know *why* Aisling Baxter was killed?"

"It turns out she wasn't in Malta to investigate internet travel companies after all. She was looking into the malign influence of

British legal firms in Russian money laundering, sales of EU citizenship and the suppression of free speech. Since she was a potential MP, that could have made her a considerable problem. Even so, it seems someone exaggerated the risk she probably posed."

"That all of us on that particular excursion posed."

"Of course, the fact that Carneghan Strake's big over there is likely significant. Especially given the links between two of its senior partners and Marchus Grubfeld. Hence, there's been a rethink on the search warrant. We're going in as soon as I can put a team together."

"But we got nothing from Annabel's visit?"

"I'm afraid not. They're heavily involved in Russian libel actions against dissidents abroad. They've partnered with a firm in Malta that sells EU citizenship to oligarchs. They've used the threat of legal action to silence a long list of journalists who have made accusations prompted by Wikileaks. All highly immoral but nothing illegal. You said you were about to call me?"

"Adrian Fenech called," he said. "I'm meeting him at the flat and I may need to get him a safe house somewhere. He thinks he's in serious danger."

"When did you learn this?"

"When I was on my way to the shuttle. I've been on the underground since then. No signal. I'm at the surface now. He claims that the journalists on Aisling Baxter's list are quietly and methodically being killed, and he's also being targeted as part of that."

"We put the list to the bottom of our priorities after Edna's investigation proved fruitless. I'll revisit it as a matter of urgency."

"But then I had a thought. Why target the journalists? They don't know anything special, after all. They're just guys with a story that was spiked by lawyers. It's not as if they can pass it on to a colleague, and it won't be spiked a second, third, fourth and nth time."

"What are you suggesting?"

"I think they were writing about the sorts of things Aisling Baxter went there to investigate," he said. "It makes sense now, especially given Ted Taylor's revelations. Why else would she have a list of their names?"

"Because she was 'under cover' in an amateurish sort of way. Someone might have given it to her in perfectly good faith, believing she was looking into what she told everyone – including you and Phyllis – she was. Internet travel companies."

"It's possible. On the other hand, maybe those journalists were writing about something else, and they're either too scared to admit it, or, whatever the whole business was and is, they're in on it."

"I'm not sure how you propose to find out, John, because they wouldn't talk to Edna, and they presumably wouldn't talk to Adrian Fenech, and if they were frightened before, the fact that they're now slowly being eliminated isn't going to placate them."

"They might not know what's happened to the other members of the list, so they wouldn't know that they're potentially next for the chop. If they realise they've got something to lose, it might make them desperate enough to speak out."

"So you think we should tell them."

"Somebody should, definitely. Even apart from getting information out of them. But that wasn't my only idea."

"Go on," she said.

"We need to find out what stories they were working on originally; if they really *were* writing about the online travel business. Talk to their editors, in other words."

"A lot of time has elapsed since some of them were even working in journalism. Do you think they'd remember?"

"You'd recall a cease and desist letter from a top London legal firm. They can't be that common."

"Okay, look, here's what you're going to do. Go to the flat, pick up Adrian Fenech and Lucy Staveley and bring them here. Even if we have to accommodate them in the lobby way for an hour or so, you'll, all three of you be safer than you probably are out there. You've made some very useful suggestions. With those, plus the search warrant, plus Ted Taylor's confession, we may have enough to finally crack this case."

She hung up. He was walking along Camden High Street now, with its jumble of never-to-be-repeated little shops huddled together in different colours like toy bricks. He saw Adrian Fenech after he turned two corners, standing on the edge of the pavement just along the road. He looked down at the ground, his jowls seemed to have drooped, he was stubbly, his shoes were several times more scuffed than before, and he looked defeated. He looked up and saw John and a light seemed to come on in his eyes. But he didn't move. He probably didn't want to give himself away.

"You should have gone in through the gate," John said, laying a friendly hand on his arm. "There's a garden with a bench. You could have sat down. I gave you the code."

"And I forgot it. Besides, looking like this, the other residents might have thought I was a tramp."

As a prospect, it wasn't entirely improbable. John didn't know many of the other people in the block, but he got the impression they were a suspicious lot. And Adrian Fenech really did look a lot like a guy whose luck had run out. Give him a bottle of meths and you'd complete the resemblance.

"I maybe need a shower too," he said. "Although I realise that's a bit of an imposition. I fear I've failed you."

"Let's not jump to conclusions," John said. "Who do you think is after you?"

"I don't know. It can't be Marchus Grubfeld because, like you said, he's been here in London."

"Where have *you* been?"

"Penzance."

"*Penzance?*"

"Sunny, picturesque, but too many tourists. Like Malta."

"At least you haven't lost your sense of humour."

They were at the gate now. John keyed the number in. It sprang open an inch. They went through, climbed the stairs and walked along the concrete landing to the flat. John opened his front door and politely gestured for Adrian to go in first.

What happened next took them completely by surprise.

Chapter 32: Things Finally Get a Bit Simpler

Adrian Fenech emitted a combined yelp and shriek and lurched backwards. He knocked John off balance.

Then the force of his reverse was tripled as something shoved him hard from the front to get past. John was thrust onto the landing's metal rail with Adrian on top of him. A blur shot out of the flat and made for the stairs.

But not a complete blur, because it quickly resolved into a recognisable figure. *Marchus Grubfeld.* And was that – *blood?* inside the flat?

He pushed Fenech out of the way.

Grubfeld had reached the bottom of the stairs, but the gate wouldn't open. It had an unpredictable latch. Unless you were used to it, you generally needed three or four tries. There wasn't enough time. John launched himself from the third step and grabbed Grubfeld's back as he sailed past him into the wall. He used Grubfeld for centripetal force to cushion his impact, and Grubfeld was flung into the courtyard with no way of escape except to get past John.

He ran backwards, jumped onto one of the planters and leapt from there to the stair rail, vaulting it with one hand and running back upstairs to the flat, where he probably had a weapon.

But Fenech came to meet him, and had the advantage of being higher on the staircase. He tried to kick Grubfeld, but Grubfeld feinted left and, although Fenech hit him in the chest, most of the impact was lost.

Nevertheless, Fenech was still an obstacle, and although Grubfeld obviously considered it for a second, he didn't have time for the struggle necessary to bypass him before John caught up. He made for the drainpipe – an old-fashioned cast-iron model

– and hauled himself expertly towards the roof, using the brackets as footholds. He grabbed the gutter closest to the top of the pipe where it was least likely to come off the wall, and pulled himself up so effortlessly he seemed to fly.

Here was a guy, John realised, who spent a lot of his time practising mock getaways, and could think on his feet in widely different scenarios as clearly and methodically as most people could think at a desk in their local library.

Adrian Fenech had readjusted, and stood with his hands tightly clasped in front of him at waist-level. John stepped high onto them, and, with his own momentum, and with Fenech propelling him upwards, landed a little above the gutter. Adrian gave him added leverage from beneath, and suddenly Grubfeld wasn't alone.

They leapt three flat-ish rooftops. Grubfeld came to the street with nowhere to run and a hundred foot drop. He hesitated then jumped. John came to the edge a second afterwards and saw him perched atop a red double-decker bus. But he didn't look secure; he looked as if he'd gone for the least worst option and it hadn't turned out well. The bus came to a halt too quickly and he toppled and fell out of John's visual field, on the far side of the vehicle.

John had also done parkour in the past. He used the rain gutter to swing down into the second balcony, the rail in front of that to land in one beneath it, and suddenly he was on the street. He cleared the bus to see that Grubfeld's fall hadn't even slowed him. He was on the run at high speed along the opposite pavement.

Suddenly John was closing on him. He hadn't experienced anything like a fall from a bus – even though that fall must have been cushioned by something – or the uncertainty of a bus roof, or even Fenech's weak kick. And he sensed he was naturally faster. If you were the over-confident type, you might not practice sprinting as part of your getaway package. You might not think you'd need it.

Grubfeld registered a pick-up truck, to his left, slowing for red lights. They'd go green any second, and it would be away at speed. He put on a spurt and launched himself into the rear. The lights obligingly turned green. A shrewd calculation.

In theory. Because getting away like that only happened in movies. In real life, what happened was that the driver saw someone hitching a ride on the back of his vehicle and braked sharp, making the stowaway lurch forward and hit the cabin at roughly 30 mph. Then the driver got out with a serious bone to pick.

Grubfeld was strong, John had to give him that. He vaulted the side of the truck, landed on his feet back on the pavement, and accelerated. He had his phone out now and was talking fast. Presumably calling for assistance, which was handy. Once they got hold of his mobile, some very useful information would probably emerge. Especially since it would probably match whoever turned up to lend a hand.

But what was he thinking? If someone materialised on Grubfeld's side, that wouldn't be a good thing. Information was only valuable if you were alive to collect it.

They crossed Regent's Park full pelt, and exited at Hanover Gate next to the mosque. Grubfeld was clearly getting tired now, but he still had a lot to give, and given his phone call, he probably thought backup was imminent.

Grubfeld clocked another bus, this one stopped to pick up passengers. Again, he seemed to instinctively gauge the margin for error. He ran and boarded it just as the electronic doors were hissing shut, leaving John several yards short on the other side. The traffic on Park Road was sparse for once and it pulled away and accelerated. In a few seconds, Grubfeld would be gone. John had stayed the distance with a bus once before, but that had been in relatively dense traffic. This one had a clear run.

He took out his phone, put all his effort into drawing level with the driver's cabin, and threw it at him as hard as he could. It made a loud bang as it bounced off the Perspex. The driver jumped, turned to see where it came from, and grimaced vehemently. He braked. He stormed out of his cabin and came to the doors ready for a confrontation. John came to meet him. At the driver's touch of a button, the doors opened from within. John ducked and squeezed past him virtually without contact.

Grubfeld had run upstairs. When John got to the top deck, he'd already kicked a window out, and leapt onto the road.

Probably useless double-backing past the driver. He'd probably picked up a baseball bat by now, and he might have helpers. John squeezed through the window after Grubfeld and landed on top of a Fiat Uno. He slid off and the chase resumed.

It was getting boring now. They'd run through the entire gamut of possible innovations, and all that remained was more of the same. Eventually, Grubfeld would have to make a stand, and they'd have to fight.

Which would probably come at any minute. Grubfeld was probably considering his specific mode of halt and about-turn now, wondering how to execute it when John was least expecting it, and make maximum use of its shock potential.

But Grubfeld didn't have a weapon. He must know he was finished unless his friends turned up pretty quickly. London was full of police personnel and some of them were probably on their way. A miracle they hadn't already arrived, except that this was a public disturbance that was on the move – and at what, from the Met's point of view, must be astonishing speed.

They were running towards Baker Street. Suddenly, John got the impression – he didn't know how - that Grubfeld's helpmates had arrived. Then a Mercedes pulled out from a side street and overtook them both. It slowed and its rear door opened. Grubfeld made a lurch, and four hands grabbed him from within. But John launched himself. He wasn't a particular fan of rugby, but he'd played it. He performed what even he could see was a textbook tackle, snatching Grubfeld's legs in such a way that he'd have crashed to the floor had he been running. It added another twelve stone to his weight, and since he was clinging to his would-be rescuers as much as they to him, it had the effect of pulling the two collaborators out of the car, leaving three men in all, including Grubfeld, stranded in the road. The car accelerated and disappeared round the corner, its driver maybe deciding to call it quits.

Grubfeld's partners were besuited and tough-looking, and they were armed. But John hadn't just tumbled from a moving car, so he wasn't disorientated like they probably were, and he had the psychological advantage of just having bested them. The first man went for his gun, but tried to get up at the same time, which was one task too many. John kicked his chin in the air, and grabbed his gun as he flopped to earth, maybe dead, who knew. He shot the second man in the shoulder and rushed at him with a well-timed head butt as he tried to adjust to what was probably a combat-ending injury. Two down.

Suddenly Grubfeld landed hard on top of him. The impact propelled the gun from his hand. It landed in the road a metre in front. People screamed and ran away, but they were half invisible.

Meanwhile, the Mercedes had done an about turn and was racing at them. Whoever the driver was, he was probably intent on killing both of them. No more Grubfeld meant no one to cause embarrassment, and no more John Mordred meant something they'd been aiming for since all this began. Two birds, one stone.

John held on to Grubfeld as much as Grubfeld to him. This was a fight for position. Release your grip first in the wrong bodily relation to the firearm, and your opponent would follow suit. But he'd also grab the gun, and you'd have lost.

John struggled as hard as he could, but pretended harder. In this sort of situation, it was chiefly about your ability to act. He manoeuvred Grubfeld into a stance where the gun was his if he could only break free.

He let go and reversed at speed. Grubfeld pounced triumphantly and swivelled on his knees to shoot - and smile. Assassins' custom: show a victorious face.

There was a loud screech of rubber on tarmac. The Mercedes hit Grubfeld with such force he seemed to concertina beneath its chassis. Not reckoning with an obstruction whose centre of gravity was so low, it flipped over, skidded on its roof and came to a stop twenty metres down the road.

Then, suddenly, there was what seemed like perfect stillness.

But was, in fact, five wailing sirens, a Mercedes car alarm, a hovering helicopter, scores of people bellowing and screaming, and an entire regiment of police officers yelling for John to keep his hands where they were and kneel down on the ground.

Heaven.

When Dina Oforka-Jones heard that a search warrant was likely to be granted, she packed as much as she could, grabbed her passport and booked a flight. Two hours later, she sat in the first class cabin of a BA Boeing 747 at Heathrow, eating a celery stick from a transparent packet. She wasn't hungry, but looking relaxed was of the essence in a situation like this. She adjusted her headrest and smiled at the woman in the seat opposite. She could tell they shared the same thought, though: *when are we going to take off?*

It couldn't be long now. Any minute.

She didn't expect to return to England, ever. She wasn't sure where she'd end up, but France was a good starting point because it was so close and she knew the language. The USA would have been preferable, but by the time she disembarked, she'd probably be a wanted woman. Some of her suspected this was why the plane had been delayed. But what could she do? Too late to get off. Just wait and pray.

She looked at her phone. *27 new messages.* She scrolled down. Some with 'urgent' in the heading. And not spam. From colleagues.

Ian had stopped calling about an hour ago. He was smarter than she was. He'd probably planned for something like this years ago, when it started.

Then she looked at her newsfeed. What she found there took a few seconds to sink in, because it arrived as a series of disconnected fragments rather than a discreet package of information:

prominent City of London solicitor; senior partner; male; found dead this afternoon; hotel room; gunshot; unexpected.

Her stomach heaved. She wanted to retch. Just as she had after that 'terrorist incident' outside Hyde Park earlier; when she'd looked at the photos on the BBC website, and the penny had dropped a horrible twenty miles into her stomach.

She noticed her junk folder was unusually full. No mention of urgent here. These were from people she didn't know, and who probably couldn't be traced. One recurrent theme. *We're coming to get you.*

She looked out of the window and saw five people striding purposefully across the tarmac towards her plane: four men with a woman at their head, all in suits, looking grim.

Of course they were coming this way.

And naturally, that was Phyllis Mordred in front.

She sighed. Thank God, really.

Ian was dead. Whoever had killed him probably wouldn't spare her, and she wasn't good at hiding. However hard she tried, they'd find her soon enough. She needed to throw herself on Phyllis's mercy. Offer full cooperation.

She jumped as someone leaned ominously over her.

The air stewardess. "Excuse me, Madam," she whispered, "I'm afraid I need to ask you to come with me."

Chapter 33: The Mystery of John

The security services became aware of the chase through Central London at the same time as the police. Information was exchanged, strategies provisionally agreed, and both organisations sent officers to where, by extrapolating the mean line of journey and factoring in distance and speed, they anticipated the action would be next. They arrived in the right place just after Grubfeld's death. Miraculously, despite a semi-airborne car, no one else in the vicinity was hurt, but then there'd been time for people to appreciate that a rumble was occurring, and, if they didn't want to get hurt, they'd better drive, walk or run away. The police still shouted for John to get down on his knees and approached him aiming guns at his chest. Not all of them were in the loop.

A few seconds later, a Chief Superintendent turned up and from that point, everything was deference and courtesy. John was interviewed at Scotland Yard in a comfy chair, with a cup of tea, and allowed to return to Thames House. He couldn't go home, because of what had happened to Lucy Staveley. Starting that evening, MI7 put him and Phyllis up at a hotel while their flat was 'refurbished and cleaned'. It sounded so clinical, yet both felt Lucy Staveley's death keenly, even after photographs retrieved in the raid on Carneghan Strake revealed that it was her who'd handed their flat key to Dina Oforka-Jones, and thus indirectly to Grubfeld. They attended her funeral four days later, a horribly tragic affair. Mrs Staveley, despite her anguish, made a point of acknowledging them.

Adrian Fenech's Aunt Julia came to fetch him from the police station where he'd been taken at the same time as John went to Scotland Yard. MI7 interviewed him about the journalists on Aisling Baxter's list, and, for caution's sake, arranged for him to 'disappear' in a manner of his own choosing. Seven days later, he and Aunt Julia left for somewhere undisclosed in Canada. John and Phyllis went to the airport to see them off with chocolates and wine.

Yet their precise status at Thames House hung in the balance. They wanted their old jobs back, Ruby Parker wanted them back, but protocol demanded a cooling off and reassessment period. Two weeks. Time enough to tie up the investigation's loose ends, for John to attend one final session with Doctor Chakladar, and for Ruby Parker to consider all the contingencies.

Paramount amongst which was Chakladar's concluding summation.

On an otherwise nondescript Tuesday morning, Ram Chakladar arrived at Thames House in a taxi, checked in at reception and was escorted to a lift which descended several floors and opened onto a silent corridor with a single door at the end. His on-site minder – a middle-aged woman in a polo-neck jumper, thin trousers and pumps – accompanied him to his destination, knocked, and opened the door for him with a formal smile when she heard the command to come in.

Ruby Parker was standing behind her desk. She gestured for her guest to sit down, and followed suit.

"Thank you for all your work so far," she said.

Chakladar nodded. "I appreciate you saying that."

Neither speaker was expressing anything more than formal noise. The psychologist was doing his job, for which he was well paid, so her thanks were unnecessary. They weren't an indication that this interview would be easy, so his appreciation was probably premature.

She picked up an A5 booklet from her desk: *The Journal of Modern Psychiatric Case Study and Clinical Analysis*, Vol. 56, no. 12. "I understand 'Patient X' is John Mordred," she said.

"Correct," he replied.

She nodded. "So it turns out that he's vastly more complex than either of us supposed."

"I regret to say, he's a complete mystery. I don't mean that in a sinister way. He's a model employee, and well suited to MI7: highly trustworthy and fully committed. I meant, from the psychological point of view."

"So you retract your claim about him suffering from an 'inferiority complex'?"

"I'm afraid that was premature, yes. After the initial few interviews, I realised he was more complicated than I'd anticipated. We're used to dealing with broadly interchangeable tough guys in MI7: cynical, seen-too-much types with a taste for fast cars, sex and danger, yet with an endearingly down-to-earth sense of rough justice. Usually committed to fitness regimes and martial arts. Often ex-armed service personnel. The subject - "

She laughed humourlessly. "I did point out at the outset that John's nothing like that."

"In my defence," he replied, "there's often a difference between what people appear to be and what they really are. And with respect, you're a lay person. There was the question of why, if he genuinely didn't conform to the usual personality type, he'd lasted so long in the intelligence services, and apparently completed so many successful missions."

"So where did the inferiority complex notion come from?"

"Discussions I had with my colleagues, regarding several remarks he made about his relationship to his sisters, to his colleagues, and to you. As I say, the conclusion we drew was premature. There's an obvious difference between an inferiority complex and simple modesty."

"I don't understand how you can describe him as a 'complete mystery'. You mean to say that, bringing to bear the gargantuan apparatus of clinical psychology as it's been developed over a century and a half, in every corner of the globe, you still can't say *anything?*"

He made a self-depreciating face. "I'm exaggerating, yes. But what you must remember is that Psychology, for all its pretensions, isn't a science in the sense that Physics or Chemistry are. It uses the scientific method, true, but as I believe the philosopher Ludwig Wittgenstein once said, it's an arena where problem and method pass each other by. That's as true today as it's ever been. And of course, we don't have access to everyone in the whole world. The minds of the minute sample of the earth's population we get to study under clinical conditions are always fairly singular to begin with."

"I'm struggling to get some concrete recommendations out of what you're saying, Ram. Underneath your exaggeration, what are your actual conclusions regarding John?"

"Okay, let me give you a list. To begin with, if I had to employ any one category to characterise his personality, I'd probably choose 'religious'. He believes in a universal language that suffuses the universe, and which he claims to hear sometimes, and whose main theme is love. He occasionally has visions of the art historian and critic, Sister Wendy Beckett, who, to the best of my knowledge is still alive and living somewhere in Norfolk. He also has imagined conversations with an Orthodox nun called Mother Thekla. Or at least, that's what she's called now. She used to work in this department, and in those days – just three short years ago - her name was Gina Fairburn. He's devoted to his family – two living parents, four sisters and their partners - who essentially see him as a man who, for whatever reason, radically failed to reach his full potential. Yet he's a languages genius, and can speak any foreign tongue like a native. His interest in fast cars and casual sex is non-existent. He supports so many charities, he's virtually penniless. He's passionately in love with his wife. He's a vegetarian who believes all animals have souls. He's not above killing people like Marchus Grubfeld as the occasion demands, and afterwards he experiences some, but not much, remorse. In The Gherkin, he recently had what he believed was a vision of God. His favourite book is Plato's *Republic,* and he doesn't think this world is fully real. Shall I go on?"

Ruby Parker sighed wearily. "You don't need to."

"Because I could."

"I'm sure we both could. None of what you've just said is news to me."

"But it does make him something of a mystery from the point of view of familiar psychological theory. Oh, he can be *made* to fit a category. As I've just said, if I had to, I'd put him in the quasi-religious class, but I don't have to. True, I was exaggerating when I said he's a complete mystery. I should have said I'm agnostic about whether he's a one off."

"Let's go back to the beginning, because I think this is becoming far too abstract. I'm sure his personality and his condition aren't entirely separate, but we asked you to look into the latter."

"His depression."

"He claims to be cured."

Chakladar nodded. "I'm normally sceptical about self-diagnosis, but in this case, I think it's accurate."

"In which case, the question is, what caused it? And what are the chances of a relapse?"

"Some of it was burn-out. But some of it was more general. Society's getting less and less equal, and people are increasingly angry across the board. Everyone's shouting at each other on the internet and everyone's mental health is suffering. That might sound political, but it isn't. And it's affecting John. He values equality. He dislikes unearned privilege and patronage. He tells me his wife cancelled his subscription to *Private Eye*, because she thought it was exacerbating his condition. I told him I thought she'd made a wise decision."

"You do know she's a passionate Conservative? Might that be having an effect? I'm not denigrating the Conservative Party, but it is associated, in the popular consciousness, with the defence of wealth and privilege."

"He takes the old-fashioned view that there are good and bad people on all sides: Tory, Labour, Brexit, Remain, Christian, Atheist, Muslim, Trump, anti-Trump. No one group's got a monopoly. And he thinks individual people are the same. No matter how apparently depraved, everyone's got a good side. My opinion? I'm not convinced he's right, but I certainly wish more people felt like that."

"And your conclusion is that he's fit to return to work, assuming we decide to re-employ him?"

"If he wants to come back, I think it would be a serious mistake to turn him down."

She stood and reached over the desk with a handshake. "That's very good to know. Thank you again for your time, Dr Chakladar. You've been very helpful."

Two weeks after Dina Oforka-Jones decided to cooperate with the police, John and Phyllis were back in their own home. There was no sign that anyone had ever been killed here; everything had been returned to its exact prior condition. Neither was superstitious, and they were used to the proximity of death. The murder, temporally fixed, tragic and irreversible, was quite distinct from the question of *where* she'd been killed, which was a mere accident of geography.

On the morning of their joint interview for the two vacant posts of Intelligence Officer Grade One, they awoke at six, breakfasted, showered and got ready. Today they didn't listen to Radio 4. John lay on the bed, fully dressed, apart from his suit jacket and shoes; Phyllis sat at the dressing table to put on her make-up.

"Nervous?" she asked.

"Nope," he replied.

"Excited?"

"A bit."

She stood up and began to pick her clothes from the wardrobe. "You must at least be interested to find out what Dina Oforka-Jones and her crew were up to."

"If they don't re-employ us, they won't tell us."

"And we'll spend the rest of our lives wondering. Cruel, but hey, that's national security. Don't be silly, John. We were an integral part of their investigation. They couldn't have done it without us. They have to tell us, if only as a matter of courtesy."

"I'm fairly certain I know."

She stopped dressing to flick an irritable glance his way. "Er, wait a minute, then. Why didn't you share it with me?"

"I didn't know you were that interested. I thought you were just pleased it was over. Besides, you'd have called me a smart aleck."

"You'd better tell me now then, because we'll be on the tube in a moment, being crushed by commuters' bodies."

"I guess you want to see whether I'm right. Ruby Parker will explain everything and you'll compare the two accounts. Which is fair enough, I suppose."

"Just get on with it," she said.

"Dina Oforka-Jones and Ian Batchelor were running an extortion racket. The Russians have been big in London for a long time, using our world-class legal and financial services to launder money. Putin's also been putting his henchmen into the EU by means of the entirely legal, but morally dubious, sale of EU passports, which is big business in Malta. Carneghan Strake have been heavily involved in both types of enterprise, and that's won them lots of friends in the Kremlin. The firm's partners are regular guests at all sorts of Russian government social gatherings, where they naturally pick up gossip – some of it undoubtedly true – about the dirty doings of some of their own clients. Dina and Ian disseminated that information to selected journalists in Britain and elsewhere – mostly junior-level bods without much stake in the industry – who each then put together a story 'revealing' it. Carneghan Strake subsequently 'heard about' that story, and informed the Kremlin. The Russians then paid through the nose for Carneghan Strake to spike it. Some of the payment went to the dodgy journalists, all of whom were, of course, in on it. From the Kremlin's point of view, Carneghan Strake was a vigorous defender of its overseas interests, so it was very upset to discover – quite recently - that it was being taken for a ride to the tune of several million roubles."

"Which is why Ian Batchelor was murdered."

"And Dina Oforka-Jones was so eager to cooperate with the police and MI7, because she would have been next. The list that Aisling Baxter received contained the names of the journalists Carneghan Strake had suborned over the years. When Dina saw it, she probably had kittens. The good thing was, no one else knew its significance. She contacted each of the journalists in turn and told them to pretend it was about internet travel companies. Only the editors of the papers they'd once worked for knew differently, but of course, they're busy people, they had no means of connecting the different members of the list – for all they knew, their journalist could have been the odd one out, the only person with an article *not* about internet travel - and they probably wanted to keep their heads down anyway."

"It's a great theory, and it fits all the facts."

"Thanks."

"Smart aleck."

They caught the tube from Mornington Crescent to Embankment, and from there to Westminster. As they climbed the steps to the surface, they picked up a *Metro* each, as per tradition, and crossed the road to Abingdon Street. They held hands. They each had a sense of being sucked back in to something they'd once imagined they could escape from, but which had turned out to be so strong it actually made them believe they *wanted* to come back. Did they?

"Have we really talked about what we're about to do?" Phyllis asked, as they passed the statue of Richard I, outside the House of Lords. "I mean, *really?*"

He grinned. "Some people might say it's a bit late for this. Forget about 'we' for a moment. Do you?"

"I do. I don't want to do fashion any more. I can't imagine why I ever did. Ruby Parker once suggested I might be in line for her job someday, but even if I'm not, I've still got real prospects in MI7. I'm a career person. Not to the exclusion of you, obviously. But I want to serve my country at the highest level. I always have. And I can't be a Conservative MP any more. The fact that I was effectively on the scene when Aisling died will always raise stupid questions about me in some people's minds. Yes, I honestly want to do this. I'm not thinking about me when I say 'we'. I'm thinking about you."

"I want to do it."

"Because you think you can't do anything else, and you want to be with me, is that it?"

"I can do other things. I can do translation."

"Bor-ing."

"Or go and work in an animal rescue shelter."

"Where you'd get unqualified love, but limited conversation. Come on, you're quite a sociable guy. And you already support most of them. You don't have to go and work in one."

"But I want to go back to Thames House."

"Why? Come on, John. We're nearly there, then we'll have to shut up. One minute without hesitation, repetition or deviation. Why do you still want to work in Thames House?"

"I suppose after a long time of working in a place, especially if it's intense, you realise that you're somehow a product of it. It's where you belong, for all its faults. I like the excitement. I miss Alec and Annabel and Edna, and all the others, and Ruby Parker's the closest thing I've got to a living grandmother. And I met you there. And it's got excitement. Sure, I realise that one day, I'll be too old for 'the field', as they call it, though it's nothing like an actual field - "

"Dzzt."

"What?"

"Repetition: field."

He laughed. "I had a dream about Thames House last night. Brian Penfold had just retired, and Ruby Parker came to me and said, 'We'd like you to take over as the new Lord of PowerPoint.'"

"What did you say?"

"I said yes, of course. It's a job. Changing the subject slightly, what about having children? I thought that's what you wanted?"

"Ultimately, yes. But you'll have to retire from active service sooner or later. That's when you'll be made Lord of PowerPoint. Then we'll have a boy and a girl, and you can work part-time and look after them."

"Which wouldn't be as bad as I suspect you're trying to make it sound."

"Right now, people respect you in Thames House. They respect you as a spy. I mean, really. I've heard them talk about you with a kind of awe as you go by. In whispers. I'm actually really proud to call you my husband. Which I wouldn't necessarily be if you worked at, say, the Donkey Sanctuary, or Acme Translation Services."

"We shouldn't assume it's going to be a straight walk back in. Chacky may still have reservations, for a start."

"If he has, what then?"

"Then I'm happy to take that desk job they offered me. I'm sure they'll be keen to get *you* back, and if the price of that's finding something for Good Ol' Johnny to do, they'll almost certainly take it. The important thing is, you're okay with me coming back."

"I am. Now shush. We're here. Walls heave ears."

They signed in at reception. Colin told them how lovely it was too see them back and gave them a silver envelope. A good-luck-in-the-interview card from more friends than they knew they had, although most had probably used aliases in case it later fell into the hands of enemy agents. You couldn't be too safe in this business.

"Wow," Phyllis said emotionally.

"One minute till we're late," John told her. "Thanks, Colin. Was this your idea?"

"Mainly," he replied. "But I didn't have to twist anyone's arm. People actually asked if they could sign it."

They got into the lift and went straight to Ruby Parker's office, where two chairs had been set out for them.

"I take it you've discussed this," she asked them neutrally.

"In great detail," Phyllis replied.

"In that case, I'd like to hear your pitch," she said. "You can give it to me separately or one of you can give me a summary."

Phyllis relayed their position roughly as they'd agreed it between Westminster and Millbank, keeping to the main facts and omitting anything sentimental. She spoke for a minute and was conscious of repeating 'secure', 'enjoy' and 'stimulating'. Although John didn't react, she guessed he'd say something later.

"I'm glad you're not taking anything for granted," Ruby Parker said when she'd finished. "Obviously, I'm happy to re-employ you. Dr Chakladar passed you with flying colours, John, so you're back on your previous footing."

"Whoa," he said. "I honestly wasn't sure he would."

"You probably won't get to work together much in future, unless you're part of a bigger team. You know my policy as regards excluding personal involvements from particular cases. But of course, I'm reasonable, and willing to be flexible."

"Thank you," they both said.

"I suppose you want to know about the Carneghan Strake case."

"John thinks he's worked it out," Phyllis told her.

"That doesn't surprise me," Ruby Parker replied, in a voice that was neither approving nor disapproving. "In that case, John, you have the floor."

He explained as he'd done earlier. Ruby Parker nodded. When he'd finished, she looked impressed, but also as if she'd half expected it.

"The only thing you really missed out," she said, "was the involvement of the murdered Maltese businessman, Angelo Bonnici. He seems to have acted as an intermediary between Carneghan Strake, on the one hand, and the Kremlin and the Azerbaijanis, on the other. He fed Dina Oforka-Jones and Ian Batchelor potentially embarrassing true stories about Kremlin-sponsored new EU citizens, and they turned them into libellous news articles, which were then mock-suppressed, and charged to

Moscow or Baku. Bonnici was killed by Grubfeld, partly because Grubfeld, we think, wanted to strike a direct deal with the Russians and become one of their dedicated hit-men. We do know they had such things. Some of the journalists on that list probably fell victim to them – that's how the Russians found out what Carneghan Strake was up to, by the way: going to the list - and it was likely they who put Adrian Fenech in such fear for his life."

"So all's well that ends well," John said.

"Not quite how I'd put it myself," Ruby Parker said, "but at least you're both safe, and the world's down a few more bad apples. I take it you can start immediately. Your desks are upstairs, broadly as you left them. I'm pretty certain you'll find nothing much has changed, for better or worse. Welcome back."

They took the lift to the surface then climbed the stairs to the first floor. Edna was waiting to greet them with a grin, and a handshake and a hug. "Great to see you both," she said. "I'm assuming you passed the interview? I really hope so, because things have been so dee-you-double-ell here."

"We've missed you," Phyllis told her.

"Obviously," she replied.

As they were about to part to go to their desks, Phyllis's phone dinged. She took it out and grinned.

"OMG," she said. "Just as I was thinking it couldn't get any better!"

"What's happened?"

"It's from my parents! They've invited us over for dinner this weekend! They're – they're actually looking forward to seeing you!"

"By 'you', you mean - "

She looked distinctly teary. "Seeing *you*, you idiot! Seeing *John!*"

"Tell them we'll think about it."

She laughed. "What? *No!*"

Edna rolled her eyes and smiled. "John Mordred," she said. "His most challenging assignment yet."

Acknowledgements and Afterword

Much of this book was inspired by the 2017 murder of the Maltese blogger, Daphne Caruana Galizia, and the outrage it inspired across the world. As always, some news articles were more germane than others. Nick Cohen's excellent piece, 'The unsavoury alliance between oligarchs and London's top lawyers' in *The Guardian* (26 May 2018) was instrumental in helping me clarify the obvious moral issues.

"If I were to describe secretive organisations," Cohen says, "that make millions from mafia states, you would imagine – what? Mercenaries? Conspiracies with Blofeld at their head? Nothing so thrilling, I'm afraid. Picture instead respectable lawyers of high status and higher income, whose love of money is now, in the words of the Commons foreign affairs committee, a matter of 'national security' … The lawyers who worried MPs worked at the 'magic circle' London firm Linklaters, whose 40 highest-paid partners received £1.57m on average last year. Linklaters decided that the attempted murder of the Skripals, Russia's shooting down of the MH17, its complicity in crimes against humanity in Syria, the annexation of Crimea, the invasion of Ukraine, support for the far right, the interference in democratic elections in the west and the suppression of democracy at home in no way obliged it to answer questions about its dealings with Moscow."

Cohen went on to point out that, "In this conflict, it's no help to think of oligarchs as businessmen. They are closer to the privileged servants of a warlord or mafia boss. Their wealth is held at Putin's discretion. If they are told to buy influence in the Balkans or fund an alt-news website, they obey."

As always, *Private Eye* was an incredibly helpful source, inspiring not just large chunks of this novel, but also an editorial contribution to Wikipedia on the Mishcon de Reya page.

"Malta inherited English libel law from the British Empire," *Private Eye*'s anonymous contributor, 'Ratbiter', says, "and government ministers and their wealthy backers make full use of its insistence that, contrary to natural justice, the burden of proof lies on the defendant. To make it nastier, you can't escape libel actions in Malta, even when you've been murdered. 'We have to fight 26 libel actions against my mother,' Matthew Caruana Galizia told the *Eye*. 'At least, I think it's 26 – I've lost count.' With such enticing opportunities for fees, English law firms piled in."

The same article discusses the sale of EU citizenship via Maltese passports. "Daphne also wrote about receiving 'harassing letters from Mishcon de Reya in London' that threatened 'to ruin me financially in a London court.' Letters from Mishcon, seen by the *Eye*, order her to remove articles discussing the lucrative sale of Maltese passports and the EU citizenship that goes with them." Ratbiter concludes by observing that, "Although three men have been charged with her murder, police and politicians have shown no interest in who the alleged killers were working for." (*Private Eye*, 4-17 May 2018, #1469).

Malta is not the only country to sell passports, of course. According to *The Guardian*, "Almost half of the EU's member states offer some kind of investment residency or citizenship programme leading to a highly prized EU passport, which typically allows visa-free travel to between 150 and 170 countries." (Jon Henley, 'Citizenship for sale: how tycoons can go shopping for a new passport', 2 June 2018). However, the scale of such sales in Malta is generating concern. As the Politico website says, "Prime Minister Joseph Muscat's spokesman Kurt Farrugia said almost 700 passports have been issued to non-EU nationals since the program's launch in 2014. Those passports have so far generated at least €200 million for Malta. Farrugia was responding to questions from POLITICO after the government released a list of more than 900 people granted Maltese citizenship last year."

Part of the concern is about just *who* is entering the EU. Politico again: "When the government published the list earlier this month of those who obtained citizenship in Malta last year, including those who used the Individual Investor Programme, it was accused of making it virtually unintelligible by listing individuals by their first names and not including their country of origin. 'We have no idea about the names or who the hell they are,' said Jason Azzopardi, the country's shadow justice minister. 'There's no way of knowing.'"

Obviously, MEP's have also attacked the scheme. The Latvian, Robert Zile, said, "Citizenship is something that has to be earned, not simply handed out to people with deep pockets", and Ana Gomes, a senior Portuguese MEP, claimed to be "disgusted" by such schemes, saying they "put at risk the integrity" of the passport-free Schengen zone. The European Commissioner for Justice, Viviane Reding, asserted: "Citizenship must not be up for sale".

In its 'Letter from Valletta' (20 April-3 May 2018 #1468) *Private Eye* lists some recipients of Maltese passports whose names were recently leaked, and who are also subject to sanctions by the US Treasury. It comments: "Their Maltese passport could help them dodge that for a while." Equally worrying, it continues: "Here in Malta we pay vigorous lip-service to the western line on Russia. After the Skripals' attempted murder in Salisbury, prime minister Joseph Muscat said all the right things about solidarity with Britain and went through the diplomatic formalities of recalling his ambassador in Moscow for a chin-wag. But no Russian diplomat in Valletta was expelled, even though the Russian embassy here has been a regional spying HQ for decades. Sergei Skripal himself was a spook based in Malta back when the Kremlin still sported red stars."

The impression of 'something wrong' about Malta has also affected the mainstream media. The recent primetime documentary series, *Mediterranean*, on BBC2, a tour of the 'dark heart' of Europe, began there. As the *Radio Times* put it on the day episode one was aired: "Simon Reeve starts in tourist hotspot Malta, which he discovers is also a front for international money laundering and organised crime. 'I was so looking forward to coming here, but there's something rotten in this country,' he says bleakly." (*Radio Times*, 6-12 October 2018).

One sad footnote to all this has been the effect it has had of shredding the credibility of English PEN (Motto: "We campaign to defend writers and readers in the UK and around the world whose human right to freedom of expression is at risk.") As mentioned above, Daphne's sons have consistently complained about Mishcon de Reya, the London law firm that they say "threatened and harassed" their mother and "sought to cripple her financially with libel action in UK courts". But as Nick Cohen points out, in *The Guardian* article already cited, "Their outrage has been heightened by the willingness of English PEN, the society of authors that is meant to defend freedom of expression, to have Mishcon's deputy chairman Anthony Julius on its board. I asked PEN to comment, but the defenders of free speech were, for once, silent."

As regards other specific references in this novel, the Polly Toynbee article mentioned in Chapter 1 is entitled, 'Squalid prisons are just the start. The entire justice system is in meltdown'. It appeared in *The Guardian* on 21 August 2018 and can be found online. The Facebook page 'Fix Malta's Roads', cited in chapter 8, is also real.

Finally, I would like to extend my thanks to Lynn Hallbrooks for her careful proofreading of the text of this and previous *Tales of MI7* novels. Without her input, they would be much less.

JW September 2018.

Books by James Ward

General Fiction

The House of Charles Swinter
The Weird Problem of Good
The Bright Fish
*Hannah and Soraya's Fully Magic Generation-Y *Snowflake* Road Trip across America*

The Original Tales of MI7

Our Woman in Jamaica
The Kramski Case
The Girl from Kandahar
The Vengeance of San Gennaro

The John Mordred Tales of MI7 books

The Eastern Ukraine Question
The Social Magus
Encounter with ISIS
World War O
The New Europeans
Libya Story
Little War in London
The Square Mile Murder
The Ultimate Londoner
Death in a Half Foreign Country
The BBC Hunters
The Seductive Scent of Empire
Humankind 2.0
Ruby Parker's Last Orders

Poetry

The Latest Noel
Metals of the Future

Short Stories

An Evening at the Beach

Philosophy

21st Century Philosophy
A New Theory of Justice and Other Essays

9 781913 851132